Sue Turbett worked in BBC TV News and Current Affairs as a Director and Producer for many years before leaving to set up her own video production business. She has brought her passion for travel and empowering stories to life in her debut novel *Eagle Sister*.

Sue lives in Buckinghamshire, and is now working on her second novel, in between hill walking, running, volunteering, cold water swimming and ag foghlaim Gaeilge.

To find out more, visit www.sueturbett.com

EAGLE SISTER

Sue Turbett

Constellations Press

First published in 2024
by Constellations Press

Typeset by Constellations Press

Printed and bound in the UK by Biddles, Kings Lynn

A CIP record for this book is available from the British Library

ISBN 978-1-917000-01-7
eISBN 978-1-917000-11-6

For Cherry and Laurie

Prologue

The gods sent the shamans a prophecy:

When a child of the sky unites with a child of the earth
a powerful alliance will be unleashed
that will harness the forces of air and land
to defeat the wolf, and secure peace.

You will honour a new queen.

Chapter 1

Spring in the year 1215 • Son Kul Lake, Central Asia

Meder's blonde mane and tail and my long black plaits fly out like ribbons behind us. Nothing feels quite as good as galloping into the foothills of the Tien Shan, the Heavenly Mountains. Back at camp, my cousins are sewing their wedding blankets and making their miserable plans, but up here, alone, I'm free: out of reach of Mother's nagging, Father's harsh hands and my cousins' vicious tongues.

I lean into Meder's mane, into his sweet mustiness. *Trrr, trrr,* I breathe, into his neck, and he slows as we reach the sheep and goats, released earlier to make their own way up to the jailoo. They're dim-witted creatures but can at least be relied on to find the lushest spring pastures.

The lichen glows rust-red as it catches the early morning sun, and a marmot family basks in the warming rays. Their lookout whistles a shrill alarm, but before they can run to their burrows, I grab my bow, load an arrow and loose it, striking and wounding the slowest. I slide off Meder's back and, tilting my pocket-knife at just the right angle, I swiftly end its life. I separate fur from flesh, cut it into pieces, and thank Mother Earth for her bounty.

I tuck the butchered meat into the front fold of my chapan jacket, and settle into a soft patch of moss under a large cliff face, watching my flock as they graze. I spot an ibex on a nearby slope, and contemplate stalking him, bringing him down for his valuable horns, but, instead, I lie back, close my eyes and take myself off to lead my army of horse archers. I am their warrior queen, and bannermen to left and right watch my every move, waiting for my signal to charge.

'*Aldiga!*' I shout the order to gallop, and the sound of the mounted army roars in my ears as the ground trembles from the pounding of myriad hooves.

I sit up with a start. The ground is actually shuddering. Meder rears, striking the air with his front hooves and squealing. I try to stand to calm him but a massive jolt hurls me sideways. Just as I regain my balance, another violent shake throws me upwards and I fall into a gulley as the ground continues to quake and judder. Only the gods can make the earth convulse like this. I reach for my amulet, sewn into the lapel of my chapan, clutch it tightly and offer a prayer: *I promise to do better, I promise...*

A thunderous rumble triggers large chunks of rock to fall from the grey and pink cliff face. I crawl under an overhang and curl into a ball with my hands over my head. Another jolt. Another loud crack in the rock. *Gods of sky and earth, Tengri, Eje, I beg you, do not take me now. Spare me and spare Meder and I will do your bidding. Please, I beg, I will do anything you ask of me!*

A slab of rock hits the ground and shatters with a deafening roar, scattering fragments in a huge arc. My stomach lurches and vomit scorches my throat as I flatten myself even lower. Then there is silence.

I lift my head slowly to see Meder circling skittishly, kicking out his hind legs. *Come boy, come to me, it's all right now.* He gradually calms and soon nuzzles my neck, nickering softly. My body relaxes, but I can see loose rocks balanced precariously on the cliff edge, threatening another landslide. We should return to camp without delay.

Easy, boy, nothing to worry about. I mount in one jump, gather up the reins and urge him forward. He stamps on the spot, flattens his ears and turns back toward the cliff. I dig my heels in sharply. *We've got to get home.* He rears again, whinnying loudly. I'm too exhausted to take control and I relax my legs, which he takes as a signal that he's won. He will not leave the cliff. Just as I raise my arm to give him a good whack across his rump, I stop suddenly at the sight of a large heap of roughly woven sticks, moss, animal bones, and plants on the ground. A nest, wider than I am tall, has fallen from the cliff during the earth tremor. This is the nest of a golden eagle.

Overhead, black choughs squawk and I scan the sky nervously. Meder lowers his head and nudges the nest. I pull hard on his reins, but then a tiny movement in the jumble of twigs catches my eye. I dismount and approach cautiously and lift a few of the sticks to reveal the mossy heart of the nest, where a small ball of dishevelled brown and white feathers wobbles feebly in an attempt to stand.

The eaglet turns its scrawny neck to look at me with big, brown eyes, and peeps pathetically. The pitiful sound melts my heart and I scoop it up. It sits, tiny and fragile in my rough hands, with a downy head, a grey beak edged in egg-yolk yellow and two shiny, cinnamon-brown eyes that stare unblinkingly at me as it tips its head from side to side.

Hello, little chick. I stroke the eaglet's scruffy feathers and feel it relax. *What am I going to do with you now? If I leave you, you'll* most certainly die. *It'll be quick and Mother Earth will embrace your baby spirit.* The bird holds my gaze. *I can't take you with me.*

Another rock crumbles from the cliff, landing too close for comfort. I look up. There is no sign of the mother. I tuck the bird securely into my chapan, mount Meder and canter off. My heart is racing as the little chick scrabbles to escape. Every now and then I jump, as a pin-sharp talon pierces the worn fabric of my hand-me-down shirt.

According to the stories, my clan used to hunt with eagles and our prowess was legendary. But we don't own eagles anymore and I don't know why.

If I take you back, I'll risk a thrashing. I can't keep you. I stop and put the eaglet back on the ground. It squeaks and then topples over in a gust of icy wind. *I'm sorry, little one.* I grab a couple of handfuls of moss, roughly form a nest shape and place the bird in it. I take the marmot meat out of my chapan and add it in alongside. There. Then a pang of guilt hits me and I imagine the tiny creature freezing to death, or being torn apart by a hungry fox. It's not the chick's fault that it's out here alone and abandoned. I can't leave it. I'll just have to take whatever's coming from the family. I tuck the baby bird back inside my chapan.

Kyuk Kyuk Kyuk
Nest heart bone
She fire kin Hold me calm
Girl-heart fierce Strong her me
Kyuk Kyuk Kyuk
Soft down smell
neat like in the womb nest

Chapter 2

I canter down the valley, following the banks of a river gushing ice-blue melt from the glacier up in the Heavenly Mountains behind me. Meder's hooves fly over the early spring flowers erupting from the cold ground where recent snow has melted: blue gentians, purple crocuses, and yellow arnica. Before long, when all the snow has gone, the jailoo will be carpeted in the silvery-white starbursts of a million edelweiss.

Ahead is camp. Nine circular yurts in a straight line so all entrances catch as much sun as possible during the day. The collapsible, red-willow lattice frames, covered in thick grey felt, house all twenty-eight members of our Snow Leopard clan. Each spring we pack up everything we own, dismantle our yurts, and move from the plains near the city up to our clan lands, here on the shores of Son Kul Lake. The endless pastures of the jailoo are where our horses, yaks, sheep and goats breed, give birth and grow fat until the end of autumn when we pack up and return to the city fringes to endure the winter.

I hope to slip in unseen with my rescued orphan. Today the clan is preparing for the feast to celebrate our recent arrival. Moving from our winter pastures, on the edge of Balasagun, is welcomed every year but the earth tremor will no doubt be seen as a bad omen from the gods, and I wonder if the meal will be cancelled.

Just as I enter camp, a group of armed men gallops out at full speed. I tether Meder, and Mother rushes up to me.

'Gulzura! Where have you been?'

I don't know why she asks me questions. I don't talk. At least, not out loud.

I raise my eyebrows. *What's happening?*

'There's been an attack. While the earth was shaking, the Balta men snatched a dozen of our best milking mares. Alik and Nurbek have gone in search.' I make a note to keep out of my eldest brothers' way. 'We've little enough to trade this summer as it is without this loss. At least none of our women was taken this time.'

Last spring, cousin Aiza was bride-napped by Kizil Clan. I will never forget the sound of her screams or the sight of a mounted marauder pulling her through the mud by her beautiful hair.

I can't see how the cycle of raid and counter-raid will ever end. It's what we do. It gives the men a purpose and the clan something to talk about every night around the fire. I draw aside the heavy, felt entrance flap to our yurt and bump into another of my brothers, Usen. I might have guessed he wouldn't be with the raiding party.

'Where are the sheep and goats?' he asks.

I freeze. I've forgotten all about them. Usen rolls his eyes, then starts to laugh, which sets off his wheezing. 'They're back!' he splutters.

What?

'They made their own way home, all by themselves, almost as if they are used to returning alone!'

I thump him playfully on his arm then pull away, realising that I can't risk a game of rough and tumble while I have a secret baby eagle nestled inside my chapan. I am thankful it's still cold enough to wear it and I pull the belt tighter as the little bundle stirs. I would love to be able to tell Usen what just happened. There are, as there are so often, many unspoken words sitting in my head with nowhere to go.

I adore Usen; not only is he kind to me but he's often in more trouble than I am. Unlike the rest of the clan, who mistake my muteness for stupidity or laziness or both, he seems to understand and actually likes my unusual, silent ways. He leaps to my defence when Alik and Nurbek blame me for their own mistakes, knowing I can't argue back. Only yesterday he returned our little brother Bolot to me after he found him alone, wielding an axe at some wood, when I should have been keeping an eye on him.

I notice cousin Ermek approaching me, ready with some criticism or question, and I turn away quickly. A little scratch inside my coat reminds me that there are matters I must see to quite urgently. Only one person in camp will know what to do: Atashka, my grandfather. There is just one problem. I don't like him. In fact, I find him repulsive.

Atashka is a shadowy shape sitting in the gloom at the back of his yurt. He doesn't sit like the other clan men: legs spread apart, taking up space, looking bigger than they really are. He sits with his legs closed, trying to be small. He lifts his head as I enter, just enough for me to see his lop-sided, mutilated face. The ugly, sunken cavern where his left eye should have been, and the vicious scar that runs down his cheek from it, make a deep cleft in his leathery, ancient skin. He smells old and unloved, but I have no one else to turn to right now. I carefully lift the eaglet from my chapan and, before I have even shown him properly,

Atashka raises himself up, instantly growing tall. For the first time I can remember, he flashes a huge smile.

'Well, well, well, what have you got there?'

His reaction takes me completely by surprise.

'I haven't held an eaglet for a very long time.' He reaches out knobbly-jointed hands to take it gently from me, then turns it this way and that, examining every detail of its small body.

'Hello, little lady.'

I watch, hoping he doesn't notice that I can't look him in the eye; his scarred, one-eyed face makes my tummy queasy.

'You have a fine, young female, with quite wonderful features. Just look at her beautiful legs! And those talons are going to be impressive when they're fully grown. She's only about six weeks old. She'll soon start to grow her dark brown feathers and then she'll look more like a proper eagle.' He strokes the little bird, and she closes her eyes and tilts her head into his hand, clearly enjoying his warm, confident touch. I'm not sure I like the fact that the eaglet is so happy with Atashka, and I make to take her back.

'Ah! So, you want to keep her, eh?'

I take a deep breath and look directly at his good eye. It is milky-brown and sad. I attempt a small smile in a desperate effort to communicate my desire. He looks down and there's a long pause as he stares into the flickering, tallow candle which casts a golden glow over him. For the briefest of moments, his disfigured face glimmers with the shiny optimism of a handsome, young man. Then he slumps down again, deflated.

'Why on earth are we even thinking of this? You have no idea what this means, child.'

I touch his forearm tentatively. I squeeze lightly, feeling his tiny, wasted muscles in my soft, pleading grip.

'Most of my life's unhappiness has been because of eagles. Take her back where you found her; with any luck the mother will return and feed her.'

Angry tears well up and flow down my face. I never get to decide anything myself. The rage builds and I am ready to kick out at whatever is in my reach. But I don't. An unfamiliar feeling washes over me. A golden glow slowly fills me from the tips of my toes to the top of my head, bringing a sense of peace and calm like I've never felt before. I close my eyes. A calming, rhythmic voice replaces the screaming, incoherent fury in my head.

Kyuk Kyuk Kyuk
God-hatched eggs Girl and bird
Fly high Wing tip to sky
Wrap rage in soft-winged curves
Kyuk Kyuk Kyuk

I look around the yurt. Where is the voice coming from?

Kyuk Kyuk Kyuk

I look down at the eaglet in my hand. *Is it you? Are you talking to me?*

We speak twin
young plume pink skin
Kyuk Kyuk Kyuk

I *have* to keep her. Atashka is my only hope. I concentrate on looking straight at him.

'Go, child, take her back before anyone else finds her here.'

I sit back on my heels. This is a different me. I adopt an expression that I hope conveys an air of maturity and an aura of confidence that will prompt him to rethink. There is another agonisingly long silence.

'Your eaglet is very young and vulnerable right now. She still needs constant attention, constant feeding, day and night.'

I sit still and wait. Long ago, I discovered that my silence often causes people around me to keep talking, revealing far more than they had intended. Sometimes, like now, they talk both sides of a conversation.

'The only way the tribe will accept this eagle is if she becomes useful. If she can be trained to hunt, they may tolerate her. But this is long, hard work. It takes strength, courage, determination to train an eagle.' Atashka reaches out again to stroke the bird.

'This sweet little chick will grow up to become a powerful killer who could easily crush your arm with her talons. She might become bad-tempered and unpredictable.' He pauses and his hand strokes the gash in the side of his face. He is sitting quite erect now, talking faster and with increasing enthusiasm.

'This is not going to be easy. It's not for the faint-hearted. If you choose this path, you'll need help.'

His indecision plays out on his face.

'I'm old and pretty useless these days. No-one wants my advice anymore. The knowledge I have is from the past. Things have changed… You know I was an eagle hunter, a berkutchi, but did you know so was your father?'

My eyes widen.

'This is going to be hard for you to hear, child, but I think it's time you did.' He settles down on his low stool.

'Many years ago, your father had a baby eagle, named Karaluk. He was lazy and days passed when he didn't train her and barely fed her. They failed to bond. Their temperaments clashed. He found it harder and harder to control her. I could have taken over but I thought it best he learned for himself. One day it all came to a head.'

Atashka looks at me, as if unsure whether to carry on. I hold his gaze.

'They were out hunting and Karaluk failed him yet again. When your father tried to punish her, she flew back to camp, swooped down and grabbed a baby, a little girl called Sabira, who was sleeping in a crib outside the yurt. Your father shot a single arrow at the eagle, hoping to clip her wings. But instead, he killed her, and Sabira fell to her death. As a clan, we vowed never to be berkutchi or raise berkutchi again.'

My throat tightens. The chick squeaks on my lap.

'Gulzura, that little baby...' He trails off. 'Now you know why we stopped eagle hunting. That moment still haunts us all.'

He takes a long, rattly breath and closes his eyes. When he opens them, I see an unexpected spark of excitement.

'I sense this little eagle is important to our people.' He pauses. 'Gulzura, you and I need a plan.'

Chapter 3

'You'll need to feed her five or six times a day yourself for several passings of the moon,' Atashka says, as I drop another piece of raw marmot in front of the eaglet. She picks it up in her little beak, shakes her head back and downs it in one. I can't believe how much meat can fit into such a tiny body.

'And you'd better not be caught using any more food that's meant for the family. I'll teach you to hunt. Marmot and rabbit to start with.'

I can already hunt. Father gave me a bow, five arrows and a single archery lesson so I could defend the flock from a wolf attack. I have spent much of my time on the jailoo practising. I am a considerably better shot than any of my brothers.

I hold another piece of marmot in my fingers and offer it to her. She snaps her beak to grab the meat.

'No, no! You mustn't let her snatch the food. You don't want to allow any bad habits. Just drop it in front of her.'

He talks so fast I can barely keep up, but I nod eagerly, for fear he'll think I'm not capable of looking after her.

'If she starts to scream for her food, we'll make a hood for her, so she can't see you when you feed her.'

We keep the eaglet hidden in Atashka's yurt at night, and each morning I take her onto the jailoo, concealed inside my chapan. Once the herd has settled, I hunt rabbit and marmot and feed her little scraps, as Atashka showed me.

I am constantly fearful he will remove the bird from me. But I am quick to learn and am rewarded by an increasingly happy grandfather who smiles when I arrive in the mornings, and even tells funny stories of the mistakes he made when he was learning to be a berkutchi. And then one day, quite unexpectedly, Atashka says it is time to tell the family.

'Did you see their faces as we galloped off with their prize stallion?' Nurbek brags over breakfast.

'I'd like to see their faces when they find out we took their breeding goats as well!' Alik roars with laughter.

'I almost got that pretty girl too, but she slipped out of my grip when my horse tripped.'

'Shame, she would have been a good catch.'

My father and brothers sit on brightly coloured, felt rugs, talking excitedly about yesterday's successful raid, and drinking hot tea with honey. Mother puts out small, clay pots of berry jam and kneels beside the dung fire in the centre of the yurt, cooking flatbreads on the hot metal dome, and glancing disapprovingly at the boys.

'The gods obviously favour us,' Nurbek boasts. 'We've got back all the horses Balta stole during the earth tremor.'

'And a few extra!' Alik laughs.

'I have something to say.' Atashka tries to cut through the chatter, but his voice goes unheard. He tries again. 'I'd like to say something.'

Everyone carries on talking. I take a wooden spoon and bang it against the steaming pot of hot water, sitting beside the fire.

'Ready?' Atashka whispers. I nod.

'I think you should all meet the newest member of our clan,' Atashka says. I open my chapan and cautiously take out the eaglet. Into the stunned silence Atashka says, 'The gods have delivered us an eaglet. Gulzura found it, the day the ground shook, and she is going to keep it. The time has come to move on.'

Bolot, oblivious to the tension, rushes over. 'Me see, want see.' His excitement quickly turns to protest as Usen reaches out and grabs him around the waist.

'Hold on there, young man.' Bolot squeals and squirms in Usen's grip.

'Gulzura, what have you done?' Nurbek snaps.

'Take it straight back to where you found it,' Alik says in his usual, dismissive manner. 'Right now. We can't have an eagle here. It's completely out of the question.'

In two strides, Nurbek is across the yurt, towering over me, jabbing his finger into my chest. 'What on earth do you think you're doing? You can't possibly keep an eagle. How would you even train it? You don't have the sense to look after a yak.'

You don't know me. You have no idea what I'm capable of. I return the eaglet inside my chapan for fear my brother might snatch her.

'She's probably going to try to train it like one of her rats.' My brothers laugh. I shrink back to the edge of the yurt. I had no idea they knew that I have tamed a couple of rats for my own amusement.

Usen puts his arm around my shoulder. He gives me a reassuring squeeze, but we both know my situation is hopeless.

Father stands abruptly and addresses Atashka. 'You know she can't keep it. You know what we promised.'

'I've told her what happened.'

'Why would you do that? You had no right. What possessed

you, you crazy old fool? The gods punished us, and we vowed to them we would never keep eagles again.'

'That was then. This is now. The gods have sent a sign.'

Father turns to me. 'You foolish girl. You have no idea what you've done and your sis–'

Mother interrupts, her voice cracking. 'It is best not spoken of. It is too much for her… too much for me.'

My heart thumps and my breath shortens. They are hiding something and I want to know what it is. *Tell me, tell me what happened.*

Atashka coughs and shakes his head at Mother. She busies herself with stretching out the flour and water dough mix for the next batch of flatbread. Everyone looks at each other; no-one dares to speak.

Wasps gather around the jams and the tea is now cold. Only little Bolot keeps eating. The chick scrabbles around under my jacket. She will need feeding again soon but I can't leave, not without permission to keep her.

Atashka speaks again. 'It will be different this time. Gulzura will learn; I will teach her. She has so much time when she's out in the mountains with the livestock. She can hunt foxes and hares and make a real contribution to the clan. This will be the making of her.'

'Ha!' Nurbek scoffs. 'She can barely be trusted with the goats and sheep. How often does she come back long after they've returned of their own accord? How many times has she let them stray onto pastures they shouldn't be on?'

I refuse to meet Nurbek's accusatory stare, but he's right. I get bored. I am easily distracted and too often lose track of the herd. I look down at my feet and try to bury myself further into Usen, whose arm is still around my shoulders.

'Enough,' Father says. 'Gulzura is certainly not old enough, sensible enough, strong enough or clever enough to train an eagle. But I think we'll keep it. It can be given as a gift or... it might be useful as a trade in the future.' He smiles, pleased with his solution, and I scowl.

'You are right, Father,' Usen says. 'It would be advantageous to have an eagle for bartering. But the chick was found by Gulzura and don't our laws dictate that it is rightfully hers? We wouldn't want to upset the gods.'

Everyone knows that Usen's knowledge of history and law is beyond question. He has never shown much interest in fighting or horses; his passion has always been for poetry, storytelling and singing. At clan gatherings he can always be found beside the elders from the wider tribe, listening and learning their stories.

'Do we want the gods meddling in our private matters?' Alik says. 'You know they take great pleasure in causing trouble for their own amusement.' There is a general murmur of agreement.

'Alik's right, we're not the gods' playthings,' Nurbek adds emphatically.

'I have been listening to you all and I have had enough.' Everyone goes silent as Bubu, our shaman, speaks. 'Upsetting the gods is unwise. How many more omens do Father Sky and Mother Earth have to send? We have suffered famine, flood, drought and now earthquake. Remember the prophecy.'

'What, the gods would give a golden eagle to a stupid girl who can't even speak?' Alik whispers to Nurbek. Bubu hears and turns angrily to them.

'The gods know things we can never know! Tonight, I will ask them. They will have the final word.'

Chapter 4

Bubu knows things. The gods and the spirits of our dead ancestors talk to her through the patterns of migrating birds, the colours of stones and the jagged lines in heat-cracked bones. No decision, from auspicious dates for raiding rival camps to the naming of new babies, is taken without consulting her and tonight, at a special ceremony, she will ask the gods if I can keep the eaglet.

I've been excused from shepherding, but I can't settle to any chores around camp so I spend the day with Atashka. He moves with no sign of his usual aches and pains. He talks confidently, as if the decision to keep her has been made. But I am not so sure.

As the sun drops, a mist rises, and families gather in their yurts for dinner. I can't eat a thing, and my stomach churns as I try not to think about what I will do if the decision goes against me. The emergence of a bright new moon indicates the time has come. Father leads the entire clan, in order of seniority, up the hill. He wears the creamy, dark-spotted, ceremonial snow leopard pelt: the only thing he possesses to show he is leader. How he came by it is unclear, as there are no stories told of him actually hunting a snow leopard.

A trail of bright, hand-held torches, made from tightly plaited straw dipped in mutton fat, leads to the sacred place where the forces of the Sky God Tengri can be reached from the earth. Bubu is already there, sitting beside a fire, clouded in the aromatic smoke of juniper, being burned to rid the area of bad spirits. She wears a headdress of eagle feathers with a long black fringe made from a yak's tail that covers almost all her face. Her shoulders are draped in a wolfskin cape, decorated with bells, metal ornaments and tiny figurines of animals.

She stands and draws a large circle on the ground with a stick, then three smaller circles within it. She gestures for me to sit in one of the smaller circles.

'Give me your amulet,' she says.

I remove my chapan, and hand it to her, putting the eaglet in my lap. She wraps a wolfskin around me, then places the jacket, along with stones, feathers and bones, in the second circle. She sits down, cross-legged, in the third. She picks up a drum, adorned with drawings of horses and eagles, draws it close to her face and starts to beat it with a wolf thighbone.

Her eyes close. She is ready for her spiritual journey to begin. Very slowly at first, she beats the drum. Her upper body moves in small circles that get wider as the drumbeat gets faster. Eventually, she takes up a clay bowl containing a secret combination of powerful herbs. She gulps the milky liquid and, after a series of short convulsions, she calms into a trance, to commune with the ancestors and the gods.

I've seen Bubu do this many times, and it is both chilling and exciting. I hold the little bird gently and make my own passionate plea to the gods. *Please let me keep her. She talks to me. I can hear her. She is special.*

Now the spirits of the ancestors are inside Bubu and she talks in their ancient voices, using words I don't understand. Then, quite suddenly, it is all over. Bubu shakes her body from head to toe like a dog shaking off the rain, rises to her knees, drinks the contents of a second clay bowl and then spits it out through her front teeth in a wide, fine spray, drenching me and the bird.

Everyone is holding their breath and no one moves. The only sound is the distant screech of an owl calling for its mate. Bubu opens her eyes.

'The gods have spoken.'

I stare at Bubu, not daring to blink.

'Our Father of the infinite Sky, our Great Lord Tengri, wants Gulzura to have a strong totem. He wants her to have an eagle by her side. Our Mother of the Earth agrees and shook the mountains to deliver the eaglet at Gulzura's feet. This is what the gods want.'

My heartbeat quickens. The clan starts to grumble. There are sounds of disapproval all around. I look to Mother, but she won't meet my eye; her body is hunched and her lips pinched tight.

'I haven't finished…' Bubu raises her voice. 'This eagle carries a strong spirit, and their bond will bring good fortune to the clan, to the whole tribe. The gods have been clear; the partnership between this child of the earth and this child of the sky is essential to our future prosperity. If we separate the girl and her eagle, the resulting imbalance could be catastrophic for us all.'

I lower my face, not daring show my joy, relief and, above all, astonishment. The little eaglet raises her eyes to meet mine.

Kyuk Kyuk Kyuk
Side by side you me fly
Air and earth
Speak heart heart
Fly high far Seek out prey

Chapter 5

As everyone leaves, and the fire burns down to small glowing embers, the doubts creep in. Surely, the gods have made a terrible mistake. The little chick senses my fear and wriggles uncomfortably under my jacket.

'Gulzura, I've been waiting for this moment ever since you were a baby.' Bubu approaches. 'When I prepared your amulet, I knew you were destined for something special. I felt the promise of a great future for you.'

How can I be responsible for an eagle? I'm not good enough to do this. She needs training. It's a man's job.

'The gods know best. There is a reason and purpose for everything they do, and we must trust them,' Bubu says, warmly. She reaches out and pulls me into her loving embrace.

'The thought of this scares you. But you are not alone.' She pulls me closer. My head cradles in her soft bosom and she breathes kind words into my unkempt hair.

'I've watched you, child. There is no reason why you can't train this eagle. If there's one thing I know about you, it's that when you decide to do something, it's hard for anyone to stop you!' She chuckles. 'Just imagine the burden on you if everyone thought you'd be great at this. Right now, everyone's expectations are so low that whatever you do, you'll shine.'

This is true. Of all the people in the clan to be given this huge responsibility, no one would have picked me.

'I have something else to tell you. It's going to be hard for you to hear but it will help you to face what is ahead.'

I tense.

'I know Atashka has told you about how Karaluk snatched Sabira. Such a tragedy.' Bubu lifts her hand to my chin and softly turns my head so our eyes meet. 'Gulzura, that beautiful baby girl, Sabira… she was your twin.'

Rage jolts through my body. Myriads of questions burst into my brain like an explosion: *What? What are you saying? I had a sister? I was a twin? Why has no-one ever told me?*

And then it hits me. I am a half thing.

I shake. I can hardly breathe. Bubu kneels beside me and lays her arm tenderly around my shoulders. The little bird squeaks and I stroke her with a trembling hand.

Bubu speaks softly again. 'Gulzura…'

My body tightens.

'When the gods spoke to me, they told me they had sent your twin sister Sabira back to you in the form of an eagle. To help you. To guide you on the journey you have ahead.'

I look down at the chick in my lap. *You are my sister?*

Kyuk Kyuk Kyuk
We twin cheek to beak lie
Stay close
Root child Sky bird
Two fly as one

'You and your sister's fates have been intertwined since you began your lives together in your mother's belly. You grew as separate bodies but you shared a soul, a single spirit, and the gods have decided that you must be back together now, a child of the earth and a child of the sky, united in a powerful alliance.'

I wipe my grubby hands roughly over my eyes and cheeks to clear the tears.

'Gulzura, the gods say the future of our clan depends on you. That is why they have returned your sister to you. No one is better equipped to help you on the journey you must take.'

I seek out the comfort of my amulet again. It fits perfectly into the palm of my hand, its familiarity soothing me.

'Have you ever wondered what your amulet is made from?' Bubu asks.

I shake my head. I have never really given it much thought. It feels like a flat stone with a raised ridge down the middle and some horsehair plaited around it.

'It's Karaluk's breastbone, wrapped in Sabira's beautiful black hair.' She pauses. 'I always believed she'd come back to you in some way. You and she used to babble together, but you stopped trying to talk the day she was taken from you. She will help you find your voice again.'

I look again at the scruffy ball of feathers in my lap and smile. *Hello, Sabira. Hello, my Eagle Sister.*

Chapter 6

She is so beautiful, wobbling in a beam of light that's filtering through a patch of thin roof-felt. Sabira is right in front of my face when I wake, her big, golden eyes blinking slowly. Her body is so tiny under my rough hand that I stop stroking and put my face against her so she can feel my warmth. She leans into me, and her soft, downy, white feathers tickle my cheek. I have already learned that a gaping beak means she's hungry. *Don't fret, little one, I'll find you some food.*

I pull on my trousers and shirt hurriedly, grab my chapan and run toward the yurt door, reaching down to swipe a hot flatbread from the fireside on the way.

'Where do you think you're going in such a hurry?' Mother has her hands on her hips and a don't-mess-with-me look on her face. 'You have *not* been released from your morning chores.'

Is that all she can say? No congratulations? No word of pride? I want to shake her and beg her to explain why she cannot be pleased for me, like the other mothers would. Instead, I take a breath and think of the women who just do as they are told for the sake of peace and quiet.

'Feeling pleased with yourself, I expect,' Ermek says.

Walking through the narrow gap between the yurts toward

the mares, milking bucket in hand, I squeeze past my cousins who move to block my way. There was a time when I was desperate to be part of their world. Watching them whisper secrets, plait each other's hair and play games that didn't include me, had left me in no doubt just how unpopular I was. On the odd occasion I was allowed to join in, their rules seemed impossible to grasp and I always got things wrong, which made them cross, and me frustrated. They rarely ventured far from camp, so their teasing and name-calling was easy to avoid out on the jailoo and when they all celebrated their first moonblood I gave up wanting a place in their world, as I still wait for mine. For a long time, I've not been bothered by what they think of me.

I hunch my shoulders, so my neck shortens and my head lowers into the top of my chapan to block out their angry, jealous whispers. But then, the realisation that, for the first time ever, I've been chosen above everyone else prompts me to raise my head with pride. An unfamiliar glow grows inside me and emerges on my face as an uncontrollable smile which feels like it stretches from one ear right across to the other: I am going to train an eagle.

'Looking pretty smug.'

Ermek has every right to be crosser than the others as she's been given my shepherding responsibilities while I train Sabira. She hates working with the livestock, far preferring needlework and cooking and the warmth of the yurt. I lower my head and push on but, however hard I try, I simply can't get rid of the grin plastered across my face, which serves to make her crosser still. Her lips pucker and her eyes tighten.

'Think it's funny, do you? Funny that I've got to go out all on my own now in the mountains with those smelly sheep and goats while you get to stay here and play with that bird?'

I walk away quickly but the venom in her voice worries me; I'm pretty sure she will try to find an opportunity to get back at me for this.

Mares milked, dung-pile re-stocked, bedding tidied away, it's time to find Atashka. I bump straight into him as he lifts the felt flap at the yurt entrance.

'I've been looking for you. We have work to do, young lady!'

He looks clean and fresh again, standing taller, more upright than I've ever seen him. The musty, sickening smell that usually lingers around him has been replaced by the fresh smell of pine. He's been in the sauna twice now in a single moon. Quite unexpectedly, my stomach lurches but I manage a smile to hide the wave of uncertainty that washes over me. Atashka looks at me just long enough to register how nervous I am, but thankfully doesn't mention it and continues his chatter.

'We have a little time before we can start to fly her. Time to gather all the bits and pieces we'll need – a tomaga, ayak-bau, a thick leather glove and, of course, you'll need a baldak!'

I have no idea what he is talking about.

He walks off with impressive speed for such an old man. I'm struggling to keep up with his huge stride and scared now, to think that I might fail and incur the wrath of the gods.

'We're going to have a daily routine and we'll schedule your chores around feeding and training. There'll be rules, and consequences if you disobey those rules – I will have no hesitation in releasing her back into the wild. There are strict time limits to stick to if you're going to do this properly. Your eagle won't wait.'

His words fly around my head in an unintelligible jumble.

He stops and puts his arm around my shoulders and leans down toward me, smiling reassuringly. I feel inclined to shift slightly so he can't get so close but manage to stop myself and then find his arm comforting in a way I had not expected.

'Does this frighten you? Well, don't worry my little one, I'm here to help you. I believe you can do this. I also believe your silence will be a big advantage. You can listen and focus on your eagle, her thoughts, her needs. I honestly think you will prove to everyone you are worthy to be called berkutchi.'

He looks so serious, as if he is talking to an important member of the clan.

'You know, Gulzura, I will hear you. Even if no-one else has taken the time or effort to try, I will watch you and listen and learn to hear whatever it is you want to say. Oh, I know you won't speak but there are other ways to hear you.'

I fidget uncomfortably. I don't know if I can do this. Me, train an eagle? Me, a berkutchi? What I do know is that I really, really want to keep that scrappy ball of feathers.

'So, what do you think?' Atashka stops and looks directly at me with a gaze so fierce that even his good eye has an alarmingly threatening stare.

I look at him with the most serious face I can compose, place my hands on my hips because that feels strong, lift my chest and nod firmly. A huge smile lights up Atashka's lopsided face and he punches my shoulder playfully, not noticing that he nearly knocks me over as he ducks through the door into his own yurt.

'Here we are, this is for you.' He struggles to bend down and open a carved and heavily chipped wooden chest. He tips the contents across the floor. 'I've always hoped that one day I would need all this again.'

A jumble of wood, leather and rusty bits and pieces is strewn across his carpet. He sifts through it but stops abruptly. With a burst of youthful exuberance, he jumps to his feet.

'First things first, we must get you into a saddle.'

I don't want a saddle. I've been riding horses since before I can remember and I've always been happy and comfortable sitting on a soft sheepskin pad tied around Meder's belly with a strip of cloth. Of course, my brothers have saddles: essential for the balance and stability they need to use a bow and arrow at full gallop – although I seem to have no trouble firing a succession of arrows at full gallop when bareback.

I shake my head and point at Meder.

'He'll just have to get used to it. You can't ride with an eagle on your arm for ever. When she's full grown, her weight will simply be too much for you on long journeys. She'll need a baldak and we must make that too.'

I raise my eyebrows.

'It's a slingshot-shaped piece of wood that attaches to your saddle. She sits on your arm and your arm rests on the baldak, so you can relax, and your arm doesn't drop off!'

It's a lot to take in.

'We need a name for her.'

Sabira, she's called Sabira. I clutch my amulet and point at her.

'Karaluk?' Atashka suggests, with a grimace.

I shake my head vigorously. *No, Sabira.*

'Oh, well, let's just keep calling her Eagle until we can think of something better.'

I huff and he smiles at me. But this is important, so I try again. Flapping my arms, I run around the yurt and then swoop down to grab an imaginary baby. I stop suddenly, mid-flight, spread my fingers out wide in front of me, clearly dropping the baby, then clutch my heart where the arrow has struck, and fall dramatically to the ground in a heap. I pick myself up and smile broadly, quite proud of my little re-enactment. Atashka's furrowed brow indicates he's trying hard to work it out.

My shoulders slump and his smile reappears.

'Don't give up, I'm enjoying this,' he says. 'Try again, we'll get there.'

I have another idea and get down on the floor to lie on my back with my arms and legs waving in the air.

Atashka starts laughing. 'That looks like an upturned beetle!'

I continue, putting my thumb in my mouth, then turn over to crawl.

'Are you a baby?' he says. I nod. 'Would you like to call her 'Baby'?'

I shake my head. How can I say she's my twin? How can I tell him she's my missing half, the part of me that that's been absent for so many years?

Then I run to my yurt, where I know I will find what I need. I grab it and return.

The circular wooden pot is in two parts of equal size – a body made of dark wood and a lid made of a lighter wood – joined by matching tear-shaped metal clasps on each half so when it's put together it's a perfect sphere. Mother says the traders who sold it to her call it 'Yin-Yang'. I unhook the clasps and twist the lid so the pot comes apart and hold one half close to my chest and the other beside Sabira. Atashka's eyes light up.

'Are you saying your other half? Your twin? Sabira?' I kneel up and raise my arms and punch the air in a victory salute.

Yes, my eagle's name is Sabira. My eagle sister.

Chapter 7

'Don't give up, Gulzura, she is making progress.'

Sabira is completely ignoring me, refusing to move from her perch, her head tucked under a wing. Training her is so much harder than I could have imagined.

'What are you going to do now?' This is what Atashka always says. He sits back to watch, testing me and making me work it all out for myself. 'What are your choices? Think it through.' And always, 'You can do this, Gulzura. You can!'

But often I can't. I get it wrong. My head hurts with all the instructions: what to feed her; how much to feed her; what to let her do; what not to let her do. I stroke Sabira and feel that her crop is full, possibly overfull.

'I think you're right,' Atashka says. 'You've overfed her, a common mistake, easily done. You'll just have to wait now until she's hungry again.'

I wrap my arms around myself. They are sore and bruised from Sabira gripping me when I forgot to take the thick, leather glove with me. Atashka sits next to me, takes my hand.

'She *is* making progress. Last moon, she was flapping and hopping about like a tetchy chicken when she couldn't catch the dead mouse you were trailing along for her. Now she gets that mouse nearly every time.'

Atashka insists we stick to training Sabira exactly as our ancestors would have done and says that if we don't, we will never earn the respect of the clan. 'Much rests on your – on our – success. The gods are watching.' I listen to him, every word, because I know it's not just the gods watching. Last night, as I was checking the sheep and goats, Alik and Nurbek cornered me.

'We're watching you,' Alik said. 'You can't train an eagle and the moment you slip up –'

'Which you will,' Nurbek interrupted.

'– we'll have her. She'll fetch a good price.'

'And I need a new knife,' Nurbek says, pulling his blade from the sleeve of his chapan and bringing it close to my face. 'Just so you know.'

They frighten me, but it is the thought of being separated from Sabira that really frightens me.

'It's time to introduce her to the ayak-bau.' Atashka passes me two metal anklets to which leather straps, which he calls jesses, are tied. 'They'll protect her legs should a fox try to bite her, while she's learning.'

The red fox is the ultimate prize – it's hard to catch, but its fur is valued above all others. I imagine Alik and Nurbek being forced to praise me for my skill as I hold a pelt aloft. The vision is quickly shattered as, despite Atashka's patient demonstration of how to fix the ayak-bau to Sabira's legs, I just can't seem to do it.

'No one has an easy path in life. Failure is a good thing, if you learn from it. Take a breath. Be patient. You know, there is never a guarantee of a bond between trainer and eagle; sometimes it just doesn't happen. But, Gulzura, the bond you have with Sabira is there, and I know it's strong.'

What he doesn't know is that we are learning to talk to

each other and we are getting better at it every day. Secret conversations in our heads. A skill no-one can see or judge.

I can't tell you how to do it. You're just going to have to stretch out those enormous wings and jump.

Sabira looks at me, squeaking and stomping up and down on the ground, spreading her wings and flapping them.

And pray to Tengri. Go on, you can do it, girl. Take courage.

Kyuk Kyuk Kyuk
Sky calls wind Wind calls me
Feel lift Wings wide Air strong
Land

Stuck Hop hop hop
Catch fly Eat fly
Head twist flick look cock side side
Hook claw kill

The first time Sabira flies properly, I miss it. The wind is squally and, by chance, she must have spread out her wings and flapped at the very moment of a gust, because what I see when I turn is an ungainly crash onto the grass a few hundred paces from where I last saw her. She picks herself up, ruffles her feathers, walks back to her perch and preens herself as if nothing has happened.

After three full moons she is unrecognisable from the chick she was. Her white, downy fluff has been replaced by dark-brown feathers. Her feet are now pale yellow. Atashka points out her first flight feathers emerging from their sheaths and I gently stroke the milky, translucent casings.

'She's ready to take to the mountains,' he says.

Chapter 8

'This is the very cliff face I used to practise from. I want you to climb to the top.'

The rocks rise almost vertically out of the grassy jailoo like wolf's teeth. Sabira hops off the baldak onto my leather glove and I lower myself down carefully from Meder. I start to remove the tomaga, the hood Atashka insists she wears to cover her eyes and keep her calm.

'Not yet. Don't take it off until you are at the top. Only then, when you're absolutely sure she has seen the lure, release her.'

I hold the jesses tightly while I make the tricky ascent, and my arm starts to throb as she grips, struggling to stay balanced. I find a narrow ledge where I can risk standing upright. Down below, Atashka gallops off, pulling the fox fur behind him on a long string. This is it. I remove her hood, lift my outstretched arm into the breeze and let go of the jesses.

Sabira rises at great speed and vanishes over the horizon. Shamefaced, I clamber back down the mountain. Atashka approaches with a huge grin. *Why isn't he cross?*

'You forgot to wait until she'd seen the lure before you released her jesses. She hadn't spotted it, so she just flew off.'

I kick the nearest stone hard, which hurts my toe. But Atashka wraps me in a big hug and kisses the top of my head.

'Don't worry, she's having fun. She'll be back, when's she's hungry enough.'

The wait seems endless and I feel nauseous with panic. How stupid I am. How could I make such a basic mistake? I start to tremble, thinking that if she returns to camp without me, Alik and Nurbek have their excuse to take her and trade her. An image of her caged, dull-feathered and hungry, won't leave my head. I have failed, I am only fit for tending sheep and goats and collecting dung. I bury my head in Atashka's coat and sob.

Eventually, I hear her, *Kyuk Kyuk Kyuk,* but my relief quickly turns to anger and frustration as she won't come, even when I call for her in our secret, silent language. Instead, she teases me, circling, landing, then threatening me with her massive claws and gaping beak when I approach. She flies off again. She's making a complete fool of me.

Kyuk Kyuk Kyuk
Stand on air's edge and lift lift
Up climb up
F L Y
Hang still in breath of gods

Flick tail twist self

Strike
Fast fall Land rush Quick green
Wind gust switch me
Tilt dip Wing tip blade flick up down
See far see far
Mouse lamb rat chough snake fox

See all with new eyes   Up high sharp eyes
Look Kyuk Kyuk
Fly clear on white sky

Go. See if I care. See if you can fend for yourself out there. You're pretty hopeless at catching your own dinner, so you'll quickly starve and then you'll come back, but I'll have moved on. I'll get another bird, a better eagle.

She returns to rest her head apologetically against my arm. I can't resist her and stroke her feathers which glisten from her adventure. A thought rips through me. *Am I losing you?* Perhaps she's got what she wanted from me and now she's ready to leave.

I here stay   We soul kin   You me one

Atashka sits down on my other side. 'Gulzura, you have a talent I've rarely seen in adults, and never in someone of your age. Making mistakes is normal. As long as you learn from them, you will become a great berkutchi.'

His hand drifts up to the scar on his face. 'I made plenty of mistakes. This was one of them. I was training a young female and I got cocky. The wind was gusting and threw her off line at the very last second. She landed badly, missed my arm and buried her talons into my face. I lost my eye and nearly lost my life. Our shaman had to work hard to put the spirits to rest and allow my skin to mend. I learned my lesson.'

His fingers trace the jagged line of the deep cleft in his face from cheekbone to jaw. 'Until you are truly tested, Gulzura,' he continues, 'you will not find out who you are.'

I wrap my arms around him and squeeze tightly. I didn't

know I could love him so much. No matter what kind of day, Atashka is there for me: steady, calm and patient.

He takes a knobbled ibex horn from his shoulder bag. 'Here, give me your arm. I expect you're a bit sore after today's activities.'

He rubs the horn up and down my aching muscles, and the tension and soreness ease away. And, for now, so do the doubts.

I learn she She learn I
Test and trust No more ties
Bound and free
Soul share

Ride warm air on chopped wind
Kyuk Kyuk Kyuk

Fix gaze Fast swoop
Prey freeze
Stretch long Straight fall
Beast run swerve stop quick turn run
Crash I to hard earth
Prey gone
I learn fast

Chapter 9

Three full moons wax and wane as Sabira and I venture into the mountains daily. The sheep have been sheared for their autumn wool, and other signs that summer is over start to emerge, slowly at first, with a heavier morning dew, and now with regular frosts, sharp enough to trigger the emergence of thick winter coats on the horses. Atashka rarely comes with us these days, although he keeps a close eye on our progress through regular inspections and tests. Nurbek and Alik continue to criticise at every opportunity and, despite my desire to fight them both, I hold Atashka's advice at the forefront of my mind: 'They're just words and you live in a world with no words, Gulzura, so ignore them.'

As soon as we are out of view, I remove Sabira's hood and jesses and release her. Without all the paraphernalia, she is calmer, more focused and the connection between us grows ever stronger. Away from the clan, we are both free: she to fly wherever she pleases and me to dream whatever I please. This is where we are happiest. Sabira regularly rewards me by returning with marmot, partridge and rabbit, treats for the clan larder that my critics cannot ignore.

This is not the behaviour of an experienced berkutchi. Sabira seems to understand the rules, though, and always returns to be hooded and tied before we go home.

One evening, as we are all settling to eat, cousin Ermek catches my eye and smirks as she stands to address the family.

'Excuse me, everyone.'

All eyes turn to her.

'When I was out on the jailoo today, collecting herbs for Bubu, I saw Gulzura's eagle. Gulzura was nowhere in sight. She has no control over it whatsoever and I think it could be very dangerous.'

'Of course Gulzura was nowhere to be seen.' Atashka speaks up for me immediately. 'The bird is well-trained and flying greater distances every day. It's good for muscle-building and stamina. And today they returned with a sand fox. An impressive catch for such a young bird, wouldn't you all agree?'

'But Gulzura had removed her jesses, I couldn't see their trails in the air. Is that allowed?' Ermek looks pleased with herself.

Alik stands. 'Did we not say that Gulzura could keep the bird only if she stuck to the rules? And, if not, the bird would be removed from her?'

'Do you question the gods, Alik?' Bubu bellows.

Alik sits down. He's failed this time, but my heart is beating rapidly; he's getting closer.

'Let's not question Gulzura's techniques but focus on her results,' Atashka says. 'Just think of the value in that pelt.' He smiles proudly at me. If only he knew the truth. That sand fox was on its last legs. Sabira had simply picked it up and brought it to me, and I put it out of its misery.

Ermek got what she wanted. Within a couple of days I'm back on the jailoo, looking after the sheep and goats again. I don't mind. It keeps me away from camp. Every day, Sabira and I range further, over hills and into valleys that I have never dared visit before.

One morning, as she disappears over the ridge, I spot a female black kite returning to her nest, tucked into the rock face. She lands and turns in circles, wiggling her body from side to side, clearly settling on a clutch. Eggs are rare at this time of year. How pleased Mother would be if I brought some home. I drive the goats and sheep toward the pasture beneath the rock face to check out the climb.

It's a bit of a scramble up steep scree and then onto a series of narrow ledges like a zig-zag ladder to the top. When I reach the nest, the mother flies off but circles nearby, whistling her shrill rising-and-falling alarm call and flicking her distinctive forked tail.

Four small, blotchy brown eggs lie in the downy lining of the nest. I carefully scoop up three and put them in my pockets, leaving one for the mother bird to sit on. Just as I glance over my shoulder to check my descent, the kite attacks me, with Sabira in hot pursuit. I thrust my arm out to strike the kite as it makes its second approach but, instead of making contact, I push hard into thin air as the bird dips at the last moment. Sabira, so close behind, hits me with a hard thump in the chest. For a couple of beats, I teeter hopefully on the tiny ledge, before losing my balance. I tip backwards and tumble down the incline, rolling over and over down the sharp scree. I land at the bottom in a patch of coarse grass.

I lie still, unsure if I'm hurt. Meder is oblivious, quietly flicking flies with his tail and enjoying the last of the summer grass. Sabira is still chasing the kite. As I sit up, I catch a glimpse of someone ducking down behind a clump of rocks. I freeze. Then there is nothing, no movement, and all I can hear is a few crows squabbling in the distance and the munch, munch of Meder and the livestock.

I must have imagined it. I get up, brush off the worst of the scree debris and check myself over. Apart from broken eggs, torn trousers and bleeding knees, I think I got off rather lightly.

I venture toward the rocks, still uncertain whether I actually saw anything. I hear a twig snap and turn fast. There is a boy just ten paces from me, arms folded, smiling broadly. The hairs on the back of my neck stand on end and a sickness rises in my throat. I'm going to have to run fast or fight.

Chapter 10

'Need any help?' he asks, chirpy and confident.

Instinctively, my right hand slips into my sleeve and folds firmly around my knife. Young women and girls are frequently snatched by rival clans, and I am not going to let it happen to me. Fighting him would not be my first choice, but I think I can be on Meder's back in a dozen long strides. The boy's horse, a dark bay mare, is nose to nose with Meder, exchanging scents, so I could grab her reins too, and then the boy would have no way of chasing me.

'Sorry I was hiding. I didn't want to frighten you, but looks like I did anyway.'

I stare hard.

'You took quite a tumble down that slope. Are you hurt?'

I shake my head. My cheeks flush, which surprises me. He grins. 'You might want to have a wash before you go home.'

Embarrassed, I forget about defending myself, and focus on wiping off the eggy mess oozing from my pockets and cleaning my sticky hands in the grass. I feel small and stupid and want to disappear but there's something about him that interests me. He looks like a nomad but he's dressed like a city dweller.

From the earliest age, we are taught not to trust city people; they are another enemy. Meder and Sabira are still unbothered by his presence, which permits me a thin veneer of confidence, although I return my hand to my knife, just in case.

The boy's face softens and he speaks quietly. 'I don't know of any more nests to raid but I could help you harvest a few wild onions. They're just perfect at the moment... if you like?'

He reaches forward as if to grab me. With lightning speed, I pull out the knife, ready to attack. My hand trembles in the air between us.

'Whoa, hold on there.' In his hand is a dead leaf that he's just pulled from my hair braid. He casually drops it to the ground. I thought he was going to kill me but he smells of fresh bread, mint and kindness.

I keep my knife in full view, just so he knows that I can hurt him if I want to. He stands with arms spread wide in front of me, and no visible means of defending himself.

'Don't hurt me. I'm sorry that you have nothing to show for your effort and bravery in collecting those eggs. I would like to help you, if you'll let me. Come on.' He turns and walks away.

I limp after him. His back is to me; in four long steps I could plunge my knife between his shoulder blades and then run. He turns to grin at me again. 'I'm Aibek... and I'm here to steal your sheep.' He winks.

I check the flock and am reassured that they are all there, peacefully grazing.

Is he playing with me? He can't be serious. Surely, he wouldn't be so stupid to tell me if he was about to steal my sheep?

'It would be polite now for you to tell me your name.'

He's either an idiot or this is part of a plan to trick me. Suddenly, my small knife feels inadequate, and I reach around for my bow. It's not there. Then I remember removing it, and the quiver of arrows, before I climbed up to the kite's nest.

'I tell you what, I won't steal them today. Let's find these onions.'

He winks again and walks off. Wild onions would be welcome – but what if he's luring me away so his clan can take my livestock?

'Come on, what are you waiting for?'

I step towards him but I keep tight hold of my knife. He looks at me carefully, slowly. 'You know, you have wonderfully enchanting eyes.'

I feel my cheeks heat up again and I don't know where to look. I've heard my cousins talk about boys: who they like, who they don't like, how they know if a boy likes them, what to do if a boy makes you blush. I wish now that I'd paid more attention, but I never really thought it would ever concern me. Thankfully, Sabira has returned from her kite chase and is circling overhead. *Help me out here, sister. Am I safe?*

Kyuk Kyuk Kyuk
He no harm No nest he
I see him there then here now
Good heart he Warm soul he
Friend you me

What do you mean, you've seen him before? Who is he?

'I don't know your name,' he says. 'I'd like to call you something.'

I look at him directly and shake my head.

'You do have a name, don't you?'

I wave my hand across my mouth.

'Oh, you don't talk?'

I'm pleased that he grasps it quickly.

'Well, I'm sure we can find a way to understand each other.'

This boy continues to confuse me.

'Have you noticed that eagle flying overhead? It won't leave us alone; I think it might be the mother of those eggs you stole. We should be careful.'

He definitely comes from the city! No nomad would mistake a black kite's nest for a golden eagle's. His ignorance helps me relax further and I smile. I point up to Sabira and then jab my finger into my chest.

'That's *your* eagle?'

I nod.

'Can I meet it?'

I collect my leather glove and a treat for Sabira from Meder's saddle bag. *Come, Sabira.* She flies down immediately and does a perfect, gentle landing on my arm to take the rabbit leg lure. Aibek is the one now looking uneasy, while the fear I felt earlier has melted in a new, warm glow of confidence. I stroke Sabira and indicate that Aibek should do the same. Just as he reaches out, tentatively, to touch her long tail feathers, Sabira snaps at his fingers, spreads her wings widely and flaps. He jumps back, his dark hair blown from his face in the gusting wind.

He looks pretty scared of you. That's enough. He's got the message. Sabira folds her wings and I feel her body soften.

'I've seen men with eagles many times in the city, but I've never seen...'

I hold his gaze until he has to look away.

'You know, I thought you were brave when I saw you climb to the nest and then tumble down that rockface without so much as a whimper. But I had no idea. You are impressive.'

A wave of pure pleasure washes over me. He's plucky too; undeterred by Sabira's show of strength, he steps closer and puts his hand out again to stroke her.

'It's all right, I'm a friend and I think you're beautiful.' He talks softly and caresses her from the top of her head down her back to her tail feathers with surprising tenderness. Sabira shuts her eyes in satisfaction.

We all turn at the sound of a horse galloping toward us.

'Oh no, that's my brother. How did he find me?'

I break into a sweat. I have no chance against two of them. Aibek leans toward me and says quietly, 'Take no notice. I don't mean this.'

He takes a big step away from me and Sabira and then, in a loud voice, says, 'Just give me the bird.'

I can't work out what's happening. *Sabira, help me!*

'Come on, girl, hand it over.'

I turn away quickly into the wind, lift my arm sharply upwards and Sabira takes off.

Aibek's brother dismounts and walks over to us. I sense his hostility.

'Hello, Aibek. Long time, no see. What's going on?' he says, looking his brother up and down.

'Ilyas. What are you doing here?' Aibek doesn't look at all pleased.

'Ma sent me to report back on how you're doing.'

'I found this girl out with her sheep and goats. She has an eagle. I thought I might like it.'

'Good idea. A trained eagle would be a very welcome addition to the Balta Clan. So, girl, where's your bird now?' he demands.

I freeze. He's from Balta Clan? This couldn't be worse. They're our arch-enemies and I'll be in serious danger if they find out I'm Snow Leopard Clan.

'She can't speak,' Aibek says.

'How do you know?'

Aibek turns pink. 'I was just talking to her, trying to get her to trust me, so I could take the eagle more easily.'

'Where *is* this eagle then?'

I glance up into the sky at the same time as Aibek. Sabira is nowhere to be seen but I know she is there in the snow-laden clouds, circling effortlessly above us.

Ilyas turns to look at the herd, who are quietly eating, unaware of the danger they are in. 'I suppose we can take a goat. It won't impress the clan, but Ma will be pleased with me if I bring a big, fat, milking nanny home.'

Aibek stares at me and I stare back. Why is he taking my side? It doesn't make any sense.

Meder walks toward me, sensing that I might need him. *No, Meder! Go away, boy!*

If they see our clan mark branded on Meder's rump I don't stand a chance. The snow leopard's footprint, four oval toe pads above a central footpad, is branded onto every one of our sheep, goats, yaks and horses, and decorates every yurt, cart and all the belongings we own. I catch Meder's eye and jerk my chin, the sign for him to turn away.

'Here, let's take this one.' Ilyas grabs one of the best milkers by her horns. Thankfully, she's grown sufficient winter coat to cover her brand mark.

'Aibek, stop being so useless, come and help me rope her.'

Sabira flashes past my left ear like an arrow, her legs extended forward and her long talons stretched wide as she flies straight into Ilyas's chest. She tears through his coat and knocks him to the ground, releases him, rises, turns, attacks again.

'Aibek!' Ilyas shrieks. 'Get my knife! This thing's going to kill me! Quick! It's in my saddle pocket.'

Aibek moves slowly. I realise that he has no intention of

helping his brother defend himself. What is going on between them that he would abandon his own brother in the face of an eagle attack?

'Aibek! In the name of our Great God, Tengri, help me, brother!' Ilyas pleads.

'I'm coming, I'm coming,' Aibek replies.

Sabira persists and Ilyas crouches low to the ground, warding off her talons. Eventually, he is bloodied and humiliated, and she rises in victory. He crawls to his horse, heaves himself onto its back and kicks it into action. As Aibek mounts his own horse, he turns and waves at me.

Come, Sabira.

Sabira tosses and turns on the wind, completely ignoring my request. She swoops down on me in a mock attack, celebrating her strength, almost knocking me over. She rises and wheels in the air again.

When she finally returns to me, she completely misjudges her landing, overshoots my arm and grabs my shoulder. Her talons rip through my chapan and my skin into the bone. There is a terrifying crunch, then a *pop* as my arm dislocates.

I open my mouth as if to yell from the excruciating pain. My voice is a tiny croak. Sabira is circling overhead. I reach tentatively to feel the damage. Although a fierce stabbing sensation prevents me from turning my head, I can clearly see my chapan is shredded and my arm hangs limp.

Meder snorts. There is no way I can mount him. I don't want to move but I can't stay. He nuzzles me, encouraging me. I reach up and tap him just behind his front leg, the signal he knows to kneel, so his belly rests on the ground. I take a deep breath and ease myself onto his back. He rises cautiously, adjusting his weight and position to help me stay balanced. Sabira settles on the baldak and I bury my face in her feathers. *I hope our punishment won't be too severe.*

The snow falls and settles in a lacy, white blanket on the jailoo as we start a slow, careful descent back to camp.

Chapter 11

I arrive in camp bloodied and shivering, like a beaten warrior returning from a lost battle. I am shaking as Meder gently lowers me to the ground outside Atashka's yurt. Sabira flies to her perch where she preens her feathers. No-one notices she has returned without a hood and jesses. Atashka emerges, rubbing his eyes, sleepy from an afternoon nap.

He sizes up the situation immediately, goes back into his yurt and emerges with a tomaga which he quietly slips over Sabira's head without saying a word. I wish he would. I deserve a good telling off. I lower my head, hoping the gesture is sufficient apology. He kneels beside me and I flinch as he touches my arm.

'I'm taking you straight to your mother. This is something she needs to deal with.'

I shake my head. I don't want to give Mother another reason to be cross with me.

'Sorry, I can't fix this. This is a job for her.'

It would be a natural job for most mothers. But not mine. In fact, I've learned not to bother her with anything. Atashka's knees crack as he struggles to stand, but he lifts me carefully.

'What on Mother Earth have you done now? Don't you think I've enough on my hands at the moment?'

I look up into my mother's narrowed eyes, pleading with her to be kind, this once. Atashka lowers me gently and whispers, 'I have no idea what's happened, but I trust you have learned something and won't repeat it.' He feigns an angry face.

'This is all part of what she must learn, Elgiza. Don't be too harsh,' he says as he leaves.

Mother frowns but reaches out and strokes the stray hair from my forehead. I can't let her find out that it was Sabira who did this to me. I reach into my pocket for what's left of the broken eggs and show her the gloopy mess.

'You fell collecting eggs?'

I nod. It's true, sort of, but I daren't look her in the eye.

'Look at the state of you!' She guides me to a sheepskin mattress. 'Here, sit down so I can see you properly.' The sharp, stabbing pain in my shoulder is now accompanied by a dull ache and while Mother is at the back of the yurt, rummaging around in some wooden boxes, I cautiously reach into the gaping tear in my chapan sleeve to feel a large, tender lump under the skin at the top of my arm.

'How many times have I mended your chapan for you this year already? It really is time you learned to sew properly.'

I nudge the blanket over the rips in my trouser knees.

'Well, at least you got yourself back here. I'll make a tea to help with the shock – you're as pale as a corpse.' She shreds little white flowers from the stalks of dried herbs into a pan of water over the fire.

Ermek bursts in.

'I've got the sheep back… again,' she gasps, breathless and smiling, beside herself with excitement.

'Oh, thank you, Ermek. Gulzura's injured. I'm not sure exactly what's happened, but it doesn't look good.'

'I saw her.' Ermek puffs up her body, smiles a perfect goody-goody grin and my stomach lurches. 'I saw her with a boy. I was collecting yarrow on the riverbank and I saw her.'

I scowl, wondering how I hadn't noticed her.

'What?' Mother drops the stalks into the pan and turns abruptly to me. 'What boy?'

I shake my head but my face heats up, betraying me. Ermek is quick to fill the silence.

'I think he frightened her. She fell down the rockface. I expect that's how she hurt herself.' My stomach stops churning as I realise she doesn't know it was Sabira at fault. I shoot her my most vicious look and she leaves with a self-satisfied grin.

'Oh, Gulzura, how many times do I have to tell you? We can't protect you if you wander too far. Who was this boy? What clan is he from?' Mother sits beside me and places two steaming mugs between us. For a brief, hopeful moment I think she just might wrap her arms around me and hold me safe and secure. But she doesn't; she undoes my plaits and hastily combs out the moss and leaves from my tangled hair.

'I know, only too well, what can happen. I never want you to experience what I went through. It wasn't...'

There's a long silence.

Her occasional comments about a previous life, and Father's drunken references to her as his *'booty'*, have often made me wonder if she was bride-napped.

'Did you know Uncle Mirlan's first wife, Sezim, was snatched?'
I didn't.

'She was taken in a raid on Balta Clan while she was milking the mares alone one evening.'

Aibek's clan.

'I remember her arriving. It was late. Mirlan rode into camp with her tied to his saddle by a rope around her wrists. Day and night, she howled like an injured beast. I tried to talk to her, to tell her it would all be all right if she could just accept her situation and make the best of it. But she wouldn't listen. Mirlan tried everything from flirting with her to beating her with a stick.'

I wince as she re-braids my hair too tightly. She stops mid-plait and is silent. I turn to see a single tear brim over the edge of her lower eyelid, roll slowly down the contour of her cheekbone and hang from her jaw. I have never seen Mother cry and I feel guilty. I lean forward to brush the tear from her chin, but she swipes my hand away and wipes it herself.

'Sezim had been with us for six full moons,' Mother continues, 'when she found out Mirlan's child was growing inside her. She stopped eating and became weaker and weaker. I couldn't bear it any longer. I was convinced she'd die.' Mother hesitates. 'This is a secret, Gulzura. Only Bubu knows.'

I nod, appreciating that she is sharing this with me.

'One morning, on the pretext of taking her with me to milk the mares, I gave her a horse and told her to go. I told everyone she had overpowered me. We never saw her again.' Mother looks into her lap. Another tear falls and she wipes her cheek brusquely. I am astonished that Mother had the courage to disregard the clan and deceive them, I have only ever seen her comply. But I am also warmed at how much kindness she showed a stranger.

'Anyway, that's all in the past now, but I don't want anything like that for you, Gulzura. I don't want you to know the pain of being taken by force, against your will, by strangers, to live with people you've never met, never to see your family again. It's a… it's a truly terrifying experience.'

Then why do you allow the men to send me out day after day alone on the jailoo, with nothing but a bow and five arrows?

She stands up abruptly, busying herself with the rug she's felting. She takes a piece of thin charcoal and I rest, watching her draw the outline of elaborate, swirling patterns on the felt pieces which she will later stitch together to make a shyrdak. Ironically, the rug in front of her now is destined to be mine and I will receive it on my wedding day to give me protection, strength, happiness and prosperity. I can't think why she's bothering; she doesn't want me bride-napped, but she's also told me that finding a clan to take me is going to be very hard. I should have had a husband chosen for me by now, but the kalym we would have to pay another clan to take me is too high. You would think my inability to speak would be an asset in a wife, but no, apparently, it's an *unmistakeable indicator* of my stubbornness and defiance. So, I remain un-promised and I pray daily to the gods that we are never rich enough for that to change.

Bubu comes into the yurt.

"Elgiza, I hear Gulzura's hurt. Can I help?"

"I don't know what the child's done this time, but I'm so cross with her. Look at the state of her arm. I've told her over and over about the dangers. Please just take her. I really don't have the time or the patience right now."

Bubu puts her arm around my waist and helps me to her yurt.

The effect of Mother's herbal tea is wearing off and my shoulder is throbbing again as Bubu prods and pokes. Mumbling, she disappears to a dark recess at the back of the yurt, then reappears with a small leather pouch of dried herbs and flowers.

'Rest here, child, while I make a concoction. I can't pull your shoulder straight without giving you something to dull the pain.'

Bubu's skills with healing herbs are legendary. She is respected among all the clans of the tribe. She pounds a vivid, green mash in a small, stone bowl. I brace myself for what's to come.

'It won't hurt if you drink this first.' She takes me in her arms and lifts the infused mixture to my lips. I sink deeper into her soft bosom as she starts to hum. The sound vibrates right through me and my heart slows to match its peaceful rhythm.

'I don't know what went so wrong today, but I can see the damage Sabira has done. Luckily, your chapan will cover the bruising and no-one need know.'

Bubu has always been able to see right through me, as if I were one of those translucent cave geckos. She must know I'll never be a berkutchi. I'm trying my best, but it keeps going wrong. My vision blurs round the edges as thoughts dance inside my head like snowflakes melting before they settle, making no sense. I don't want an eagle for a sister anyway; I want a proper sister, who can hug me, someone to play and laugh with. I'm not good enough. Maybe the gods will take Sabira back. My eyes prickle and then tears well up and fall down my hot cheeks. The thought of losing my eagle sister makes a panic rise from the pit of my stomach. Bubu hugs me closer and kisses the top of my head.

'Gulzura, listen carefully. The gods were clear when they spoke. You and your eagle sister are bound together. I don't know when and I don't know how, but I do know the future of our tribe depends on you, and she has been sent to guide and protect you.'

She sounds like she's talking in a cave.

'Sabira is the part of you that you lost as a baby. She completes you.'

Sweat prickles my forehead, my vision narrows to a pinprick and I close my eyes.

Kyuk Kyuk Kyuk
Earth God Sky God made we

Bound tight two Bird girls us Eagle twins
Flex claws feet
Spread wings arms
Feel strength rise

Heels up, toes down, push off, arms out wide, fingertips spread.
Then rapid ascent as I crash into a strong updraught. I am flying.
Soaring high and free with a wind jostling and bumping me like a
leaf swept along on a river in full spate. We are together, my sister
and I, we are flying side by side, speaking the language of eagles.

Flick wing Twist self Drop tail
Air-dive Sky-swoop
Head still Tail flick Check Look down

Land shifts
Leaf rock sand lake merge and part
Streams rip red earth
Ridge-high black scree crease and fold
Snow blue meets stone

I see me
Bird shape in sky lake
Then wind-whipped
Gone

We fly the seam that links the gods to men

Below me, I see three brown hares chasing each other in an
elaborate dance that finishes with them in such a tight circle it's
hard to tell where one ends and another begins. I am filled with

a sensation of unlimited power and I fly higher and faster. Sabira joins me and our wing tips brush. Another movement on the ground catches my eye. A rabbit. It is a very long way off, but I want to catch it and I want to kill it. I pull my wings in tightly to my side and stoop toward the ground. There is no cover for my prey, not a single tree, its only hope is to get back down into its tunnel. But this rabbit, contentedly nibbling chamomile flowers, doesn't know what is coming. Instinctively, I turn, so the sun is behind me and I swoop so low that the grass brushes my chest. I push my legs forward, stretch out my talons and land with a thump on the animal's back. Right at that moment, I see a fox. He is a hesitation too late and I take the prize from under his nose. My talons grip; the tips easily pierce fur and flesh, crushing tiny bones as I ratchet them ever tighter. Sabira is on the fox in a beat, one foot on his muzzle to hold his mouth tightly shut, the other clamped onto the scruff of his neck. The fox twists, trying to shake my sister off but it knows it's lost. I spread my wings, mantling my catch, and the rabbit shivers a final twitch.

I surface long enough to realise I have been dreaming, but fall straight back to sleep. A lone, grey wolf circles a city's walls, hungry and mean. The city is on fire. The screams of its people rise from every direction. I am caged and cannot help them. The wolf bares his fangs and howls. I claw frantically at the metal bars as the fire gets closer. I start to choke and cough as thick smoke fills my cage.

I wake gasping. The smoke from Bubu's fire is blowing directly into my face.

Chapter 12

Days on the jailoo are running out fast. In two days we'll be heading for our winter home on the city outskirts. Flocks of bar-headed geese honk goodbye, flying in formation. As I walk Meder, his hooves crunching the frosty ground, I imagine how exciting it would be to fly with them to new places. The livestock, too, sense the time here is limited, and wander further in search of grazing. I roam with them until I recall Mother's warning and quickly try to drive them closer to camp.

The animals scatter, unwilling to be corralled. We need to get back; I am vulnerable here. Then I hear a high-pitched whistle, and twenty of our sheep come running toward me, followed by Aibek, weaving back and forth on his horse, rounding up my herd. *Is he going to take them? Lord Tengri, protect me.*

'Good morning. I saw your herd scatter to the four winds and thought you might need a hand. I can go, if you want?'

I put on the sternest face I can summon because, yes, I want him to go.

'Or shall I help you round up the rest?' He's smiling.

I know perfectly well how to round up my own livestock, but they're all agitated now and I'm going to struggle to do it alone in a hurry. I check for Sabira, certain she will come immediately if there's any threat. I nod. Aibek and I form a pincer movement and the herd is quickly reunited as one flock. He dismounts. I gather in Meder's reins, heels ready to kick him into a gallop.

'I've been hoping I would see you again after the incident with my brother.'

I scan the area to see if Ilyas is nearby.

'Oh, don't worry. He wouldn't dare come out here again after the way your eagle scared him off.' He laughs.

He reaches into his pocket and pulls out two apples.

'Would you like one?'

I hesitate, wondering if this might be a trick.

'I found a tree a while ago, picked as many as I could and stored them in my cave. You're welcome...'

They look delicious and I am hungry. I dismount and choose one and he smiles so I put it back and choose the other, then indicate that he should eat the one I've left. He takes a bite and I'm reassured there's no trickery. He sits down, and I sit just close enough to study him but far enough that I could outrun him if he lunges for me.

'I'm no threat to you.'

I keep my face expressionless.

'I've seen the Snow Leopard banner flying over your camp and the sign is branded on your horse's rump, so it wasn't exactly difficult to work it out. But, I am no longer with my clan, and I could do with some company now and again.' He gives his apple core to Meder.

'I have watched you this summer, a girl out here all alone every day. I suppose, at least, you've got your eagle.' He glances up at Sabira, who is circling overhead. 'With her guarding you, I'm sure you'll be fine.'

His words kindle a warm glow inside me. I move closer to sit on a moss-covered rock, almost within arm's reach of him.

'It's not safe out here. Have you heard the news of the Mongol emissary?'

I shake my head. I have no idea what he's talking about.

'There are rumours that a massive army is assembling in the east, with a cruel and blood-thirsty leader. He sent an emissary, a man called Toq, to our Gurkhan Kuchulyg to negotiate for peaceful trade. Our great Gurkhan' – he sneers – 'rejected the offer. Not only that, he also had the emissary's guards beheaded and Toq's beard and head shaved clean as a baby's bottom!'

I put my hand to my mouth.

'The poor boy had to return to his Khan defeated and humiliated.' He gives a laugh and I laugh too, although I'm shocked at such shameful treatment of a guest.

'Anyway, the point is that you should be very careful. If what I hear is to be believed, that army is on its way, and they're savages.'

I try to imagine what I would I do. Despite my skill with a bow and arrow, I doubt I would come out very well.

'You see that mountain, the one that looks like the head of a de-horned yak?' He points. 'That's where my cave is. I'll be back next spring. Come and see me there.' He gestures with open arms.

'In the meantime, take this, so you don't forget me.' He hands me a small, black stone attached to a leather thong. I turn it over to see an engraving on its perfectly flat, shiny surface.

'It's a snow leopard entwined around a Balta axe. I did it. I had the idea after we last met. I don't want our clans to fight.'

He has a kind heart, but no clue how much hatred there is in Snow Leopard Clan toward Balta. I hold the stone briefly to my heart and then slip it over my head, tucking it inside my shirt.

As we leave, a double rainbow appears in the valley below us. Two perfect arcs straddle the shores of our great lake like a bridge: an auspicious sign from the gods.

Chapter 13

Winter comes with snow that transforms the land. The river freezes; the yurts tremble in the biting winds. Our camp, outside the city walls, is cramped and muddy, and we struggle to survive. City people don't want us here. Even when we are trading with them, we are treated with dislike and suspicion, and I am happy for once to obey father's ruling not to enter the city walls.

Despite Atashka's warning that Sabira is too young to start training on fox, I am impatient. I deliberately irritate everyone around camp so they beg Father to let me ride out with her. Everyone knows the value of a red fox pelt and now is the perfect time to hunt, while they're visible against the snow.

Fox flash bright on white
Tuck wings close Dive sharp steep
Fox snarl snap bite
Screech Keee Keee

The loss of a talon puts a stop to all hunting for the rest of winter. I am trapped in the camp, unable to escape constant criticism. Atashka reassures me again that she will learn, that she simply got over-confident, that it's nothing to worry about. I look at her deformed foot and feel guilt for putting her in that situation, for expecting too much of her, for being selfish. Each night, I think of Aibek and clasp the little engraved stone tight in my palm.

In spring, we return to the jailoo. New growth is everywhere: the grass, the flowers, the shrubs; even on my body. Hair appears, soft and fuzzy, in my armpits and where my legs meet; my nipples are tender.

Despite my status as a berkutchi, I remain the lowliest member of the family. I am required to keep up an endless supply of dung-cakes – scooping up the piles of yak, horse and cow pats, mixing them with a little water and dried grass, moulding them into discs and putting them in rows for the sun and wind to dry, ready to burn. It's a hateful chore. As soon as I have replenished the dung-cake pile, I release the sheep and goats from their overnight pens and drive them out onto the jailoo. Sabira follows overhead, ensuring I am well away from prying eyes before I meet Aibek. He spent winter in the city. We were so close to each other, separated only by the ramparts. I bet he had an easier time than I did.

We share the food I secrete in my chapan, and as spring moves into summer, we spend the time riding and play-fighting, and he tells me stories. He teaches me hand-to-hand sword skills and wrestling, on horseback and on the ground. He takes great care not to injure me, but I still have to find ways to hide the scratches and bruises. I teach him how to fire a bow and arrow at a gallop. He makes me a big pile of arrows. We laugh; we dream of adventure together, and I have never been happier.

Boy kind heart

Atashka keeps an eye on Sabira and me, offering tips and advice whenever he feels the need. I am quite certain he knows about Aibek and in my heart I thank him daily for his silence.

The harvests are poor, and we are back in the shadow of the city even before winter takes a hold. This year, Sabira proves invaluable in providing regular supplies of meat. Finally, we come home with a red fox.

Hunt catch kill
Soar scan seek Bleak white land
Prey-sharp sight Gods with us
Shock sharp from blue up-wind
Dive from sun
Strike
Hit
Thrill

Hold fast fox
Hook deep hot flesh pierce heart
Wild life fight
Blood glut Eyes glaze Breath stops

We share the skill
One day you too will kill

When we return at last to the jailoo, there are big changes. My breasts swell, my moonblood comes and I am, at sixteen summers old, a woman. Bubu celebrates and shows me how to make a tea to ease my cramps, but my body hurts and I feel changed and I don't like it. The milking mares notice that I smell different, Sabira notices when I cry unexpectedly and Aibek, too, notices a new awkwardness in me.

Itch twitch
Pluck down
New plumes grow sleek dark
Strong for fly high wide far
Girl kiss stroke soft sing
Thrum thrum thrum my bones
I rest in warm neck-curve
Heart kind strong
Gods know Gods warn War comes

The clan does not notice. All anyone can talk about is that war is coming.

Chapter 14

While everyone prepares for the spring celebrations, I am out with the herd. The light rain has turned to hail. Great pea-sized drops of ice sting my skin and cold water drips down the back of my neck. I'm about to push Meder on up the hill toward the rocky outcrop where I hope to find Aibek warm and snug in his cave.

One of the ewes delays me. She's in labour, bleating pathetically, straining with every contraction. She's exhausted, so weak she can't push out her lamb. It's too early. It won't survive. 'There, there...' I whisper and ease my hand, then arm, slowly and carefully inside her, up to my armpit, to find out what the problem is. I feel immediately that the lamb has its legs bent in the wrong direction. I shift my weight and wedge my feet against a rock, then I grip the lamb's slippery limbs and, with all the strength I have, I pull. It slides forward and, a couple of contractions later, it's out. The mother turns to lick her newborn but the tiny creature is cold and lifeless. I pick it up by its back legs and rub hard up and down its limp body, blowing little puffs of air into its mouth, and then I feel a little wriggle. I lay the lamb down and rub again, getting more warmth into it. Luckily, this mother is desperate to bond and she joins in, licking her baby's face over and over, as the rain beats down. The lamb revives and lifts itself up to wobble on four long legs, right next to its mother's full udder. Instinctively, it nuzzles and finds a teat to latch on to.

Once it's safe, Meder and I press on. Outside Aibek's cave, I hear the sharp crack of a rock fall, then another, and my heart beats hard and fast. It could be Aibek; it could be a wolf or a bear or a snow leopard. Just as I turn Meder away, I hear singing from the cave.

'Hello there, Eagle-Girl!' Aibek emerges. 'Quick, come in and dry off.' He hugs me and pulls me inside. This is the first time I've been into his cave, and as I become accustomed to the dark, I make out strange markings on the smooth walls. I gaze around at the incredible scene that unfolds: deer, horses, goats, hunting scenes, figures of men with bows and arrows, stars and moons, groups of people in a circle – all carved into the walls from ceiling to floor. My fingertips trace the tiny indentations chipped out of the clammy rock.

'Astonishing, isn't it?' Aibek says.

I stare up and down the rock walls.

'Our ancestors, did this... a very, very, very long time ago.'

Meder has wandered into the cave to stay dry and nudges up beside me. I take the blanket off his back, place it on the damp rocks and sit on it.

'Can I share?' Aibek says.

I shuffle over to give him some space. He lies back and I lie back too, enjoying the warm feeling that comes when our arms occasionally touch as I turn this way and that, trying to take in the vast panorama of people and animals that spread across the cave.

'Do you see that man, over there, with the spiky hair?'

I look where he is pointing and see a stick figure with a halo of spikes coming out of his head.

'Well, that's Ilyas when he returned to camp after he met your eagle.'

I giggle as Aibek prods my leg.

'Would you like to know why I'm living here?'

I turn to look at him.

'My father has always made it very clear to me, for as long as I can remember, that I didn't belong in the clan. You see, I'm not my father's son.' He hesitates and starts to pick at a hole in the sole of his leather boot. 'My ma was taken by your clan when she was young, but she managed to make her way back to my father. She was welcomed back, but then he found out she was with child.'

Thoughts whirl around in my head. *Could Aibek's mother be Uncle Mirlan's first wife? If she is...* everything suddenly clicks into place and it's there, right in front of me: *Aibek is my cousin.* I'm glad I can't talk because I wouldn't know what to say right now. I stare at him and he continues.

'He vowed to kill the baby as soon as it was born but Ma pleaded and begged and finally persuaded him to keep me. He agreed on condition that it – that I – would be banished on reaching manhood. I did everything I could to prove myself worthy of a place within the clan. I did terrible things, things that I later regretted, things that the gods punished me for.

'Ma feels guilty that I've been condemned to a life as an outcast. She promised she'd send Ilyas with food parcels every week, but he doesn't come anywhere near that often. I think he just eats it all himself. He has no interest in looking after me. If I survive, I could challenge him as clan leader.'

I reach for the skin of water tied to my belt and take a gulp. *Aibek is family.*

'Ma prepared me as best she could, ensuring I learned

everything I would need to survive alone. I spent my first summer in exile in this cave. And then, when winter came, I moved to the city, to Balasagun. I lived with a group of orphans who, in return for a few pelts, took me in and taught me everything I need to know about surviving in the city. I go there each winter now.'

He continues to talk but I hear nothing more. I just stare. He's my enemy – I've known that for two years – but he's also my family. Should I kill him or embrace him? I feel Sabira nearby. *What do I do now? Can I trust him?*

Kyuk Kyuk Kyuk
Boy kind heart
He not see clan foe   He see you
Kyuk
Hold you in his heart nest

Meder shakes his head and stamps his hooves in alarm. I sit up, immediately on guard, as he turns and shoots out at full speed. The sound of his hooves disappearing downhill is replaced by a deep growl that resonates menacingly around the cave. I look at Aibek who is stiff-backed and alert. My skin goes cold and my breath shortens: there is only one creature I know who makes that sound... a wolf.

Aibek jumps to his feet, and his eyes widen as he comes to the same conclusion. He reaches round slowly for the bow and arrow on his back. The growling gets closer. I smell the animal's doggy wet fur and, clutching my amulet, I send a quick thank you to the gods that this is a single wolf and not a pack. I heard once about a nomad clan that tamed wolves as pets, but I know for certain that what I can hear now is no pet.

It stalks closer and I can see its head. Upright pointy ears;

rusty coloured fur; a copper muzzle with shiny black nose. But it is its mouth that causes the hairs on the back of my neck to rise in alarm: teeth bared, lips curled back revealing black skin, shiny with saliva, a pink tongue and a ragged collection of sharp, yellowing teeth. The wolf creeps further into the cave, revealing its gaunt, hungry body. Ten pink nipples protrude from her belly. She will undoubtedly be fearless in her effort to provide for her offspring.

Aibek raises his bow. 'I can't kill her; she's got pups that need her. I'll just warn her off.'

His arrow skims the wolf's back. She flinches and snarls, taking another step toward us, then lowering her body and folding her back legs under her, preparing the burst of power needed for an attack. Aibek draws back his bow quickly on a second arrow; he has no choice now but to aim to kill.

Rain slants warm air

See kits play
Scoop skim squeak squeak scare
Kyuk Kyuk Quick!
Girl cry fright

Kyuk Kyuk Kyuk
Slice air tilt tail tear wind

She deep in cave

Fly in sharp strong twist turn
Flex
Smack wolf head hard

Wolf yelp yelp Jaws snap snap
Miss Bite air
Grip hold Claw crush
Pierce fur Find flesh Dig deep
Lift

Fly back quick
Sharp whip smart flash gold
Grasp wolf jaw

Wolf want free I grip grip

Want kill want end wolf
Girl kind heart call no
I yield
Wolf run run Girl boy safe

Chapter 15

Twenty-two camels, attached to each other with a rope from a wooden peg in the soft flaps of their nostrils, move like a snake over the ridge and down toward our lakeside camp. Laden with exotic cargo from distant lands, they are accompanied by four equally exotic, pale-skinned men with delicate features. These traders buy and sell a vast range of luxuries and necessities along a route that starts far in the east and ends even further in the west. Silks, spices, jewels, furs, metals, textiles, weapons, porcelain, perfumes, wine, tea, medicines, musical instruments... They come to us for the horses, bred from the heavenly stallions of the Fergana Valley, for these horses are larger, stronger and have greater stamina than any other.

Chores increase when the traders arrive, but the change in routine and the excitement of strangers among us makes everyone happy. The smaller boys gather to watch and learn as the sheep are slaughtered and butchered, and the women and girls chop, slice and stir the lamb, onions and noodles in a huge pot over the fire to create beshbarmak.

Mares' milk is poured into a goatskin that has been smoked over a juniper fire, and the old men take turns to shake the bag, so it ferments into kumiss, which has the power to make grown men groggy and foolish.

As the sun sets, Father summons the clan to dinner. He paces up and down; it's been a long while since the traders last visited and the women have been complaining to him that we are short of many basic essentials. We need rice, tea, herbs, spices and medicines and everyone knows he's not traded well in the past. The merchants are shrewd, highly skilled in the art of negotiation, and they know that in massaging his swaggering ego, they end up with a deal very much in their favour.

He's already being loud but thankfully the traders are too polite, or too hungry, to notice as they settle down to eat. After a ritual welcome involving a prayer to the gods and much kumiss, Bubu declares we may eat.

My father serves the halved, roasted sheep heads and the tastiest pieces of sheep's tail fat to our special guests and everyone else tucks into the beshbarmak.

In every way, the traders are as different from our clansmen as bees are from flowers. The traders sit quietly, talking in hushed tones, dressed in exquisite blue and red embroidered silks, their pale skin framed by neatly plaited hair, oiled smooth. Our clansmen are rough and strong, with wild hair and untamed beards, wearing animal skins, talking loudly of their battle scars and the next fight. And yet, strangely, like bees and flowers, they are wholly dependent on each other. The traders' fragile looks and calculated silences are a clever strategy. Our clansmen think them weak. And this gives them power. There is no doubt they will get exactly what they want at exactly the price they want to pay.

We all reach inside the pot with our right hands to grab the meat, bones and noodles, while the traders each use two thin wooden sticks they've brought with them. Even though I've seen this before, I can't help staring. *They have perfectly good hands – why make it so difficult?*

For a while, all I can hear is the sound of cooked meat being sucked from bones. Then Usen says, 'There are rumours circulating of a big army sweeping west.'

Bao Li exchanges a glance with his fellow traders. Usen should have let the men finish eating first. He smiles apologetically, but Bao Li's gaze sweeps the room to make sure he has everyone's attention. He knows that he's not just here to trade; there is an expectation that in return for our hospitality, he will share news and gossip.

'The rumours are true,' he says. 'A huge force is coming, and you would be wise to sit back and let it. It's bigger than anything you will have ever encountered before.'

The room goes silent. Meat juices drip from hands as everyone hangs on the trader's every word.

'I have heard accounts of their tactics. They are ruthless. They destroy anyone – man, beast, woman, child, nomad and city dweller alike – that opposes them.'

'Pah, we'll make them regret it if they dare to venture this way,' my father blusters. Everyone ignores him.

'The story is extraordinary,' Bao Li continues. 'A young man from the steppe – far, far from here – was abandoned by his tribe as a child, left to die along with his mother and brothers. Somehow, he survived and has now managed to unite hundreds of tribes, and created an army larger and more powerful than anything we've ever seen or heard of. They call him Genghis. Genghis Khan. The speed at which he has conquered vast swathes of land to the east is staggering, and now he's turning his attention to the west.'

I tremble. Atashka, sitting close beside me, whispers, 'We'll be safe,' but I don't believe him.

Uncle Mirlan asks, 'What can we expect? How do we prepare?'

'My strong advice to you is: don't even think about fighting him – you cannot win against Genghis Khan. As I said, he has a reputation for destroying almost everything and everyone in his path, killing, looting and burning entire cities. He has evil cunning and the devil on his side. You will be annihilated if you so much as lift a finger against him.'

The clan sits in silence, the remains of the meal congealing in the pot. Everyone looks to my father, hoping, just this once, for strong guidance and reassurance.

He shrugs. 'We only have your word on this. I'm sure it can't all be that bad. Let's just wait and see. We've been fed stories like this in the past and they've come to nothing.'

Bao Li shakes his head and sighs. 'What you don't seem to understand, Jyral –'

My father isn't listening. 'Anyway, we're strong, we don't cower... we're the greatest clan, we always fight our way out of trouble... we can resist this. What would our ancestors think if we surrender before we've even tried to defend ourselves? Where's the honour in that, eh?'

Bubu nudges Usen. He kneels up and talks loudly enough to drown out Father's rant. 'But, Father, this story corroborates everything I've been hearing in the city. Gurkhan Kuchulyg sent Genghis Khan's envoy packing, and has been gathering a force to fight ever since. Can you imagine how outraged the Khan would have been when his emissary returned shaved bald, and, I've heard, with his tongue cut out? We do not want to be involved in that fight. We should make preparations for an honourable surrender as soon as they appear. That way, we can save ourselves.'

'You spend far too much time in that pit of evil,' Father responds angrily. 'Don't you have anything better to do than gossip like a woman with your city friends? You're useless. You're never here to help, and now you're willing to hand the tribe over to this invader without so much as a thought for our ancestors and everything they've fought for. Get out of my sight, boy.'

Bao Li has had enough. 'I'm tired now. Let's talk more tomorrow. That is, if you wish. But I will say one last thing on this subject tonight: You are facing a period of great upheaval. Everything is about to change.'

Chapter 16

Mother raises her head from under the mare she's milking. 'Gulzura, take the camels for a drink while the traders rest.'

I obey at once. I love the camels. Most of them are shy and sensitive, although there's always the odd, aggressive one that will spit a foul-smelling, green liquid-paste directly at you if you dare to go near. The traders love them dearly and often discuss at great length their beauty and whether one camel has more attractive features than another. They also give them names which amuses everyone in the clan, although I think it makes perfect sense. I lead the camels in a long line to the lake edge and sit with them while they refuse to drink until the water has warmed up. Finally, they suck up enough water to last them the rest of the day.

Sabira watches carefully, flying lower and lower on each circuit, to get a look at these strange beasts.

With the camels hobbled safely in their compound, I sneak into the main yurt, where the traders are busily unpacking their wares, and crouch down in the shadows beside a large pile of silk bolts. I watch, hoping I won't be sent out, as they carefully unpack the intricately carved camphor-wood chests and spread a cornucopia of delights onto the rugs.

The traders know that it is the silk that attracts everyone's attention, even if we can't afford it. It is, they say, the main currency for buying anything and everything from Xi'an, far to the east, to Constantinople, far to the west. It is admired across forests, deserts, mountains, boundaries, tribes and civilisations I struggle to imagine.

The youngest trader catches my eye and smiles. He pulls out a leather pouch hanging from a cord around his neck, undoes the tie and pours out the treasures he's been keeping safely close to his body. There are pearls with a milk-white lustre, and pieces of orange and red coral that look like tiny trees carved with intricate patterns. The traders tell stories of a great sea where men hold their breath to dive deep under the water to harvest these riches. Our clan can't possibly afford any of these and I don't touch them, scared my rough fingers will damage their delicate perfection. Instead, I turn to look at the luxurious bolts of silk – blue, green, red and black – piled high. At first, I did not believe this beautiful cloth could be made by tiny worms but I've heard the story so often now, I know it must be true.

I spit into my palms and wipe them down the front of my chapan, checking for any green slime left from feeding the camels. I consider them clean enough and reach out tentatively. The smooth, cool fabric conjures up a life far removed from mine on the jailoo.

'Gulzura, what are you doing in here? Get out – we have business to do,' Nurbek snaps.

'There's dung to be collected. Stop idling about and get onto it,' Alik joins in, looking nervously at Nurbek.

I let my fingers linger a moment longer, stroking the lustrous fabric, reluctant to leave. 'Gulzura! Now!' they shout in unison.

I get up and stomp out, passing Father and various other men who are entering to start the trade negotiations. Back in the main yurt I refill all the little clay burners with yak fat. Atashka arrives, brandishing a piece of soft leather.

'Gulzura, come here, child. I want to show you this.' He beckons me to sit beside him as he lays the cloth on the floor and brushes out the folds.

'It's a map!' He's beaming from ear to ear. I have no idea what this is. I only see black, meaningless scratchings on the surface of the leather.

'Look – it shows where things are on the land, so the traders can find us even if they've never been before. This is us here.' He points to a little circle. 'And this is Balta Clan.' He points to an identical circle just a finger's width away. How can they be so close to us?

'And these pointy marks, they're the mountains between us.' He's so excited. 'Rivers look like roots running over everything, from mountain glaciers down to the lake. It helps make sense of everything around us.'

I like the map and spend a large part of the afternoon crouched on my haunches at the lake edge, scratching marks in the soft mud with a stick. I try to make lines and shapes to represent what I can see around me and what I know is beyond what I can see, and quickly discover it is much harder than I thought. But, by the end of the day, I am pleased with the patterns that have hardened in the mud, showing our camp, the mountain where I found Sabira, the place where I first met Aibek, and the great summer pastures of the jailoo where Meder likes to gallop.

Much depends on tonight's feast; any mistakes can lead to higher prices or, at worst, no trade at all. We have prepared olovo: sheep's lungs marinated in mares' milk, spices, salt and oil, then cooked with potatoes and onions. It's a complicated dish, where the mixture is spread onto a slab of pastry, rolled and then steamed. Tonight, it is the centrepiece to honour our guests.

The sound of slurping and the occasional belch signals everyone's enjoyment. Our men drink the kumiss, not noticing that the traders drink only water.

'So, *how* do we become his ally?' Usen won't let the topic of last night's conversation go.

Bao Li smiles. 'The Great Khan will send a messenger one day, out of the blue. You will be told how much tax you must pay – as a small tribe with little of great value, the tribute will not be a burden. One in ten sheep over one hundred? Maybe a few more. Maybe a few less.'

'Ha, little of great value! You insult us.' My father speaks out. He's already slurring his words.

'I'm sorry, I had no intention...' Bao Li bows down in deference, not wanting to spoil the negotiations which are, according to the gossip, going very much in his favour. 'Let me explain. The Great Khan is not really much interested in the physical assets your clan possesses. What he wants from you is allegiance. If you give him this, you will be recognised and rewarded with a life of peace and security. Believe me, he's tough but fair. Should you choose to resist, there is absolutely no doubt, as I said last night, that you will all die.'

'He's nothing but a savage barbarian. We've seen off his like before and we can do it again,' Father shouts.

Bao Li glances around, clearly sensing the growing unease. His brow furrows.

'There's something you should know about Genghis Khan. His brutality is not the full story. One of his clever tactics is to encourage the spread of rumours. You might be surprised to know he always prefers to frighten his enemies into surrender, so he doesn't actually have to fight them. If everyone believes he's unbeatable, then everyone simply capitulates. This has proved hugely successful.'

'So, he's a coward! Ha! And we're supposed to respect him?' Uncle Mirlan scoffs.

'Yes,' Bao Li says emphatically, looking straight at Mirlan then turning to Father. 'The Great Khan is a genius, a superb military leader, a man of great, original and creative thought. While on the one hand, cities that arrogantly thought themselves impregnable have been razed by his army, on the other hand, poor nomads, no different from any one of your clan, have risen to become Generals in his army. He rewards those who are skilled, loyal and faithful. He has no time for the rich and powerful.'

Father huffs and belches.

Usen speaks out. 'Well, I think I have more respect for this Mongol than I do for our so-called leader, Gurkhan Kuchulyg. He is a cruel oppressor who usurped the legitimate ruler and has no thought for anyone beyond himself. How could it be worse?'

Father stands up unsteadily, knocking his drink over. 'That's dangerous talk, boy. He's our leader and we must show him our loyalty.'

'Why? What has he ever done to deserve it? There's much unrest in the city; people talk of rising up against him. Maybe this is the right time to banish the tyrant. We deserve better.'

There is silence. Everyone knows that Usen is right but not one of them has the courage to defend him in this arena. Usen is undaunted. 'So, what's the Mongol Khan like, then? Have you met him?'

'Ha! No, I've never met him, but I know people who have,' Bao Li continues. 'You must understand, it's true that he's killed many, many people, often in ways that are too horrific for me to speak of. But, quite remarkably, he's brought peace in his wake. Hundreds of tribes, spread across the steppe, have stopped fighting and raiding each other. He's introduced laws that ensure equality for everyone, no matter your kinship or status. You earn his respect through deeds rather than rank or birthright.'

'What about religion?' Usen asks. 'Many of my fr... Many of the Muslims in Balasagun have had their mosques destroyed by Kuchulyg. They've been rounded up and tortured and now they practise, in fear of their lives, in secret, in each other's houses.'

'The Great Khan really doesn't care who you worship, just as long as you pay your taxes to him. Oh, and he has an explicit edict banning the use of torture.'

I want to stay and hear more about this contradictory leader – good and bad, kind and brutal, fair and ruthless – but it's getting dark and the camels won't feed themselves.

I find my favourite, a young, white male called BaiBo, settling down so close to the traders' yurt that he is in danger of pulling the entire tent down as he starts to roll inward on it. I rush over to grab his halter and pull him up. As he rises with a loud grunt, a saddle bag falls out onto the grass from under the ground flap of the yurt. A strange drawing carved into the underside of the leather opening catches my eye. Another map? It is a circle, and in the circle are three hares chasing each other. It reminds me of something, but I can't think what. I pull the bag out to take a closer look.

'Can I help you with anything?'

I jump back. The trader who had kindly shown me the deep-sea treasures is approaching rapidly. I drop the bag, hoping that, somehow, he hasn't seen me holding it. Turning pink with embarrassment, I lower my face and then raise my eyes with as contrite a look as I can muster. His face softens. He lifts the bag from the wet grass where I dropped it and wipes it dry on his sleeve.

'Do you know what this is?' he says.

I shake my head.

'These are hares. Do you see that there are three of them?'

Does he think I'm completely stupid?

'Well, now, how many ears are there?'

He really does think I'm stupid. I hold up six fingers.

'You haven't actually looked, have you?' he chides me, but with a kindly smile. Then I look closely and see that there are just three ears shared between the three hares – each has two ears, but one of those ears is shared with the hare next to it, so there are only three ears in total. I smile and my shoulders shake in silent laughter as I realise it's a clever joke.

'Well, it would be funny if it weren't in fact a serious symbol. It's...' He hesitates, looking around to see if anyone can hear. 'There are a great many people who believe life under Genghis Khan would be preferable.' He stops and bites his lower lip. 'I'm not sure I should...'

One of the advantages – although sometimes it's a disadvantage – of being mute is that people tell me things, safe in the knowledge that I won't, I can't, tell anyone else. So, I look interested and wait. It's often difficult for a speaking person not to fill the silence.

He continues, 'I like you, Gulzura. I've watched you and your eagle and there's something about you, something I can't really put my finger on. You impress me. If you've found this, the gods must want you to know that this symbol, these hares chasing each other, is a sign you can trust and, wherever you see it, you can ask for help.'

In a flash, it comes to me. I remember where I've seen the

hares before. They appeared in the dream I had when Bubu was healing my shoulder. The wonderful power and confidence I had felt then, when the three hares had looked up at me as I was flying overhead, washes over me once again, with an excitement that sends a thrilling shiver from my head to my toes. I commit the symbol to memory.

Chapter 17

'I *suppose* she can come with us.' Nurbek nods in my direction. 'That eagle of hers might prove useful in picking up a few of the runaways.'

'Unless we just take the eagle and leave her behind?' Alik suggests.

'I don't want the bird without her. I don't want to be responsible for it if it gets out of control,' Nurbek argues.

'Well, *I* don't want to be responsible for *her*,' Alik says. Just at that moment, Atashka walks in and assesses the situation in the space of a breath. 'I will take responsibility for Gulzura and Sabira. You have no need to trouble yourselves with them.'

They exchange glances of relief. 'Gulzura, you can only come if you stay close to Atashka. Is that clear?'

I nod, hardly daring to meet Nurbek's eye in case he changes his mind. My heart is racing; I am going to the great hunt. Our leader, Gurkhan Kuchulyg, has summoned all the clans of the Kara Khitai tribe for a game hunt that will double as a practice for war; his aim is to turn us into battle-ready warriors.

It's still dark as we set off. Heads down, we ride into a wall of driving rain which eases as dawn breaks pink and gold on the horizon. I am soaked to the skin, hungry and shivering, as we arrive at the meeting ground. I release Sabira to get her own breakfast, so she's not tempted to take any game meant for the hunt.

'You'd better get some food inside you too, before it all kicks off.' Atashka offers me some dried deer meat from the roll pack tied behind his saddle. I take a couple of strips, even though my stomach is in knots, and start to chew as I look around. The others have all gone off to greet and pay their respects to allied clans. I turn to Atashka, hoping for an explanation as to who is who and what is going on.

'You see right up there?' Atashka points with his riding whip to a plateau above the plain.

'He's there – do you see him? – in the middle, skulking like the coward he is under that ridiculous canopy.'

The Gurkhan Kuchulyg is sheltered under a bright-yellow, silk-tasselled umbrella, held up at its four corners by miserably damp servants. Sitting astride a white stallion, with a saker falcon on his forearm and a couple of lean dogs either side, he looks out over the wide plain below him at the vast gathering of his tribespeople who have assembled on his command.

'Imposter…' Atashka spits into the dirt. I'm surprised at the vehemence in his voice and look around to make sure no one can hear his treachery. 'Do you know why he's so unpopular?'

I do, he's told me more than once before, but I look interested as I know how much he loves to tell this story.

'He's not one of us. He was a Naiman, an outsider, who usurped our last great Gurkhan – had him, his family and entire household killed. Then he imposed his beliefs on everyone, destroying everything we stood for. He's brutal, a tyrant, and I advise you keep your head down and stay well out of his way.'

I nod as if I mean to do as he says but actually, I'd like to get close up to the Gurkhan, just to see what a tyrant is really like.

'There's a rumour, you know,' he adds, 'that there's a girl in the city who is the last Gurkhan's daughter. I'm sure Kuchulyg would have had her eliminated by now if it were true.'

A girl? What kind of man sees a girl as a threat?

Atashka continues, 'Just for today, we'll put aside our arguments and disputes with our enemy clans and we'll unite to show our Gurkhan that we have all the skills he needs for a successful hunt, and for a big war.' He pauses. 'And then we can resume our quarrelling later.' He winks at me.

I look around, trying to take it all in. I have never seen the whole tribe gathered in one place before and I can't decide if I'm trembling with excitement at the party atmosphere or with fear at the noise and unpredictability of the vast crowd. Clans congregate under their banners which billow in the strong breeze on high poles. I see Wolf, Hare, Falcon and then I see the axe symbol: Balta Clan. My heart jumps.

I start to feel light-headed and lean down to rest my head on Meder's neck. He's calm and still, only his ears flick around, picking out sounds that interest him from the cacophony: loud greetings between friends and families; dogs barking and yapping; hooded eagles squawking on the arms of the berkutchi who are bragging about their latest catches; young swaggerers proclaiming loudly how bountiful this hunt will be and how they will personally catch boar, deer, hare, red fox and even a bear.

'Hello, Eagle-Girl.' Aibek's voice cuts through the din. I couldn't be more pleased to see him, although he's hiding his face under a huge, floppy hood. I grin broadly and his horse gives me a welcome nicker as I give her a good scratch at the top of her shoulder, exactly where she loves it most.

'So, young man, you know Gulzura, do you?' Atashka smiles

as Aibek bows courteously from the waist. He looks directly at me, wide-eyed and happy. At last, he knows my name.

'When did you join the hunt?' Atashka asks.

'Oh, I've been hanging around for a couple of days, just watching from a distance. I have to say I'm not too impressed with what I've seen so far. If the rest of your clan have half Gulzura's skills, you will certainly be able to teach some of the others a thing or two.'

I glare at him.

'Gulzura's skills, eh?' Atashka fakes a concerned look. 'That doesn't surprise me. And what's the mood like today?'

Aibek glances around to see who is within earshot and nudges his horse closer to Atashka.

'To be perfectly honest, people are pretty fed up. They're tired and hungry and I don't think they're any better than when they started. It's all been a bit shambolic.'

Atashka leans in towards Aibek, obviously warming to him.

'Well, at least you and I have one thing in common,' Atashka says, as quietly as he can. 'Our contempt for our leader. You know we should be practising this every year, not just immediately before we need to fight.'

'I heard that the city's bankrupt, that he's embezzled enormous sums from our taxes. This can't continue...' Atashka trails off, distracted by the sight of Nurbek, beckoning him urgently. 'Gulzura, don't go anywhere without me.' He trots away.

'Well, *Gulzura*. You have a name at last! I will be shouting it from the mountains when this is all over, so you'd better come when I call.' Aibek laughs, then his face visibly pales. 'I've got to go, Gulzura. I mustn't be seen by my clan. That's why I'm hiding inside this hood. Please take care of yourself, stay safe.' He nudges his horse right beside me, leans forward and whispers into my ear. 'I've missed you. I'll see you again as soon as I can, I promise.' His hot breath on my cheek makes me blush and sends a tingle right through me, and I realise that his promise can't come soon enough.

The party atmosphere does not hide an underlying nervousness in the air and, as I wait for Atashka to return, I catch snatches of conversations from all directions.

'...he's raised thirty thousand troops to defend Balasagun from that Mongol horde...'

'...sent spies to find out what was going on in Genghis Khan's camp but not one has returned. He doesn't seem to care. He thinks he can win this war on arrogance and a sense of superiority alone...'

I glance over towards the tyrant and a flash of light blinds me as the sun reflects on his metal armour.

Kyuk Kyuk Kyuk Look see sharp

My eyes focus with a surprising new clarity and I spot a weakness. There's a gap between the chest and leg plates and it would take me less than a blink of an eye to fire an arrow into that sweet spot at the top of his thigh and watch him bleed to death. My little bow looks shabby and ineffective in comparison to the gloriously polished and superior weaponry of the Gurkhan's guards, forged by the best blacksmiths in the land. Still, it's a thought that lingers in my head.

The hunt starts with a ritual from Kuchulyg's shaman, calling on the gods to be generous and thanking them for their bounty. The clans ride out to create a huge circle, stretching so wide you can't see one side from the other and then, on Kuchulyg's command, the circle starts to close in, slowly trapping all the animals caught in the middle. Atashka and I become hungry and tired but we cannot break ranks. To do so would immediately bring a vicious punishment from Kuchulyg's guards, who are watching closely for any signs of dissent.

Towards the end of a chaotic day, throughout which there was little direction, no-one seemed to know what anyone else was doing, and we failed again and again to maintain the correct formation, the circle tightens. A rope with felt strips attached is passed around to create a simple pen, ensuring no animals make a last-moment dash for freedom. It is only at this point that Kuchulyg comes down from the plateau, and the game that hasn't managed to escape during the lengthy periods of mayhem and confusion is driven directly toward him. I stay close to Atashka, unsure what my role is now.

'You've done well, child. Your riding and archery skills have been noticed and are the subject of much chatter and gossip all around.' He smiles his pleasure and I smile back, reflecting on how much fun Meder, Sabira and I have had chasing down and killing a great many animals that escaped the ring. We canter forward and then, by chance, find ourselves close to the Gurkhan and his men. He is admonishing a young water-bearer, who has accidentally spilled a few drops on his shiny armour.

'What are you doing, boy?' he shouts. He raises his whip and brings it down with a crack across the boy's back. 'I'll get the dogs on you if you do that again,' he yells, and then turns to a mounted guard beside him. 'Do you know you have to almost starve a dog to death to get it to tear a man apart these days?' He laughs. No-one else does. 'Get out of my way. Let me at the beasts.'

He gallops into the centre of the ring, sending courtiers flying in all directions. I dismount and approach the boy, holding out my hand to help him up. He takes it, but nervously flicks his eyes around to see who is watching.

'No damage done this time, ta,' he says.

I turn to remount Meder.

'I wouldn't go that way – they're gonna release the bear,' he warns. I frown my incomprehension.

'The bear for Kuchulyg to catch. So he can show everyone what a great huntsman he is.' The boy brushes himself down and stands in front of Meder, stroking his whiskery muzzle. 'Hunt master bought a bear, right? Blunted its teeth, removed its claws, drugged it, so now it won't harm a fly. He's going to release it, all sly-like, into the commotion right in front of the Gurkhan – and then the Gurkhan's going to kill it and look like a proper hero. Only it's a sham. If the bear weren't really old and ill, I'd have let it go so it didn't suffer. It'll have a quick end, anyway, I'm sure.'

I turn to see where the animals are being driven. When I turn back, the boy is gone.

Kuchulyg swaggers in front of us with the air of an all-conquering hero. He dismounts and faces the bear on foot with nothing but a convincing act of fearless courage and a small sword. He lumbers around a bit, circling the beast, taunting it with his sword, then kills it quickly with one upward thrust into its throat right in front of everyone, as the water-bearer predicted. The crowd whoop and cheer.

Atashka and I wait patiently on the periphery as the carnage continues. A free-for-all bloodbath unfolds in front of us as hundreds of terrified creatures are slaughtered. Men desperate to make a kill trample over others running away. As the game is collected up by Kuchulyg's men, the Gurkhan bellows, 'Take it all to the Palace.'

There are gasps of disbelief all around.

'You deserve nothing. We need all the food we can get in our stores in case the Mongol pig dares to lay siege to our city. We will show the swine that we will never be defeated.'

'But we were promised the spoils of this hunt,' a man next to me complains to his neighbour. 'We need the –' but before he can finish, a lash from Kuchulyg's whip lacerates his face. A line of blood trickles down his cheek and neck and soaks into his cotton shirt.

'If anyone else dares to contradict me, I will not be so lenient. The next traitor will be fed to my dogs at the end of the day as a lesson to you all.'

The crowd shrinks back. Some of the clans have been here for over a week, with little to eat, and now, with nothing to take home, they're angry and resentful but powerless.

The Gurkhan continues, 'I hope we have a few spies among us to take the message to the Mongol pig that we are ready. We will annihilate him should he dare to step foot on our lands.' The men exchange surreptitious looks of doubt but cheer loudly.

If this is a display of Kuchulyg's prowess, then I don't think the Mongol Khan has much to worry about. If this is supposed to build our morale and create an army, the Gurkhan has failed.

Men round up prey
Trap beasts Blood runs hot
Hares leap dash deer boar run
Call keen cry
Fox blaze

Sabira comes out of nowhere, plummeting through the air, wings tucked tight, straight into the bounty of dead animals. She grabs a particularly plump red fox and flies out. *No, Sabira, no, no, no!*

The onlookers are stunned. But not Kuchulyg. He aims quickly and looses an arrow at Sabira who is flying directly toward me with the fox now dangling from her talons. I open my mouth wide and yell a silent scream as the arrow misses her by a hair's breadth. Kuchulyg, embarrassed at missing such a large bird at close range, kicks his horse sharply in anger. Sabira brings her catch directly to me, landing on the baldak. My breath shortens to rapid gasps.

'Don't move,' Atashka whispers, terrified.

Kuchulyg gallops over, his face puce but his voice chillingly calm. 'Give me the fox.'

I wrench it from Sabira's clutches and pass it to the servant. 'Now,' Kuchulyg commands, 'give me the eagle.'

Atashka kicks his horse forward to put himself between me and the Gurkhan. 'Please don't take the eagle, my Lord.' He addresses Kuchulyg slightly askance, to hide his bad eye. *Sabira, go!* She spreads her wings and pushes off to rise vertically.

Kuchulyg raises his bow and knocks an arrow but then changes his mind.

'Let it go,' he orders, as if he is in control of Sabira. 'I'll send my huntsman out for it later.'

'The eagle is important for our clan,' Atashka says. 'Important for my granddaughter here, who's trained it.'

'What's a girl doing with an eagle?' the Gurkhan scoffs, not looking at me. 'It would look so much better on my arm. I'd certainly teach it who was master.'

'My Lord, my granddaughter's... a great job... a strong bond... than I've ever witnessed before...' There is no doubt in my mind that it would be better if Atashka just shut up.

'Well, she isn't doing such a great job now, is she? That bird stole one of my red foxes – where was her control then?'

I feel nauseous with fear. I hold my breath, watching the struggle behind Kuchulyg's harsh gaze as he weighs up his options.

'All right, old man, you win. Go!'

I am weak with relief. Kuchulyg smiles, picks up his reins and turns his horse away. The crowd grumbles quietly, disappointed to be denied a spectacle. But in a blink of an eye, when everyone's dropped their guard, Kuchulyg wheels his horse back, pivoting the beast a half circle on its rear hooves, unsheathes his sword and plunges it directly into Atashka's chest. A moment later the sword is out and blood flows freely from the gaping wound. Atashka slides silently off his horse.

No! Without thinking, I draw my bow quickly and aim at the small sliver of exposed thigh at the top of the Gurkhan's leg. But before I can loose the arrow, Aibek gallops in at full speed and knocks me sideways. The arrow releases into the ground beside the Gurkhan. Aibek grabs Meder's bridle. 'Not now, Gulzura!'

I leap off and land on my knees beside Atashka, placing my hands tenderly around his face. A man pushes forward through the gawping crowd. 'Let me through, I'm a shaman, I can help. Let me see him.'

As the crowd parts, a thunderous voice booms out.

'He's old, he's no use to anyone, don't waste your time. Get over here! Right now! My hands are sore and chapped and in need of your attention.'

The shaman hesitates, raising his eyes to the gods briefly; then, with a look of utter misery, he turns to the Gurkhan. I put my lips on Atashka's rapidly greying cheek and breathe softly, hoping he can hear my thoughts.

I love you. I love you. Do not die. Do you hear me? I love you. Do not die.

Chapter 18

'Prepare yourself. The gods will take him very soon,' Bubu tells me softly. She has attended him without rest for three days and nights, brewing ever stronger herbal potions to alleviate the convulsions that engulf him in agonising waves. I lift the blanket, crawl in beside him and take his ice-cold, bony hand into mine. His chest rises and falls, rattling and wheezing. Exhausted by the effort of breathing, he is slowly suffocating. He squeezes my hand weakly and my eyes prickle.

'My job is done... the gods want me now.' His mouth barely moves and his voice is so quiet that I have to lean in closer to hear him.

'Be happy for me... I will be at peace...'

I press my lips to his sunken cheek, hoping I can manage a few whispered words. Nothing. Silence. But the words scream in my head: *I love you. I love you. Don't leave me. Who will guide me?* And then I beg: *Take me with you. I don't want to be here without you. Please.*

'I will watch over you,' he rasps and then sighs a final, untroubled breath. Silent sobs shudder through my body and I gulp in air like a drowning fish. The tears give scant release from the pressure inside me, and I shake from head to toe. I shake with anger, and I shake because I know what I have to do: I must avenge Atashka. I must make Kuchulyg pay for what he's done. Atashka's voice whispers in my head: *If there's just one lesson you must learn, it is to be patient.* I don't know how a nomad girl gets close to a Gurkhan, but I will work it out, I will bide my time and I will find my moment.

I cannot sleep. I toss and turn, trying to ease the pain from the burning lump in my chest and escape the vision in my head of a blindingly bright blade thrust hard and deep into Atashka's frail body. It repeats over and over, and each time it pierces the cloth of his threadbare chapan, the sound of metal shattering bone gets louder and the glint on the blade gets brighter.

The rhythms of everyone else's breathing indicate it's only me struggling tonight. As a pinprick of light through a thin patch of felt in the yurt roof marks the first sign of dawn, I quietly leave my bed and tiptoe over my sleeping family to the door, still in my light cotton shirt and trousers. Sabira hops out of the yurt behind me and flies up into the freezing air. Meder greets me with snorted puffs of steam and we gallop off. I sit back, letting him choose the path as I let the fine drizzle soak me.

Meder finally stops in a bowl-shaped depression. Steep, rocky crags form a near perfect circle all around, as if an angry god has punched the ground with his almighty fist. Booming crashes and low grumbles of thunder bounce around the mountains. The gods must be displeased. I shiver uncontrollably and collapse as I dismount, my chilled legs unable to support me. Meder pushes his head against my back, encouraging me back on my feet, but the fearsome hand gripping and squeezing my heart renders me helpless. I can't go on. I just want the pain to end now. I wrap my arms tightly around my shins, rest my head on my knees and rock back and forth. I am beyond being able to bear it.

Atashka, I beg you ask the gods to take me now. I am not fit for their purpose. Let me join you.

Meder nuzzles closer, his steamy breath warming the back of my neck. The rumbles of thunder get closer and the rain gets heavier. Inside, I howl with fury. *I couldn't save him. Why him? Why not me?* My mouth opens and closes, emitting nothing more than a raspy breath. *Lord Tengri, I need him. I can't continue my task for you without him. Why did you take him?* The pressure continues to build inside me like a dammed river, and I feel as if I am going to burst. I claw at my wet shirt, wanting to reach inside my chest and tear out my broken heart.

There is a deafening crack of thunder overhead and I flinch as a forked bolt of lightning strikes the ground directly in front of me: a blinding light from the heavens to earth. *Eternal Father of the Sky, what do you want of me?* Something deep inside me sparks and kindles: a tiny flicker at first, the mew of a newborn, which expands, raw and wild, until my body can contain it no longer and it bursts out of my mouth as the howl of an injured beast.

'Aaaaaaaaargh!'

I stop. The sound bounces back from the walls of rock around me. 'Aaaaaaaaargh!' it echoes. This is me. I hear me.

'Noooooooooo!' And again, it repeats, 'Noooooooooo!' The noise reverberates round and round, repeating over and over, a little quieter each time.

This is my voice. And it is glorious. Meder cocks his ears and whinnies.

Kyuk Kyuk Kyuk
Girl shout roar
Shout rage from heart wound

Roar pain from soul gash
Feel force loud words speak strong
World sit up
Hear new voice

I sit motionless, astonished. 'Hello,' I try in a whisper. 'Hello, me.'

Sabira wheels high above, calling her thin screech in encouragement as she descends.

'Hello, Sabira,' I squeak, as she lands right next to me. 'I… talk.' I smile and stroke her back.

'I sound… like you.' I laugh. I've always been surprised that eagles, the most magnificent and powerful of all birds, produce only shrill, feeble yelps, more like a puppy than a predator.

'I'm like you now.' My voice cracks and disappears.

Sabira rests her head under my chin and nestles close to feel the warmth and comfort of my pulse. The rain stops and a gap opens in the black clouds. A single beam of sunlight shines down into the valley. The gods have given me back my voice. *What will I owe them in return?*

I whisper into Meder's ear, 'It's time to go.' He nickers and I hug him tightly around his neck, breathing in his familiar, grassy smell. 'Choo, choo,' I trill, as he picks up speed to a comfortable, happy canter to warm us both up.

I am lost in thoughts of how I might reveal my new voice to everyone, when Meder skids to a sudden stop. In a small valley below is a lone horse, with a strange-looking rider slumped over its neck. I urge Meder on to get a closer look.

I'm wary but it soon becomes obvious that the man is either sound asleep or barely alive. I try to call to him but my unfamiliar voice fails me, and it comes out as a little more than a squeak. I ride closer still, confident that Sabira is overhead, keeping an eye in case it is some kind of trap. I try again. 'Hello.' It's barely more than a whisper and I feel annoyed that my powerful, new voice has all but disappeared already. The rider doesn't move, so I dismount and approach, poised to reach for my knife, though I'm not sure my frozen hands could hold it tightly enough. The chestnut gelding seems pleased to see me and, as it trots forward, the rider slithers off, landing in a heap with a grunt of pain. One of his legs is bent back at an angle that can only mean it's broken; an exposed thigh bone protrudes through his trousers and there's a trickle of blood from a deep gash in the side of his head.

'Hello.' It sounds so ridiculous, but I can't think what else to say. He starts to mumble so I lean down to put my ear closer to his mouth.

'I'm dying,' he moans. 'I... message.'

No words come to me. Just an inner, bitter laugh at the cruel humour of the gods. Giving me a voice with one breath and then a dying man in the next. *What do they want of me?*

I put my hand tenderly on his shoulder and lean toward him again. 'What... can I do?' I whisper.

'Take message... pocket.' He is drifting in and out of consciousness and I think hard about what Bubu would do in this situation. *Keep him awake.*

'Look at me,' I say. 'Do not die.' But he closes his eyes and I run my hands over his clothing, looking for a pocket. He's wearing what would once have been a luxurious and very expensive leather and sable coat that is now covered in dirt and almost shredded, so that it barely covers his silk undergarments. I try to turn him.

'Aaaarrgh!' he yells.

'Sorry.' I search more carefully and find a pocket containing a small, suede pouch. I untie the leather lace and take out a piece of paper with dark ink scratchings on it. I recognise it is writing but, as I have never learned to read, I don't know what it says. Usen offered to teach me, thinking it would be useful if I could write down all the things I wasn't able to say. I liked this idea, but Father said it was a waste of time – why on earth would I need to read and write when I spend my days with sheep and goats? – so I never learned even a single symbol.

'I can't read,' I whisper.

'Take it… very important.' He closes his eyes and his body sags.

It's a mystery to me how those dark marks speak and I promise myself I will learn the secret one day. I fold the paper back into the pouch and see the sign. The three hares symbol is inked onto the soft suede

Chapter 19

A blood moon rises the night Atashka and the messenger are sent on their journeys to the heavens. Yak-fat lamps light a long procession, led by Bubu. Our strongest men carry aloft the washed and rug-wrapped bodies. I sit beside two earth mounds, marked by stone cairns, arms wrapped tightly around my knees and head bowed in silence, as the other women keen. They didn't like Atashka and the howling of their fake grief only adds to my anger and heartache.

> *Gods greet men*
> *No need to grieve*
> *Old man he guard you now*
> *His teach done You me fly*

Two sheep are slaughtered and plates of mutton dumplings, horsemeat sausages and kebabs of fatty sheep's tail are laid out. I am not hungry and don't care that, as the least important and therefore the last to serve myself, I end up with little more than scraps. Usen, as usual, takes far more than he can eat and, when no one's looking, slides a few choice pieces onto my plate.

Father attempts to give a speech. 'A great, great man... two great men... a man we admired and respected,' he slurs. Some of the clan snigger, others hang their heads in shame, embarrassed at such a show on this solemn occasion.

'I can hear you.' Father snaps at his nephews who fail to disguise their disrespect. I sit in silence, not ready yet to reveal my voice. My hand fiddles with the suede pouch in my pocket while I decide whether or not to show Usen. He's the only person in the clan who can read, but I'm worried I will be in some kind of trouble for simply having it in my possession. I decide to do it now, quickly, before Usen picks up his komuz to accompany Uncle Sabit, who is now telling a traditional story that everyone loves to hear. I extract the paper and slip it into Usen's hand.

'What's this?' His eyes scan the vertical rows of inky lines, circles, hoops and tails. He blows out his cheeks, frowning. I try to snatch the paper back. But he's too quick and stands up, holding the crumpled scrap aloft.

'Father, Father! I have some news,' Usen shouts above the raucous laughter that has erupted at the end of Uncle Sabit's story.

'I haven't finished. As I was saying, a great man –' Father picks up, mistakenly thinking that he's still got more to say.

'Father, please, this is urgent.'

'Go on, then, if it really can't wait.' Father sits, obviously relieved, and pours himself more kumiss. All eyes turn to Usen.

'Gulzura has just given me this. I think she must have been given it by the stranger we've just buried.' I nod once in agreement.

'It's a message from Genghis Khan.' Usen waits for the gasps to subside. 'Shall I read it out?'

There is a loud 'Yes', and a 'Well, no one else here can read!' and several 'Get on with it!'

He holds the scrap of paper in both hands, arms straight out in front of him.

To the Gurkhan Kuchulyg,
Honourable Leader of the Kara Khitai,

I want peace with you. Surrender to me and there will be
no war. Swear fealty and there will be no retribution for the
treatment you meted out to my emissary, Toq. Resist and you
will be annihilated, along with every man, woman, child and
beast in your city. I do not seek war. The choice is yours.

Genghis Khan

The yurt erupts, everyone shouting to be heard above each other.

'Silence!' Father yells over the din, suddenly sober. 'We must destroy this message immediately and pretend we never saw it. The Gurkhan will surely kill whoever delivers it.'

'We cannot leave the people of Balasagun to die at the hands of Genghis Khan,' Usen pleads.

'Why not?' asks Nurbek. 'Those city people hate us and you can bet they wouldn't come to our defence.' Alik, predictably, nods in agreement.

'Your loyalty should be with us here. Clan and family first, always.' Father looks at Usen sternly.

Uncle Mirlan comes to Usen's defence. 'But it won't just be city people, will it? We're *all* going to die if Genghis Khan arrives. The Gurkhan won't allow the tribe's nomad clans to surrender. He'll expect us to join his army and fight for him. If we don't, and he survives, he'll have us slaughtered anyway.'

'Mind you, if we do join him and fight, we'd all be slaughtered, judging by the state of our army at the last hunt,' Uncle Sabit says.

'So, we all die whatever happens,' Mother says quietly.

'Elgiza might be right,' Uncle Mirlan says. 'The traders warned us – Genghis Khan has a terrifying reputation. They said he has succeeded many times in defeating tribes much more powerful than ours.'

'You believe traders? Huh!' Father sneers, his voice getting higher.

'Yes, I do. They had no reason to lie. I've no confidence whatsoever in Kuchulyg's ability to lead us to victory against the kind of army that we'd be up against,' Mirlan says, slamming his fist down and knocking over his beaker of kumiss.

'The Gurkhan's a dangerous half-wit who's done nothing to win our loyalty.' Uncle Sabit joins in. 'I can't see that we'd be any worse off under a new leader.'

'I think the situation is quite clear,' Usen says. 'It really doesn't take a genius to see that Genghis Khan will destroy us if we fight but leave us in peace if we surrender. It is that simple, particularly if we offer fealty and a few sheep.'

A ripple of nervous conversation circulates.

'How can it be any plainer?' Usen says. 'It is our duty to persuade our Gurkhan to be reasonable.'

There are now more mumblings of agreement than dissent around the yurt and Father, sensing the change in mood, steers a new direction. 'I hear you all.' He shifts uncomfortably, picking at the bones in front of him, clearly thinking how best to backtrack on his earlier decision. Father's judgement has been called into question time and again and his claim to the leadership of Snow Leopard Clan rests heavily and simply on tradition. The eldest son of the past leader becomes the new leader when the gods decree it. This is how our ancestors did it, so this is how we continue to do it. A discussion around swearing allegiance to an enemy of our tribal leader represents a huge threat to his own position.

Mother puts her hand on his sleeve. 'Why not let Usen take the message? He knows the city and its people well.'

'He's not favoured by the gods... unpredictable,' Father mutters. He turns to Alik and Nurbek. 'You're my strongest sons. You'll deliver the message.'

'What? And leave the clan undefended at this dangerous time? I don't think so,' Alik says, defiantly. 'That's a terrible idea. All of you will be left exposed and vulnerable if we go,' Nurbek adds.

'You'll need both of us here to guard the horses. If we lose them, we'll have nothing. We will starve to death. What about Kursanbek? He's more than capable of doing it,' Alik says, pointing at our cousin.

'You can't expect me to abandon my mother.' Kursanbek is outraged. 'She's already lost her husband and eldest daughter in raids. It's unthinkable to leave her to face another threat all on her own. How could you even suggest such a thing?'

And round and round it goes. One after another, each of the men explains why they can't possibly be the one to take the message to Kuchulyg, until it comes back again to Mother's first suggestion.

'Usen, you clearly feel very strongly about this,' Father says, looking tired and like he just wants the situation resolved. 'And, you're the one who spends the most time in the city. *And,* it was your idea. It's decided! You will deliver the message to the Palace.' Father sits abruptly, pleased with himself, unembarrassed by his obvious lack of leadership. 'Whatever happens after that is out of our hands. Now, someone pour me another drink.'

Usen gets flustered. 'But I can't.' I hear a faint wheeze as his chest tightens.

'Why not?' Mother asks. 'You're the expert on city life. You spend enough time there. You are the only one who would know how to get this message to the Gurkhan.'

'Yes, but… I think Kuchulyg will recognise me. He certainly knows my friends, the people I mix with, and he has spies everywhere. They are… well, they're mostly ummah and he wants all trace of them erased. If I present myself to him, there's a strong chance he'll imprison me and torture me to make me reveal where they're hiding. You know he's destroyed our' – he coughs – 'their mosques, murdered the Imams and driven their religion underground so they're forced to pray in secret. I can't be seen by him, there's too much at stake.'

'The little runt wouldn't last long under interrogation,' Alik mutters under his breath and Nurbek fakes a wheezy laugh, mimicking Usen. I scowl. Father puts his head in his hands.

I could do it. I could deliver the message, and in the witnessing and re-telling of Kuchulyg's humiliation at the hands of a much more powerful leader, I would be honouring my vow to avenge Atashka. I have been patient and my moment has come. I take a deep breath, open my mouth to speak… but nothing comes out.

No one even notices; they continue to bicker among themselves. I try again. Nothing. I feel for my amulet.

You speak now Soar like bird
Words hit hard Shock

'I'll go.'

The words burst out quite a bit louder than I was expecting. The chatter stops instantly, followed by a moment's silence as everyone takes in what has just happened and then a clamour as they all talk over each other again.

'When did you start to speak?'

'I knew she could talk all along.'

'How did you get your voice back?'

I sink down, unable even to begin to answer the deafening interrogation and, thankfully, Usen moves to put his arm around my shoulder. Mother is frozen, wide-eyed, and I cannot tell if she is shocked because I speak or because I have offered to go to the city, or both. Whichever, she does not look pleased.

'This is incredible. I'm so happy for you,' Usen says softly. 'Let's talk later, when they've all calmed down a bit.'

Father brings the mayhem to order. 'Silence! Everyone! Let's hear the girl speak.' Everyone looks at me, and I can feel my throat shrink and tighten shut.

'Well, come on, girl, surely you've got a lot to say after all those years of silence?' he laughs.

I concentrate hard and say the words in my mind a few times before I force them out of my mouth. 'I... will... go.'

Mother interrupts immediately. 'That's ridiculous. How could you think such a thing?'

The argument forms in my head, but my voice fails me, and the words just won't come. I screw up my face in anger and frustration, then lower my head, flushing red hot.

'What use would she be anyway if we send her and she just goes dumb every time someone asks a question?' Nurbek says.

'Actually, Nurbek, you know, that might be an advantage.' Father smiles. 'Even if they force her, it's unlikely they'll get any information out of her.'

He laughs but no one else does. The rest of the family sits uncomfortably, contemplating the shocking idea that Father is willing to send his only daughter on such a risky mission. I'm not surprised. Father had always thought my silence was stubbornness and that, like a horse, I needed breaking in. He starved me once, insisting that I could only have food if I asked for it. After five days I became so weak that I couldn't get out of bed. Bubu had to intervene and insist I was fed. One day, I will put my lips right up next to the folds and crevices of Father's ugly ears and I will scream as loudly as I can, so it is the last thing he ever hears.

'Brother.' Uncle Mirlan rises to speak. 'You cannot send Gulzura. We must choose one of the men. This is not a task for a girl, let alone a girl with her... her difficulties.'

No words come to me to defend myself as they continue to talk about me like I can't hear them. *I am more than capable of doing this simple task and I will prove them wrong. They have no idea what I can do.*

They not see They not hear
They squawk like crows
Gods give you flight

Bubu, who has been sitting back quietly observing the mayhem, rises to her feet and a hush descends.

'The gods have chosen this moment to return Gulzura's voice to her. This is a sign. An omen. However' – she hesitates and looks down – 'this is an important decision. The burden on the bearer of this message is great. We must be certain we choose the right person.' She pauses again. 'I will consult the gods to make sure I understand their wishes and we do the right thing.'

Everyone moves aside to let Bubu through. 'Give me two shoulder blades,' she commands, pointing around the floor where the bones of the two sheep, stripped of their meat, have been cast aside. 'I must have one from the right and one from the left.'

Two large, flat, three-sided blades are passed to Bubu, who

carefully cleans them of any remaining fragments of sinew. She feeds the fire with a few small juniper branches and puts the bones directly on the flames, droning an incantation to the gods.

'Father Sky, Mother Earth, show us the way. I pray for your direction. Who should take this journey and deliver the message? Who should risk their life to save the clan?'

All eyes watch the bones crackle dry and then scorch black in the flames. Bubu extracts them, chants again over them and then examines each of them. She traces her forefinger along the jagged cracks and over the scorch mark patterns, muttering as she does so. Finally, she holds up the two bones, one in each hand above her head for all to see. The two blades look like the wings of bird and, as Bubu starts to move, she flaps the wings as if they are flying. Despite the poor light, it is very clear that the right shoulder blade has a large white split running straight down its centre.

Bubu stops. 'The gods have made it clear,' she says. 'The Eternal Great Way is revealed on the right blade. The gods have chosen.' Everyone holds their breath. 'Gulzura will make the journey.'

The yurt erupts, my heart beats fast and my head spins. I can't tell if I'm excited or terrified. No one can argue now. Bubu's word is direct from the gods and it is always final.

'It is decided.' Father looks hugely relieved and claps his hands. 'However, I insist Usen accompanies his sister. Once you've got her inside the city, you can hide out, but you must ensure she stays safe. And that is *my* final word on this matter.'

'But Jyral, husband.' Mother puts her hand on Father's arm.

'Enough, woman! The decision is made!' he shouts and shakes her hand away abruptly, staggering slightly and belching as he heads for the door. He passes Usen and bends down as if to whisper in his ear, but stumbles and blurts out, 'Keep her safe, boy. I want her back in one piece, if you know what I mean. I've got an important marriage lined up for her.'

Usen puts his arm back around me to quell my shaking and whispers, 'We can do this. I'll keep you safe, I promise.'

Wind change chop churn World yawns wide
We brave fly
Rule skies side by side Wings touch close
Prey we flush Prey we kill

Chapter 20

'Come on, Gulzura, we must get going,' Usen shouts. He's putting the double-sided saddle bag containing everything we need for our journey on his horse, but I want to find Bubu, so I duck down on the other side, hoping he won't see me. Mother comes out of Bubu's yurt as I approach. She reaches out and takes my arm.

'Gulzura, I just... I want to say something before you leave.' She's biting her lower lip. I look down, uncomfortable in her awkwardness.

'I was so pleased to hear you talk last night. Quite a surprise for us all.'

I smile.

'I want to give you something to take with you, to help you, on your journey.'

She has already given me new trousers and a tunic, while muttering about the awful state of my clothing. She opens her fist and pushes something small, cold and sharp-edged into my palm. A dark red gemstone sparkles in the middle of my dusty hand.

'I've been keeping this safe for a special occasion. I have a feeling you might need it. And if you don't, well, you can always return it to me when you come back.'

I want to ask where it came from? How did she come to have

it? But my throat clamps tightly shut. She is still holding my arm, so I don't move.

'I was taught that we don't choose our lives, that the gods have a plan for each and every one of us and it's futile to resist. But I've changed my mind over the years. It's too late now for me, Gulzura, but not for you. Be brave and fight for your dreams.'

I look up to see a sadness welling in her eyes. I feel like I've been nothing but a nuisance to her my whole life.

'I've tried to be a good mother and Lord Tengri knows the gods have tested me but' – she pauses and gulps – 'after Sabira died, I stopped enjoying being a mother and now it's as if I don't know how.' She squeezes my arm and, mistaking it for a sign of kindness, I lean forward for a hug or a kiss. She pulls back abruptly and I tug my arm out of her grip and push through Bubu's yurt door as the tears start to pour down my cheeks.

'Ah, I've been expecting you.' Bubu is hunkered down over her chest of dried herbs, lifting, shaking and sniffing various leather bags. The yurt is fuggy with a wispy, yellow smoke rising from the fire. My eyes start to sting and the unusual smell hits the back of my throat, making me cough.

'This is the one.' She stands and turns to me. 'Your mother's talked to you, then?' I nod and she wipes the back of her hand gently down my cheek, smoothing it dry before bending low again to lift the heavy lid from the pot on the fire. Acrid fumes spew out as she adds the dried herbs, making me cough again.

'Stay back. You shouldn't get too close to this concoction while it cooks. I want you to take it with you, when it's prepared. You mix it with water for a powerful drink. It will paralyse a full-grown man for a short time – time enough for you to make an escape, should you need to. It'll take a moment to heat through. Let's sit together while we wait.'

I hesitate, thinking how cross Usen will be if he's delayed any longer.

'Usen,' I whisper in a wheezy rasp and then cough again.

Bubu smiles. 'Oh, don't worry about your brother. I've asked your mother to keep him occupied with a couple more tasks before he goes.'

I smile, noting once again how she gets what she wants with such little effort. I fold my legs beneath me and settle onto the rug beside her. She bottom-shuffles herself tight beside me. I slowly open my fist and show her the jewel. The red stone glints like a crystallised drop of blood.

'I'm glad she has given you this. It has great value and a strong spirit. You will need it. The gods won't be there for you at every twist and turn of your journey. Mortals have to use their own defences sometimes, even when the gods are on their side.'

She takes the jewel and, rising up on her knees and closing her eyes, starts to chant. She raises her arms up high above her head and sways in a gentle, slow circle, round and round. The chant is over quickly and she sits back down. She takes the hem of my chapan and rips the seam apart with her hands, then leans back, passing me a needle.

'Here, child, thread this for me, please. My eyesight is not what it used to be.' I take the end of the sheep's wool yarn and put it in my mouth to gather all the wispy fibres together. Then, aiming the spit-wet point through the eyehole, I thread the little ivory needle in one and she sews the hem back with the ruby tucked inside.

'You'll need this too.' She hands me a small cloth bag with long ties. 'I want you to keep your amulet, Genghis Khan's letter, the powder and any other treasures' – her eyes flick to the lump under my shirt where the carved pendant from Aibek lies – 'in this bag, under your clothes, close to your body.' She cuts my amulet out of my jacket and sews the seam back neatly too. I put all my treasures into the bag and she shows me how to tie it around my waist, then checks on her herbs.

'They'll take a while to cool, so, let me tell you a story. A story your mother would tell you, if she were able. Your father's family found it very hard to arrange a suitable match for him. Family after family within the tribe turned him down as a potential husband. It was humiliating for everyone – but understandable. He was irresponsible and had an uncontrollable temper. Who was going to give away a precious daughter to that brute? So, the only option left was to kidnap a bride for him. A bride from far away, so far that she wouldn't be able to return home, ever. Your mother's family was wealthy – she had silk dresses, ate from fine porcelain crockery and had a multitude of servants. She lived in a big house in a city and had grown up believing she was superior to the grubby, unsophisticated nomads. You can imagine how frightened she must have been.'

I nod. The thought of being forced to live against my will with another clan sends a chill right through me. I remember Mother once showing me a piece of shiny fabric that she kept in a box. The moth-eaten remnant of brocade felt like nothing I'd touched before; quite solid but with a soft, silky texture. It was bright red with multi-coloured flowers, clouds and geometric patterns, all arranged in complex designs and motifs. Dominating the front were two large creatures breathing fire. Mother had explained they were dragons – mythical creatures who represent power, strength and good luck to people in the east. 'Not that they brought me any luck, eh?' she had scoffed. She had snatched the fabric from me and bundled it up rather more hurriedly than I had thought necessary.

Bubu tips the cooked herbs onto a flat stone and rubs them vigorously back and forth with another, crushing them into a fine powder.

'Your mother tried to escape many times and your father's brothers tied her like an animal to the frame of the yurt while she screamed and fought. Your grandfather hated what was happening and argued endlessly in her defence, but no-one would listen to him, of course. Finally, after spring, summer and autumn, she lost the will to fight any longer. It was only then that she was introduced to your father. He was good looking and, actually, surprisingly sweet with her... to start with at least. She decided to accept her fate and learn to live as happily as she could with him but it was hard – she missed her sisters and mother and the life of luxury she had been ripped away from. She confided in me that she often dreamed that her brothers were out, day after day, looking for her and that, one day, they would find her and take her home to a rapturous welcome. But even the dreams faded after a few years and she got so busy raising children that eventually she forgot all about being rescued.'

I've heard random things about Mother, throwaway lines in conversations, occasional references to events I didn't understand but this is the first time anyone has put those overheard snippets into a story for me.

'Bubu, does she love me?' I ask tentatively. Bubu looks up after she tips the powder into a tiny packet.

'Oh, my child, yes, she does – I'm quite certain of it – deep down. But your mother doesn't know how to love you like the other mothers of our clan love their children. Her ability to love, or to hate, for that matter, was damaged and then, when Sabira was killed, she... well, she is broken.'

Broken is fine, broken can be fixed. Like a broken cart axle, a sick yak, or a snapped bow, you just need to find the right person to mend it.

'You see, Gulzura, we are all guilty of hiding things we don't want other to see. We all have secrets.'

Chapter 21

The mare casually flicks flies with her tail as I close my hand around her downy teat and draw down firmly with my thumb and first finger. Usen has chosen his horse well and she lets down her milk easily. The drink is sweet and refreshing as I squirt it directly into my open mouth.

'We're not staying long. We need to get over these mountains before dawn.' Usen takes the other teat as I finish.

We are resting on the north side of the lake, below a wall of rock that rises almost vertically to disappear into the blue-black sky. Even the thousands of stars and large waning moon can't cast enough light to illuminate the seemingly impenetrable barrier that sits between us and the plains. Our usual route to the city is much more straightforward but, for speed and secrecy, Usen has brought me a different way. These mountains looked so tame and manageable from the comfort of camp on the south side of the lake, but here, close up, they scare me and I would like nothing more than to turn back. I wipe my sleeve across my milky mouth and go to Sabira, who is resting on the baldak. *I don't think I can do this, sister. The gods have chosen the wrong person.*

'Come on – the sooner we get over the pass, the sooner we can get settled, eat and hide out for the day. I don't want to get caught in the open in daylight,' Usen says.

I envy his confidence and certainty. I'm starting to think I was chosen for this journey because I am dispensable. The clan doesn't need me; the younger children can shepherd the goats and sheep.

'This is the hardest part. Once we're over the top, it's pretty easy for the next three days,' Usen says. 'Are you all right to keep going?'

I'm not, but I nod.

Usen points toward a small cleft in the wall of rock and sets off. The horses pant loudly, heads down, working hard to negotiate the narrow rocky path that zigzags up and up and up. The moonlight comes and goes as clouds whip across it and the landscape deceives me in silhouettes and shadows. A flock of sheep is a rocky outcrop, a chough is a cairn and a lone traveller is a gnarled tree stump. Meder places each hoof carefully to avoid treacherous holes and obstacles, but I hold my breath when his back legs start to buckle under him as he briefly slides backwards on a patch of scree. I am disorientated by the rich smell of juniper, wild rose and sage, and alert to the sound of a shuffling hedgehog, the frozen stare of a fox and the mournful howling of a distant pack of wolves. Thankfully, Usen is in no hurry to talk and we carry on in silence through the night to the crest.

The descent is considerably easier; a long, undulating, wide path winds gracefully down to the floor of the next valley. The sun rises, gilding the mountains behind us rose-gold and my nocturnal fears disappear with the fading stars. *Thank you, Mother Earth, for delivering another day.* Sabira, who's been napping on the baldak, wakes, stretches her wings and lifts off in search of her own breakfast. *Don't forget we're hungry too, sister.*

'Choo, choo,' I whisper and Meder breaks into a gentle canter. Seeing the wide path stretch out ahead, I urge him past Usen who, unable to resist the opportunity for a race, kicks his horse on. We gallop joyously, just as we did when we were children, until Usen pulls over to a small grove of apricot trees nestled in a dip.

'This looks like a good spot. Water, shade, and well-hidden,' he says.

'Good boy, Meder.' I pat his sweaty neck and lead him toward the river.

Usen stops in his tracks in front of me, beaming. 'I've waited all night for you to talk. I can't tell you how pleased I am to hear your voice.'

I realise the thoughts in my head have come out of my mouth.

'Mmm,' I say, sheepishly. Usen lifts me off the ground in an enthusiastic hug and twirls me around.

'It's amazing! Fantastic... wooooo hooooo!' We laugh together until he starts to cough and has to lower me to the ground.

'When did it happen?' he says, once he has caught his breath. 'How? I mean what? I have a million questions...'

I open my mouth but only a raspy murmur emerges. Usen stares eagerly, eyes wide, and I try again. Nothing.

'No hurry, Gulzura, you'll talk when you're ready.' He turns to untack his horse and I do the same. Bridles, saddles, sheepskins and saddlebags are strewn across the dusty ground. I pick a clump of dried grass and brush Meder, leaning my forehead against his belly.

'I just found it.' I close my eyes, hoping more words will come. 'Atashka died. I was angry. It came...' The words trail off in a whisper.

'I'm so pleased for you, Gulzura,' Usen says softly, 'and I'm so pleased for us because now we can talk about everything and I can't wait to hear you – in your own time.'

High pitch warm breeze blow
Hang in air Sharp stare
Wings tucked tight Drop down fast
Twist turn true
Scan side to side
Lone plump beast
Crush skull and spine Share kill

It's an idyllic spot; the ground is covered in soft, short grass and any noise we make is drowned by the river babbling over smooth boulders. I hobble the horses and pick my way through the patches of pale-pink lilies, wild geraniums and sea buckthorn that line the riverbank to find a secluded spot. A turquoise pool has formed in a kink in the river, and I strip. The pebbles are slippery with green weed, so I lower myself quickly into the icy meltwater, gasping at the shock. Soon my breathing calms and a warm heat builds deep inside me. I edge my way beyond the pool to a smooth black boulder which I hold tightly and let the fast-flowing water massage my back and shoulders, washing away the dust and grime.

Goosebumps break out as I haul myself out of the river and lie on the bank. Hidden by the reeds and blue irises, I close my eyes and let the sun dry me.

Aibek drops straight into my thoughts. I haven't seen him since the hunt so there was no chance to say goodbye, or let him know where I'm going, or even share my new voice with him. My chest tightens and tears prick my eyes. I couldn't bear to lose him, as well as Atashka. I shake my head clear. *Think good thoughts.* Maybe I'll bump into him in the city. *That's ridiculous; of course, he won't be there.* He would always choose the jailoo over the crowded city in the blistering summer heat.

'Gulzura, Gulzura?' Usen interrupts my thoughts. 'Our meal is ready, where are you?' I dress quickly and join him at the fire, where a marmot and wild garlic stew is bubbling in a pan.

Sleep doesn't come easily in the daylight. I toss and turn, falling in and out of strange dreams that merge my desire to avenge Atashka with my desire to see Aibek. The noise of hundreds of chattering birds descending from the sky to roost in the trees for the night is our wake-up alarm. As the sun sinks over the horizon, the birds finally fall silent, and we gather up our belongings and set off again. Usen sings softly as the horses fall into a gentle, syncopated rhythm. Although I don't understand many of the words, the rise and fall of the tune is comforting. Usen follows the meandering river closely until he finds a section where we can swim the horses across the current to continue on the opposite bank.

'We keep heading north,' Usen says as the horses shiver-shake the cold water from their bodies. I shrug. I don't know how he knows this.

'How?' I squeak.

'You see the group of stars that look like a cooking pot with a bent handle?'

I stare up at the sky, struggling to make anything out in the wide band of milky light that straddles the heavens like a lacy belt. I look back at Usen and follow his pointing finger. And there it is, a cooking pot.

'Yes!'

'Well, just follow the line of the two stars on the right-hand side of the pot, up and up and up until you come to a single star that's much brighter than all the others. That's the North Star – and that's what's going to guide us to Balasagun.'

I am in awe of Usen's knowledge. I can't help myself from looking up every now and again, just to check it's still there and we are still following it.

Early the next morning, Sabira joins us.

Dawn hunt best prey

Ride
Grass brown crisp dry
Stone dust grit

Glide low heat haze
Breath squeeze raw
Stress storm   Wild rain
Cool wash clean preen
Air clear
What see
Stop Hide Wait

The landscape ahead looks empty.

Kyuk Kyuk Kyuk
Girl Stop Hush
Side eyes look Kyuk Kyuk

'Usen.'

He is too far ahead and doesn't hear me. I canter up beside him and grab his reins.

I point to the ridge on the right. 'There!'

'What?' he says. I swallow and try to summon a voice with

authority. What would Atashka sound like when he had to tell me something urgent?

'Danger....' I stare at him to emphasise how serious I am. 'Important. Follow me.' I kick Meder into a gallop and head off up to the ridge.

Usen groans, 'We don't have time for this,' but he follows anyway.

'I can't see any danger,' he says, before he's actually looked. We dismount and crawl on our bellies through the long grass to the edge which looks down over our next valley. Directly below us is a small hunting group, young men, having a bit of fun. We'd have blundered into them, had we not been warned.

'I know them!' Usen looks surprised. 'They wouldn't be kind to us. How did you know they were there, Gulzura?'

'Sabira told me,' I whisper.

'What?'

'We talk.'

'That's incredible. How?'

I don't have the words to explain that I don't exactly hear her, that I just seem to know, in my head, what it is she wants me to do.

'You know them?' I want him to stop asking about Sabira and tell me how he knows the riders in the valley.

'Yes.' He rolls over and lies on his back. 'They are Balta clan and if they see me, I'll be in big trouble.'

I bob up to look, foolishly hoping that maybe Aibek's with them. He's not. Then it strikes me: how does Usen know them? He certainly wouldn't recognise any of them from the raids, because he's never joined a raiding party.

'How?' I ask.

'You mean you don't know?' He laughs. 'Oh, little sister,

you must be the last person in the land not to know about my shameful past.'

I blush, then lean up on my elbows to look directly at him. 'Tell me...'

'I had a, let's say, an *encounter* with them and... well... it didn't turn out as I expected.'

'What happened?'

'Not much, really, but the whole sorry story ended up with me disappearing to Balasagun. I couldn't face the clan, and I dreaded what Father might do to me, so I thought I'd start a new life in the city.'

'How did you do that?'

'I lived on the street for a while and then a group of kind people found me, the ummah, they changed my life. They took me in, clothed me, fed me and taught me to read so I could understand their special book, the Qu'ran, the word of Allah.'

'Allah?'

'He is their one god. But in the city, Gurkhan Kuchulyg has outlawed the worship of all gods except Lord Buddha, so they have to practise their beliefs in secret. The ummah treated me like family.'

'Why did you... come home?'

Usen sighs. 'I don't know. Life in the city is incredible. I learned to write, sing, play komuz, but I think, in spite of all that, I was missing the jailoo. Believe it or not, I missed the family too, *even* Nurbek and Alik.' He laughs. 'City life can also be hard when you look like we do. Even though I found friends and allies, being a nomad among city people is... well, it's tough.'

I am not at all sure I understand, and I'm quite certain there's a large part of his story missing, but the sun is rising fast and my eyelids are drooping with exhaustion. 'Sleep?' I ask.

We check that the young men of Balta clan have left the valley and find a shady overhang under the ridge to sleep out the day. Despite the shade, I wake sodden with sweat, my fringe glued to my forehead and beads of salty water running down my face and pooling in the little dip at the base of my throat. I was foolish not to believe Usen when he'd told me that the summer heat on the plains was hot enough to cook an egg on a rock.

Meder can't resist licking the crusted salt on my hairline as I lie looking longingly at the snow-capped mountains far behind us.

We ride through the night again, and as dawn breaks on the morning of the third day, the outline of the city emerges, floating in the shimmering haze on the distant skyline. My heart beats faster. Balasagun: my destination and my destiny.

'Let's make camp and rest for a few hours. We'll head for the city later this afternoon when it's hottest and everyone's having their sleep.'

We unpack the horses, tether them, eat our remaining strips of dried meat, drink fresh mare's milk and bed down. Usen falls asleep at once but I cannot. I have wished for adventure, to see new places and meet new people, for so long. But, now it's within reach, I am not sure. *Oh, Great Lord Tengri, why have you chosen me? I have no experience, no knowledge of city people and their ways, no skills for what I might face. I can deliver a breech lamb; I know from the colour of the clouds if it will rain or hail; I can make a syrup for a cough from coltsfoot leaves. But what use is all that in the city?* I look to the sky for a sign, but there is nothing. What if the gods are just playing one of their cruel jokes and this turns out to be another punishment for our clan to bear? I can't do this.

Gods see you girl quick smart
Rare
We fly to do gods' will

I let Usen sleep a while but as soon as he stirs, I move next to him.

'I can't do this,' I say.

He yawns and stretches.

'I can't do this,' I say louder, and he sits up.

'It's going to be all right. I promise.' He puts his arm around my shoulders and pulls me close. 'The city is a great place. Don't be scared. My job is to keep you safe while you find a way to deliver the message. I'll contact my friends and we'll help you. We may have to hide but we'll be there when you need us. You must remember we'll be looking out for you, always.'

'How?'

'There's a network. A sort of secret organisation. Many people believe that life under the great Mongol Khan would be preferable. I can't talk too much about it, it would be better if you didn't know.'

His words resonate in my head. *Many people believe that life under the great Mongol Khan would be preferable.* I have heard almost those exact words before. Where? Suddenly it comes to me.

'The sign of the three hares?' I say.

Usen spins round. 'What? How do *you* know about the Three Hares?"

I start to explain but quickly realise that the trader had actually told me very little.

'I first heard about the Three Hares when I was with the ummah,' Usen explains. 'They talked of a group of people opposed to Kuchulyg. I think the idea came in with one of Genghis Khan's spies, who encouraged an underground resistance in order to smooth the way for the Mongol Khan's arrival one day.'

'How?' I ask.

'I'm not sure. I never met anyone who claimed to be one of them but I did see the results of their random acts of disruption, a steady trickle of small irritations to Kuchulyg's life. One day, the back wheels on his cart came off; someone had loosened the pins. Another day, disgusting smoke engulfed the Palace; several people lit noxious fires when the wind was in the right direction. Nothing too obviously rebellious and anyone involved would always have a legitimate excuse if asked, but the sole purpose was to disrupt his everyday activities. It's not just ummah; there are street orphans, tradespeople – even, I'm told, members of his court – who carry out small daily acts of subversion.'

I understand subversion. I've used similar tactics on cousin Ermek.

'It's good you know their secret symbol, but it will be well hidden and when you see it, be careful. Don't ask too many questions or you might be mistaken for a spy. In fact, it would be better if you don't talk.'

Chapter 22

Balasagun introduces itself well before we arrive at its gates. A bustling hum emerges from within the towering ramparts that embrace the city like a snug scarf. The closer we get to its smooth, cliff-like walls, interrupted only by crenelated watchtowers, the more the noise crescendoes. A huge, stone archway with wooden doors rises directly in front of us, menacing and impenetrable. I feel very small and wonder again at the sense of my mission, particularly as Usen has mis-timed our arrival and everyone is clearly wide awake and very active.

'We're later than I'd hoped and their afternoon sleep is over. We'll head round to the East Gate. It's a quieter entrance, and don't forget what I told you. Don't speak. We're here to replenish supplies as we're running short in the mountains. If they search us, just let them – they'll find nothing of interest on me or in the saddlebags and they won't bother with you.'

I nod, hoping Usen hasn't misjudged this too. I press the palm of my hand to my body belt and feel the shape of my amulet, praying for help to disguise my terror.

'I was afraid too when I first came to the city. You get used to it.' Usen smiles.

Even this smaller entrance has vast gates, decorated with elaborate brass fixtures in the shapes of stars, flowers and animals, all placed within a complex web of intertwined, curling lines. What must the Palace be like if they lavish such extravagance on a side gate? I can't stop staring; it is all so much grander than I could ever have imagined.

A guard approaches and Usen explains we have come to buy provisions. He yawns and nods us through, barely glancing at me. We dismount and lead the horses into the city. Immediately inside is yet another wall, even higher than the first and beyond that, a huge tower made of intricate geometric brickwork patterns that seems to ascend right to the heavens.

Seeing me open-mouthed in awe, Usen stops. 'That used to be the minaret, where the muezzin sang out the call to prayer five times a day, until Kuchulyg banned it.' I feel quite giddy as I look up at a guard at the very top, poised ready with his bow and arrow. I tuck myself in close beside Meder but am quickly disorientated by the racket from so many people, carts, animals, children, rushing every which way. I look down, trying to quell the panic, and am almost run over by a couple of boys pulling a hand-cart full of honking geese.

'Oi! Watch where you're going!' one of the boys yells.

Usen takes my hand and leads me into a busy marketplace.

'I really don't want to leave you,' he says, 'but I'm going to stable the horses and then track down my friends. I'll be quicker alone. You stay here. Do *not* move and do *not* speak to anyone. Promise me!'

I nod.

'I will be back for you in the blink of an eye.'

Before I can tell him I am terrified, he takes Meder's reins from me and is gone.

I look up and catch a glimpse of Sabira: a tiny, suspended speck. *Don't leave me, sister. Stay where I can hear you.*

Kyuk Kyuk Kyuk
Round round round
No sight Cry caw Too loud

I back into a wall, trying to make myself as small as possible in the narrow strip of shade it offers. The smells are overpowering – baking bread, rotting meat, clean washing, molten metal, fermented fish, dung, sweat and sickly-sweet aromas I can't name. In every direction, people go about their business, brushing past, not seeing me. They dip, swerve, duck and move every which way to avoid bumping into each other. There are traders with baskets and barrows of plump chickens, fresh vegetables, exotic flowers, pots and pans; people with bales of cloth on their heads piled so high I wonder how they remain upright; others pulling reluctant goats behind them. On one side of the square alone I see a beggar kicked by a passing nobleman, a cow stealing apples from the back of a fruit stall, and a donkey hee-hawing loudly in complaint as carpets are loaded onto its back.

I look up again. *Where are you?* There's no reply. All I hear is the clamour of the crowd; shouting, chatting, laughing, swearing, banging, clattering all merge into one unbearable cacophony. I have never seen so many different kinds of people – a woman with skin the colour of milk, so pale her veins show through, and hair the colour of summer hay that shines silver and gold as the sun bounces off it. And there are others whose skin is the colour of charcoal, with magnificent hair the colour of mountain ravens.

How do people live like this? The mud-brick buildings packed so tightly together and precariously balanced on top of each other don't look safe. The heat, smell and noise overwhelm me and I feel faint. I look around for somewhere to sit, where I can wait for Usen. I take a few steps and I am swept up with the crowd along a series of narrow, winding streets and suddenly realise that I am quite lost. *Sabira! Where are you?*

> *Lost in maze*
> *Cleaved by noise by not see clear*
> *Our bond cut*
> *Wait I seek you*

I stare up. There's so little sky, small patches of blue between rooftops, and I can't see her. *Sister, where are you?* I run, turn, run back. There's no sight of her and my stomach churns. I am alone; no Meder, no Sabira, no Usen. Sweat trickles down my back and I stagger as dizziness washes over me. I sway forward and crash into a girl carrying a fully laden basket of dung-cakes on her head.

'Hey, watch where you're going! Look at you, walking in one direction and looking in another. What do you think you're doing? I really don't need this, today of all days. Well, come on! The least you can do is get down here on the ground and help me, can't you?' She speaks very fast and she is very cross.

'Sorry.' I drop down on hands and knees to help her collect up the fallen dung-cakes and she doesn't stop talking.

'Careful! You've broken enough of them already; I don't need any more in pieces, thank you. Any idea how little I get even for whole cakes? I don't know what they're feeding these yaks at the market, but their dung is not as sticky as I'm used to and the cakes have come out brittle, break as soon as you look at them, so you need to be real careful and gentle. I won't get paid for broken dung-cakes, you know, and then Bortboi and Nurdeen will be cross. Yajub won't say a word, but I don't want anyone thinking I'm special. I need to make sure I contribute the same as everyone else – it's not fair if I don't and, to be honest...'

I stop listening. She is thin, dressed in a brown, cotton dress with a stained, cream apron on top, tied tightly around her waist by a piece of coarsely twisted rope. Her eyes shine like blue crystals from her dusty, pale face and her chestnut hair hangs in a tangled ponytail. There's something quite funny about how she talks in a torrent of words about people and places as if I am completely familiar with her life. As soon as her basket is full again, she's off, still babbling. I watch her walk away, admiring how elegantly she balances the heavy basket on her head. She turns to look at me and I venture a small smile. She raises her eyes to the heavens and returns.

'You're new here, aren't you? You look like a lost lamb. Where are you going?'

'The Palace.'

The girl almost chokes. 'What? You are kidding me, right? No one walks into this city and straight into the Palace unless they're summoned by our glorious leader or they want to have their head chopped off.'

'I must.'

She doesn't give me a moment to explain before she's off again.

'Must you now? Well, that's just not happening. If you want my advice, for what it's worth – and, actually, I'd say it's worth quite a lot, as I've been living in this city since the very day I was born – I'd stay well clear, and if not well clear, well hidden.' She puts her basket on the ground and continues. 'A beauty like you wandering the streets alone, you'll be prey to all sorts. You'd be a prize catch for the slavers, or the brothel, no doubt about that; they'd see you as a good little earner, I'd say. It's a good job you bumped into me first, now I think about it, though it would have been a whole lot better if you hadn't actually sent my dung-cakes flying. Better still, if you had not come to the city in the first place...'

'I *must* get into the Palace.' The words are quiet but she hears them and stops.

'You haven't got a clue. Poor, little, lost lamb.' She comes close and whispers, 'Your best bet's to turn right round and go back where you came from. This is a brutal place for a nomad girl. Trust me, I've seen enough here to know. Go home.'

'I can't. I have a message to deliver, a promise to keep,' I persist, encouraged by my voice which I think is sounding almost normal.

'What under the great blue sky could possibly be that important?' she says. 'Go on. Tell me. I can't wait to hear this! I do like a good story.'

Her tone is now mocking and quite unfriendly and I'm wondering if I dare trust her. Everyone has warned me that I must be cautious, that city people have clever ways to deceive, that young women are vulnerable to all kinds of harm. I put my hand reassuringly on my amulet. *Sister, where are you? I need you.* There is no reply.

'It's nothing... I'm fine. Thank you.' I force a smile but she's not convinced.

'Are you sure? You look pretty lost to me. You can trust me, you know. I've helped others like you.'

She would say that, wouldn't she, if she were trying to trick me?

'Really, I'm fine,' I say.

'Well, suit yourself. I'm already late and I don't want to miss out on selling this load today, so I'm off. Good luck.' She is gone in a flash.

I walk around desperately looking for the spot where Usen left me, but I feel like a minnow swimming up a river in full spate, forcing myself forward through the determined throng in the crowded streets. How does anyone know where they are? I settle on a step behind two women, packing up their stalls.

'How've you done today?' the orange-seller asks.

'Business is good right now. People seem keen to get their hands on my walnuts!' The two women laugh uproariously.

'Let's hope it stays that way, eh?' She looks over her shoulder, then lowers her voice. 'I hear the Three Hares are doing their best to disrupt things again. Honest, I can't take another downturn. We don't want the Gurkhan ordering the destruction of all our market stalls again.'

'That bunch of fools; nothing better to do with their lives than upset everything for the rest of us. They've no idea how their stupid behaviour destroys the business of ordinary, hardworking people.'

'They're nothing but cowards, lurking in the shadows, never revealing themselves.'

I slide away quickly, confused and wondering if anything in the city is as I had been told it would be.

I know the sun is setting when the ochre, red, yellow and cream bricks lose their brightness and turn a uniform, dull beige. Sharp shadows soften and then disappear and the streets begin to empty as people finish their business, traders shut up shop and everyone goes home. I am alone, with just the feel of my heart pumping hard in my chest. I hold my amulet in one hand and Aibek's pendant in the other for comfort. I hope I am where Usen left me. Why hasn't he come? Where am I to go? My self-pity turns to anger towards those who sent me. They were too scared to come and now I know why. This is an ugly, frightening place. I've been sent on a mission I can never accomplish. Nobody cares where I am, or even if I live or die.

The city at night transforms into a very different place. The crowded, tiny spaces are now empty and large, the noisy streets silent except for the occasional dog bark, cat yawl and scurrying rat. The bustling crowds have dwindled to a few lone people rushing home and, now and again, a group of rowdy young men. The cool and quiet after the searing heat and chaos of the day should be a relief but it feels sinister and threatening. I squeeze myself into a gap between two buildings, calmed a little by the fact that I can see into the street while being pretty well hidden from any passers-by.

'Are you alright?' Kind eyes greet me as I look up to see a round-faced, plump-cheeked woman bending over me. I try to smile but tears well up.

'Oh, my little angel, don't cry.' She reaches forward and takes my hand in hers. A pleasant, flowery perfume wafts from her silky-smooth skin.

'Are you alone?' she asks. A look flashes briefly across her face, and I see something I don't understand and don't like. Then she smiles.

'You really shouldn't be out here on the street on your own, you know.'

'My brother,' I whisper.

'I thought you were alone.'

'I'm lost. I'm waiting for him.'

'He's not going to be looking for you now, my lovely, now it's dark. It's almost curfew.'

'What do you mean?'

'You're not from these parts, are you? We have orders from

the Gurkhan to stay indoors between the night bell and the morning bell. Anyone caught out is arrested. At best, they're imprisoned for a few days; at worst, they're hung by their feet in the main square to set an example. And, if it's not the guards, the Three Hares will have you and that will be the last that anyone sees of you.'

The bells ring. Loud chimes reverberate and echo along the alleyways.

'Come on, come along, that's for night curfew. Time to get you inside. You look like you need a good meal and some rest. I'll get my husband to send word out to find your brother as soon as it's daylight.'

She tugs on my arm and I sense an urgency in her desire to help. She's right; Usen can't be out looking for me now, and I need somewhere safe for the night. I can't be caught by Kuchulyg's guards on my first day. She leads me through a maze of small alleys until she ushers me into a house lit by more lamps than I've ever seen in one space. As I glance around, I see other signs of her wealth – silk cushions, exotic hangings, a bird in a cage, pieces of carved metalwork that seem to serve no purpose other than to decorate.

'Sit here, my lovely. I'll get Cook to prepare something for you. Are you thirsty?'

'Yes. Thank you.' I haven't had a drink since Usen left me and my throat is parched from the street dust.

'I'm Ruhsora, by the way, and here's my husband, Emil.' She gestures to an equally rotund man, who is approaching with a big smile across his ruddy face.

'Well, what have you got here, my petal?'

I squirm under his searching gaze.

'I found this little dove all alone on the street, so I've brought her here for safety.' They exchange the kind of look adults give each other when they are hiding something. I glance at the door and work out how quickly I can get there if I need to.

'Well, she's certainly pretty.' Emil pats my leg. 'Go get her a nice drink, now.'

His clothes are striking: a yellow, silk jerkin, richly embroidered; a wide, leather belt studded with sparkling jewels; long, black leather boots embossed with elaborate, geometric patterns. But my eyes are drawn to his magnificent moustache which lies, neatly trimmed and oiled, across his upper lip and beyond to beautifully symmetrical, upturned tips. He is clean and rich, yet I shudder as he sidles closer.

'No need to fret now. You're in the best hands. Shh, shh, there, there, little one.' His scent is cloying, and I hope I don't cough.

Ruhsora returns with tea and still no one mentions looking for Usen.

'What about... my... brother?' The words falter.

'Oh, don't you worry about that, my lovely,' Ruhsora says. 'I'll make sure my boys go out and look for him as soon as the end of curfew bell is rung.' She gives me a hug and I feel her hand dip into my pocket. I freeze. She pulls back, brushes a stray hair from my forehead and kisses me so tenderly on the cheek, as if I were a much-loved daughter, that I think I must have imagined the hand in my pocket. I'm so tired.

A lamb stew, with vegetables I don't recognise, is served, along with nuts and a delicious fruit called a date, which I've never eaten before. My mind turns, for the first time since I left, to my family. I picture them eating: Father slurring his words, my uncles discussing how to breed the perfect yak, Alik and Nurbek loudly boasting of their latest feats and Mother quietly serving them all. I doubt anyone has given me a second thought.

I can barely keep my eyes open.

'I'll take you upstairs,' says Ruhsora. I don't understand what she means, but I follow her as she leads me along a corridor and up a set of timbers, each one higher than the one before, until we reach a floor above. The thought of sleeping in a room suspended over another makes me nervous. But it is cosy, with felt carpets, and I collapse gratefully onto a soft mattress. The last thing I remember is Ruhsora pulling a silk throw over me.

Chapter 23

The morning sun shines stripy beams of light through the grid of metal bars over the window. A deliciously cool breeze wafts in and I stretch out, thinking how lucky I am to have found such kindness. I rise, wash in the water bucket provided, and go to the door. It's stuck and I push harder, lifting the latch up and down to release it, but it won't move. I knock, hoping to attract someone's attention.

'Hello,' I call out.

I put my shoulder to the door and, with all my weight, push as hard as I can against it. Still, it doesn't budge.

'Hello,' I say, a little louder. I hear footsteps coming up the stairs and stand back as a key clanks in a metal lock, and the door opens.

'Good morning, my lovely. How did you sleep?' Ruhsora asks.

'Well. Thank you.'

'Come, join us for some breakfast.' She ushers me down to a table laden with a vast selection of foods. 'Come, sit down, my little dove, and eat up.'

I tuck in willingly to fruits, bread, honey, jams and cold meats, all washed down with green tea. Emil joins us at the table.

'Are you looking for my brother?' I ask him.

'All in good time, young lady. Now, first things first –'

'I'm sorry, but I really must find my brother.' I get up. 'Thank you so much for your kindness, but I need to go now.'

'Hold on there. We need to talk about payment.' Emil gets up and blocks my way.

'Oh. I don't have any money. I'm sorry.'

'Oh dear. Oh dear.' He shakes his head. 'What, nothing?'

I shake my head too, and whisper, 'No.'

'That's a shame, that is. We'll have to come to some kind of agreement then. You don't think we'd give you all that food and a bed for the night out of the goodness of our hearts, do you? We're not a charity.' He laughs.

I hang my head, embarrassed and annoyed with myself for assuming that they were indeed acting out of the goodness of their hearts.

'Hear that, Ruhsora? The girl thought it was all free!'

'Oh my, the poor little dove doesn't understand city ways.'

Ruhsora guides me firmly back to the table. 'Well now, let's see what we can do for each other.'

Something inside me says this may not be a good idea. *Sabira, are you here? Come to me. Come.*

'How about you do some work for us? Just a few light duties until you've paid for the board and lodging. How does that sound?' Ruhsora is smiling.

'Oh no, I can't stay. I'm sorry, but I have to find my brother. He'll be very worried about me.'

Ruhsora's soft face turns hard.

'I promise I'll bring you the money as soon as I find Usen. He'll know who can lend it to us. I'm quite certain I'll get it quickly and return to you immediately. I promise.'

'We don't know you. Never met you before. How can we trust your word? No. That won't do at all,' Emil says.

Emil whispers into Ruhsora's ear. She looks me up and down, and then turns to him, nodding.

'What duties would you like me to do?' I don't think I have any option but to comply.

'That's more like it. You can start today, serving our visitors with drink and food. You can do that, can't you?' Emil says.

It sounds easy. 'Yes, I can.' I will talk to the guests and ask them to look for Usen while I work off my debt.

'Good girl; that's the spirit.' Ruhsora pats my leg.

She shows me where everything is kept, and when the guests start to arrive, around mid-morning, I begin running back and forth to the kitchen, making sure the visitors, all men, are quickly served the drink and food they order. It is all very easy and surprisingly pleasant, until a long-nosed, greasy-haired man with dirty fingernails pinches my bottom as I walk by. The sudden stab of pain startles me and I drop a full tray of drinks.

'Watch what you're doing!' He stands abruptly, wiping his fingers over a large wet patch on his trousers.

'I'm sorry.' I bend down to help wipe his trousers with my apron front. He grabs my wrist painfully and twists it, trying to pull me closer. I dig my feet in and resist.

'Ooh, got a little fighter here, have we?' He tugs hard and I topple forward straight into his lap. 'Hey, Emil!' he shouts. 'How much for this one?'

I freeze. Emil comes over and I relax, assuming he will demand the man let me go.

'Now this one is very valuable to me, Bekjan. She's untouched, so I don't think you can afford her.'

'Come on. How much? I'd pay a fair sum.'

The two men move to sit at a small table in the far corner and Emil calls Ruhsora to join them. I shake from head to toe. While

I clear up the mess and continue serving other visitors, they sit with their heads close together, talking for what seems like a very long time. Then Ruhsora comes to me.

'I want you to take your apron off, go back up to your room and tidy yourself up.'

'Why?' I ask, to delay the inevitable.

'You're going to earn all the money you need to pay us back. You'd like to do that, wouldn't you?'

'Not like this. No!'

'Oh, my little dove, just do as you're told and it'll all be over quickly enough. And then you can go and look for your brother.'

If this is the only way I am going to escape this place, I will have to bear it. I'm not the first woman to be forced like this. I will just have to do whatever is needed, pay my debt and leave. I make my way upstairs and wait in my room. *Sabira, come to me!*

The door opens and Bekjan walks in.

'Well, it seems it's my lucky day.' He licks his lips and puts his hands out to reach for me.

I back away and frown at him.

'You can put up a fight if you want. That might be quite good fun, now I think about it, but I'll have you in the end, don't you worry.' He lunges and I side-step at the very last moment so he trips over his big feet and falls forward.

Sabira! Come, help me, help me!

Bekjan gets up and rushes at me; I duck under his outstretched arms and he spins quickly, grabs my dress and pulls hard so I fall. I land heavily on top of my jacket and feel a sharp prick in my thigh. The ruby.

'I can give you something,' I say.

'That's more like it. You can give me exactly what I want.'

'I have a gem. It's very valuable.'

His eyes widen. 'What kind of gem?'

'You can only have it if you leave immediately after I give it to you.'

'Let me see it first.'

It's risky, but I rip open the hem of my jacket and the little ruby falls into my palm. His eyes light up.

'Let me be very clear.' I look directly into his eyes. 'You can have this only if you leave me alone.'

He picks up the jewel, holds it up to the light between his filthy finger and thumb and examines it closely.

'Hmmm. This would buy me many young girls like you. But you know, a bird in the hand and all that.' He hands it back.

'I am not untouched. Emil is mistaken. You're wasting your money on me. I am not worth whatever it is he will make you pay. Take the ruby and buy yourself much more fun than you'll ever get from me.' A pang of guilt hits me as I realise that in saving myself, I am condemning another innocent girl.

He takes the ruby again.

'You're spoiled? Really?'

'Yes.' I lower my head, imagining the shame if that were true. 'And...'

'Yes? And what?'

'I think I might be poxy. I have a rash, it's very itchy...'

I scratch between my legs.

'All right.' He puts the ruby in his pocket and leaves. My legs tremble, then buckle underneath me with relief, although my eyes flood with tears at the loss of the little ruby. The gem my mother had kept for so long and entrusted to me, that Bubu said would protect me, has gone and I've been in the city for exactly one day.

Chapter 24

'What did you do to him?' Ruhsora asks angrily.

'Nothing.'

'Why did he leave without getting what he wanted?' she persists.

'Maybe he just changed his mind.'

'The girl is trouble,' Emil says to Ruhsora and they leave. I press my ear to the door after they lock it.

'I agree. No point keeping her here. I say we sell her on.'

'She's quite a beauty. Should fetch a good price. I'll see to it in the morning.'

I have managed to escape the frying pan only to be tossed into the fire. I have one night to come up with a plan. I howl out with anger and frustration.

Ruhsora comes in with a hot drink. 'Calm down, little one. It's all going to be all right. Just you see. You are tired. You should try to rest.'

I don't lift my head. I can't bear to look at her.

'Here, take some tea.'

The mint-and-honey is soothing and I drain the beaker in one, only to get a strong aftertaste of a herb I don't recognise. A wave of tiredness washes over me; it feels like I'm wading through mud as I move toward the mattress. Then my head starts to spin and I lose my balance and am immediately racked with an intense stabbing pain in my stomach. I wrap my arms around myself and bend in two to alleviate the searing spasms that are coming short and fast. I'm so dizzy I can't seem to balance to sit up. I double over again and retch. I retch again and this time I vomit, then collapse as my vision starts to close in, like I'm disappearing down a dark tunnel, and then there's nothing.

I wake with my cheek pressed to a cold floor, the taste of acid in my mouth and a blinding headache. A sharp wedge of daylight is coming in through a tiny window high above me. This is not the room I was in before. I try to move but my legs and arms are bound tightly and I can only wriggle helplessly on the stone slabs. I hear the door open. I close my eyes and go completely limp.

'How are you planning to get her out of here?' It's Ruhsora.

'She's small enough to go in one of the large baskets,' Emil says. 'I'll pile a bit of hay over her. Anyway, I'm not worried about that. What I am worried about is the fact that she was sick. Are you quite sure she's kept enough of that tea in her? I need her unconscious until at least midday.'

'It's pretty strong stuff and look at her – dead to the world.' I feel a foot nudge my leg. 'I'd say she's going to be out for a while. We've never had any other girl wake up, have we?'

The door closes behind them. My heart thumping in my chest tells me I am very much awake. I have to get out. I twist and turn my bound hands, back and forth, again and again. My skin burns as the rope digs in, but my only hope of escape is to continue. Eventually, the rope becomes loose enough for the tips of the fingers on my right hand to reach into my left sleeve and feel for my knife. They're a pretty incompetent pair for not checking my chapan, or maybe they just relied too much on the tea that didn't do its job. The doorlatch clicks again. I push the blade back, close my eyes and relax my body.

They bundle me into a basket and heap hay over me. The sweet smell takes me straight back to the jailoo and the end of summer when hay is harvested to get the horses through the winter. I will *not* be trapped here; I *am* going home. I wriggle my hands again and ease out the knife with my fingertips. Terrified that I might accidentally cut my wrist, I slowly saw the blade backwards and forwards over the rope. It breaks, and I cut the rope around my ankles too. I push the knife back into my sleeve. I try to make sense of what's happening outside the basket and hear a voice in the street.

'Dung-cakes! Dung-cakes! Best dung-cakes available now!' It's the voice of the girl I bumped into yesterday, and I hold my breath as Ruhsora comes back in.

'We're running low. I'll get some. That girl always sells good and cheap.'

A door opens and I hear the sound of the street.

'In here, girl. I'll take a basketful but make sure you pile them nice and neat. I'll go and get your payment.' I hear Ruhsora leave the room and the girl starts to count out the dung-cakes. I push up fast and hard and burst out of the basket in an explosion of hay, and the girl steps back in alarm.

'What in heaven's name are *you* doing here?'

'Shhh!' I hold out the knife in front of me, unsure whether this girl is going to help me or not.

'You have got to get out of here,' she says. 'This is no place for you. There are rumours about these people. Abductions, missing children, slavers.'

I know. I nod.

'Quick, put the hay back in the basket and the lid on. Then

you run, all right? Out of the door, turn right, turn right again, and wait for me.'

I obey her instructions. I've no better option.

I lean against the wall, holding my breath, until she comes round the corner, pocketing the money Ruhsora has just paid her.

'Run!'

She darts expertly around people, animals, traders, beggars, and I follow. On reaching a quiet square, she collapses in a heap and I drop down next to her, both of us with chests heaving, panting for breath, barely able to speak.

'You're one lucky girl,' she gasps, looking at the burn marks on my wrist as I rub them.

'Thank you,' I say. 'I'm so stupid.'

'No, don't say that. I can just about remember what it was like to be all alone in this city. I was lucky. So lucky. A kind woman took me in when I was a small child. Well, lucky until she died. And, now... well, now I have friends and we look after each other. I'm Mara. What's your name?'

'Gulzura,' I whisper. 'I am Gulzura.'

Mara pulls out two small loaves from her sleeves. 'Bet you didn't see me take these while we were hoofing it through the streets, did you?' She laughs and hands one over. I am astonished: how did she do that while we were running for our lives?

'So, Gulzura, you'd better tell me what you're doing here.'

In between mouthfuls of hot fresh bread, I tell her my story. The words don't always emerge as I would like them to, or even in the best order, but she listens patiently. Her eyes widen when I tell her I want to speak directly to Kuchulyg, but she says nothing. As I reach the end, I pull out the small, suede pouch and hold it out to her.

'I was told this would keep me safe. But I've heard things and now I'm not sure. Do you know this?' I point to the three hares.

Mara's eyes dart right and left – and she puts her hand immediately over the bag to cover up the symbol.

'Put that away,' she whispers. 'I do know it, but you mustn't just show people like that; it could get you into trouble. Luckily, you're safe now. You've fallen into the right hands. Trust me,' she says and takes my hand in hers. 'I will try to find out what's happened to your brother. Usen, you said?'

'And Meder?' I ask.

'Yes, of course. Now, what does he look like?'

I tell her about his arched neck, white socks and how his quarters shine gold in the sun and she bursts out laughing.

'You're sure this is your *brother*?'

She squeezes my hand and smiles. 'I will put the word out. Don't worry, we'll find them both. And... I can get you into the Palace.'

Chapter 25

Mara's home is a ramshackle affair, made of mud and straw daubed over a tightly woven, wooden frame wedged in the gap between two more substantial and much taller mud brick buildings. The front door doesn't fit very well, and the roof of interwoven palm branches looks like it would blow off in the slightest breeze. As soon as we walk in, though, it feels homely. The floor is covered with felt carpets and the walls are decorated with coloured hangings, just like a yurt.

'Everyone else is out, so we'll have the place to ourselves. You know, we all work and make money wherever we can. Here and there. We know this city and how to make a living better than anyone.'

Mara talks so fast I can barely keep up. 'Tea?' she says.

'Yes, please.' I put on a pretend-angry face. 'You won't drug me?'

'I don't need to. You're stuck with me now.' She laughs.

I settle on the floor and feel for my amulet in my hidden waist-belt. *Are you with me, sister? Can you hear me?*

But all I can hear is snatches of Mara still talking in another room.

'How are you feeling?' She passes me hot tea and a bowl of meaty stew and doesn't wait for an answer.

'Right. If my plan's going to work, you'll need to look like me. We won't get into the Palace with you looking like some sort of rustic good-for-nothing just emerged off the steppe, will we? I mean, look at you: trousered, booted and smelling of yak butter. That won't do at all; no, it won't. Let's get you out of your country-boy clothes.'

I put on a brightly coloured skirt and shirt. They fit surprisingly well. Mara unplaits my long pigtails, brushes out my hair and then ties it all back with a couple of red ribbons. I sit on the floor, feeling radiant, with her hands running over my head and through my hair. I don't want her ever to stop.

'Right. Now you look the part, you've got to sound it too. You don't say much, do you? That's a good thing. We're not going to have to worry that you'll say something out of turn. Not like me, eh?'

We laugh until my tummy hurts as I try to repeat a few phrases in the odd accent of the city people. My voice is weak and squeaky at the best of times, but now it's completely out of control and I have little command over the croaky sounds that emerge. Mara isn't cross, though; she finds it hilarious, so I keep going just to amuse her.

'Tell you what – perhaps you'd better just keep your mouth shut. I'll say you've lost your voice or something. There'll be no need for you to speak; I'll do all the talking. You just keep quiet.'

'I can do that!'

'You're lucky I have loads of dung-cakes that have finished drying, ready for sale right now. I've got to know a couple of the lads at the Palace stables and they let me have the manure. Can you believe they just throw it out? It's the best you can find anywhere in the city. The Palace horses eat only the finest hay and oats. You could say the Palace produces the very best turds in the land!' She roars with laughter. She's rude, she's risky and she excites me.

Behind her home, hundreds of perfectly round, perfectly uniform dung-cakes are drying on every flat surface of the three courtyard walls. They are nothing like the random-shaped lumps I used to make at home.

'They're beautiful,' I say, and Mara laughs.

It doesn't take long to peel the cakes off the walls and fill the baskets. Working together is fun; Mara chatters on about so many things I don't understand. She doesn't care that I don't speak and neither do I, I just enjoy being beside her.

Just before we leave, I slip back inside, and take my knife out of the sleeve of my chapan. I tuck it into my waist-belt, and feel better for having it there.

Looking every bit the city-girl, basket in hand, I follow Mara into the maze of streets, heading for the Palace fortress at the heart of the city. Wearing a skirt is much harder than I could have imagined; it seems to wrap itself round my legs, or trail under my feet, and although it's much cooler than trousers, it makes me feel quite vulnerable. I don't want to complain – Mara has done so much for me already – so I silently vow to get used to it.

The main Palace entrance is majestic; nervousness rises in me.

'We don't go in the front. Goodness, who do you think we are? We're not Princesses!' She winks and smiles. She leads me around the massive walls that protect the Palace fortress and we approach a small, wooden door, tucked out of the way at the back. It is guarded by the same black-clothed guards I saw around Kuchulyg at the hunt. A sudden jolt of pain in my chest from the memory of that day stops me in my tracks. I don't think I can do this. I'm not ready. Maybe we could go back to Mara's house and play with our hair, cook bread, sing and do friend-things for evermore.

'The guards are sometimes a little wary of newcomers, but don't worry – I have a plan up my sleeve. That guard there, he fancies me, so I'll flirt a little and tell him how you're new here and how I'm teaching you and that you're a bit shy, so I wanted to bring you when it's not quite so busy, or something like that. Anyway, whatever happens, you just stay quiet and hang back a bit. When I signal, come forward. Once he sees your full basket, he'll let us in. No problem.'

'So easy?' I'm astonished that a place as important as this has such a weak spot.

'Ha ha! Yes, if you rely on young guards deprived of female company. They've got this huge weakness when faced with an irresistible distraction. Men are ruled by that little bit of gristle that hangs between their legs. Once you know that, as a woman, you're invincible.'

I am shocked and thrilled, and my adoration and respect for Mara grows another notch stronger. A tingle of exhilaration runs right through me at the realisation that a new world of possibilities seems to be opening up.

We enter the Palace exactly as Mara predicted and drop our dung-cake loads in a heap in a vast, domed, basement storeroom. A slender, muscly man, with not a single hair on his head and glazed in a sweaty sheen, is quietly directing a couple of children and handing out coins in return for the ever-growing dung-cake pile. He stops immediately he sees Mara and hurries over to her.

'My Lady Maraim!' He bows and Mara tuts.

'Sanzar, you are a joker.' She punches him playfully on his arm, then whispers, 'My friend and I need to go upstairs for a short while.' He looks around, then turns back and nods.

'He's one of us,' Mara mouths to me, and leads me toward a set of timbers like the ones in Ruhsora's house. Just as she lifts her skirt to put her foot on the first wooden step, she almost collides with a man hurtling down toward us, brandishing a long, leather whip.

'I need dung-cakes in the kitchen fires now!' he booms, as we dive sideways to avoid him.

Mara turns to me. 'Great. We'll get to the upper floors that way.'

'You, you, you and you!' His long finger points directly at me and three others, but not at Mara. 'The rest of you, clear off!'

I take her hand and pull her with me, back toward the stack of dung-cakes.

'Oi, you, I didn't say *you*, did I?' he shouts and raises the long whip over Mara with a look that says he wouldn't hesitate to use it.

'Now!' he bellows, and pulls back the whip ready to lash out.

My heart sinks. She's going to leave me. I put my hand to my waist for the reassurance of my knife, but somewhere between Mara's house and here, it's disappeared. I am bereft.

'You'll be fine. Keep looking, keep watching, don't talk to anyone. I'll make sure we find your brother.'

She peels her hand out of my tight grip and is gone. For the second time in three days, I am alone with no plan.

Chapter 26

I find my basket and refill it. Sanzar comes to help. As he leans down, he mutters quietly, 'I'm here for you if you need me.'

Then, just as quickly, he's off, helping the others. We line up and follow the man with the whip up the staircase. He leads us along narrow, low-ceilinged passageways and I feel like a marmot in its burrow. Just as I think I can't bear the heavy basket-load any longer, we pop out into a large multi-domed space, bustling with people. Meat is being butchered, chopped, stewed; vegetables peeled, sliced, mashed, and a stew is being seasoned in the largest cooking pot I've ever seen.

'Stoke up the fires, then stack the spare beside it. Nice and neat,' Whip Man shouts. 'When you've done that basket, you can do three more each. Got it?'

No one dares speak.

'When you're finished, go back down to the storeroom and get your money.'

No one dares move.

'What are you waiting for?' he bellows.

The other three set off toward a corner fire each, leaving one for me. I stumble under the weight of the basket, but make it over to the fire, glancing at the others to see exactly what they're doing. I must not get this wrong or I'll quickly be found out as an imposter. It's fiercely hot and a steady trickle of sweat drips in salty beads down my face, neck, chest and spine. I feel faint and scared. The other children are returning for their second basket before I've finished my first, so I hurry to catch up. Whip Man is called away and leaves us to continue unsupervised. No one pays me the slightest attention.

I return to Sanzar with my empty basket after neatly stacking the final pile of dung-cakes.

'Do you still need to get into the Palace proper?' he whispers. I nod.

'Go now. There's a change of guard and the new lot won't know you're not supposed to be here.' He gives me a complicated set of directions and instructions, using words the meaning of which I can only guess at: cold kitchen, brewery, treasury, grand hall. He talks of sharp lefts, up wooden stairs, down stone steps, courtyard corners, past turrets and towers. I am barely familiar with these terms. My head spins.

I head off, trying to remember which stairs, which corner, which passageway, what any of these things mean, and am soon completely lost. In desperation, I pick up and follow the wonderful smell of clean washing that leads to a laundry.

I sift through a couple of piles of neatly folded clothes, selecting a dress, cap and apron that I think will make me look like everyone else I've passed so far. I dump my dung-smelling clothes in a basket. For the briefest moment, I clasp my amulet and say a quick prayer to the gods. *Protect and help me. I don't want to fail you.* Then, as I leave, I grab a stack of linen. Walking with a straight back and a quiet air of purpose, I become invisible except to other servants who walk past with only a polite nod of the head, which I return.

'Oh good, about time! Where have you been, girl?' A woman

pushes me through a wooden door into a large bedroom. 'I don't think I've seen you here before. Are you new?' She looks me up and down. I nod.

'I don't know, servants come and go so fast these days. Well, don't just stand there, help me change the bed linen and get this room cleaned. I'm well behind with it all this morning.'

And just like that, I become a housemaid in the Palace.

I barely sleep on my first night on the floor of a room full of other servants who are too exhausted to chat. The Palace creaks and groans with sounds I don't recognise and the onslaught of so many new experiences races through my mind, scaring me with all the possible alternative outcomes to the lucky one I've landed.

It turns out that I am very good at cleaning, tidying and changing bed linen. Quick, quiet and highly capable, is how Adel, the woman who took me on, describes me. I smile as I think about how Alik and Nurbek would describe me.

Over the next few days, the confusion of corridors, halls, courtyards and rooms starts to fall into shape in my head. In the main Palace, where the Gurkhan, his wife, the Khantun, and the family live, there are two large courtyards and four smaller ones, each elaborately decorated with exquisite tilework: glistening panels of flowers, exotic birds, diamonds, stars, and an endless variety of patterns in deep sky-blue and turquoise, highlighted in yellow and dark red. There is perfect symmetry across the large spaces, with an equal number of tiled window-frames and doorways leading to an equal number of rooms off the covered walkways.

Adel seems to enjoy my company, despite, or maybe because of, the fact that I barely say a word. She chatters and I listen intently, waiting for any clues about the Gurkhan's whereabouts and habits. In this way, I learn about the stables, the kitchens and bakery, the treasury, how the guards operate their shifts, who might be friendly and who to watch out for. The most exciting and unexpected thing I learn is that there is a network of secret passageways throughout the Palace, which Adel encourages me to use, to ensure we never accidentally bump into the Gurkhan himself. Doors that, at first glance, look like part of the wooden panelling, open to reveal dim corridors or narrow staircases. I quickly learn where they go and discover how I can listen in on conversations while remaining entirely concealed.

I am bewildered by just how much conflicting information I hear. The Three Hares are either the saviours or destroyers of the city, and the Gurkhan is either a hero or a villain, with equal numbers of fans and enemies within his walls, and the frustrating bit is that I cannot see who is saying what.

Although I think I'm becoming a good spy, as the days pass, I feel increasingly like a prisoner. I don't appear to be making any progress toward meeting the Gurkhan and delivering the message, and I cannot leave until I have.

I ask Sanzar to tell Mara I'm safe, and my spirits soar when he tells me that Usen and Meder have been found. But, I still don't know if I can trust him. Is he Three Hares? If he is, how do I know they are on my side? If they are on my side, is that a good thing?

Contact with Sabira is intermittent and unpredictable, and I don't get a chance to talk over my worries with her. Every night I cradle my amulet and pray to Lord Tengri that she doesn't get bored or frustrated and simply fly back to the mountains without me, and that she stays safe from our enemies – whoever they are.

One day, I linger in one of the small courtyards. It's deliciously cool, despite the searing heat all around. A fountain in the centre flows into four narrow channels, each running at right angles, dividing the garden into four beautiful flower beds. Each is filled with a wonderful array of perfumed trees and colourful plants. Birds sing in wire cages and panels of mosaic tilework in turquoise, dark blue, green and gold cover the walls. The beauty of this small oasis briefly distracts me. How wonderful that someone created these small sanctuaries in such a dusty place.

'What are you doing?' A guard approaches.

I open my mouth, and nothing comes out.

'Come on, girl, answer me. What are you doing here?'

I exhale slowly through pursed lips and try again. 'I'm sorry, I'm new. Lost. I'm looking for the laundry,' I say, hoping he can't see my hands trembling.

'Well, you can't hang about here. The Gurkhan is on his daily walkabout and he won't want his peace disturbed by low life such as yourself. Go on, get out!'

I scurry off, barely able to contain my excitement at the new knowledge buzzing in my head, and it doesn't take long for a plan to take shape.

'Wouldn't it be nice if we put fresh flowers in the Khantun's bedroom? Shall I see if the gardener can provide some?' I am cleaning with Adel and she looks up, clearly pleased.

'That's a lovely idea. The frangipani is smelling particularly sweet at the moment. Go now and see if he'll cut you a few stems.'

The gardener is in one of the larger courtyards. He's delighted to have someone to talk to and spends time explaining all the flowers, shrubs and trees in his tender care. He introduces me to his *children* as he calls them: jasmine, roses, lilies and ylang ylang. Around the edges of the quadrangle: orange, pomegranate, olive and almond trees.

'Adel suggested frangipani,' I say.

'Ah, yes. The most radiant and captivating of all flower scents. Hard to describe. Hints of vanilla, spices, almonds... sensuous, enticing... perfect for the Khantun's bedroom, I would say. Good choice.'

He cuts six large blooms and ties them with a piece of vine.

'May I come back for more? I think there are other places in the Palace to show off your beautiful flowers.'

'I'd be delighted. Join me any time.' He smiles, pleased his work is appreciated.

I make daily visits to the courtyards, getting to know the gardener and his plants. He's happy to talk and I'm happy to listen. I ask questions, all about the plants and flowers to start with, and then slowly I start to ask about the Palace, the people, and, finally, I pluck up the courage to ask about the Gurkhan's daily stroll.

'Does he come here at the same time every day?' I ask casually.

'Yes, he's quite regular. I can tell if he's in a good mood or a bad one, just by the way he walks, the speed of his gait, the heaviness of his footfall. Once or twice, he actually stops to smell a flower, but most times he just passes through with his entourage. I keep my head down.'

'If I was quiet, could I see him?' I ask, looking carefully to see his reaction.

'Would you like that?' He sounds excited.

'Yes.'

'I think the best chance would be in his secret garden. The place he goes to be completely undisturbed. I can hide you in there if you *promise to* stay well-hidden and not make a sound.'

'I promise,' I lie.

Chapter 27

The gardener is talking to me, but I'm not listening. This is it. This is the moment I've been dreaming of. But now it's here, all I want is to go back to the jailoo and forget about the stupid message.

We are in the Gurkhan's private courtyard, the one he comes to alone. It's shady and cool with lemon, orange and almond trees around the edge, and at its centre is a large day bed. With a carved wooden post at each corner set atop a stone tortoise, it's luxuriously draped in red, sheer silk with gold threads which shimmer in the light breeze. The gardener sets a bowl of fresh fruit beside the bed. He fills the water jug from a fountain, and adds fresh mint.

'He's coming. Quick – behind the hibiscus, like I showed you.'

I squat down between the red-flowering shrub and the tiled wall. The guards walk across the courtyard, two ahead of Gurkhan Kuchulyg and two behind. There is a scribe alongside him, scratching notes with a quill on parchment secured to a wooden tablet. I grit my teeth, seething with hatred. I remember Atashka, I remember his slow and agonisingly painful death.

Kuchulyg walks slowly, hands behind his back, with the same arrogant air that I recall from the hunt. He is dressed more informally today, in a loose-fitting silk robe of emerald-green, bound in yellow and blue embroidered strips. He has a fat nose bent sideways, grey-flecked hair and piercing blue eyes. He lifts his head and his nostrils flare, as if he's sniffing me out. I take a deep breath. I rush forward, into the gap between him and the front guards, and face him square on.

'Excuse me... excuse me.'

He stops and looks directly at me, shocked. His lip curls in a snarl. 'Seize her, you useless fools!' His voice is deep and throaty.

A guard twists my arm sharply behind my back. Another lifts me off my feet.

I kick and wriggle, making it as hard as possible for the guard to hold me.

'No! Let me talk. I have to tell you something important. Let me go. LET ME GO!' I sink my teeth into the guard's bare arm when Kuchulyg speaks.

'What have we here, then? A little wildcat. Put her down and let's hear what's so important that she thinks she can take on one of my guards.'

The guard drops me to the ground while the other three stand ready, towering over me, swords drawn. I pick myself up slowly, not wanting to give them any reason to attack, and brush my hands down the front of my apron, checking to feel that the message is still in the pocket. I keep my head bowed respectfully low, not meeting the Gurkhan's eyes.

'My great Lord... Oh Lord... Sir...'

I have forgotten how to address him and his guards snigger.

'I found a messenger in the mountains. Injured. Dying. He gave me this. For you. It's very important. From Genghis Khan and...' My hand is shaking as I hold out the paper. Kuchulyg snatches it. It takes him only seconds to read it.

'Pah! I'm not bowing down to the Mongol pig. Did he not get the message when I sent the little runt Toq back, shaven and shorn, curly tail between his legs? I'm not scared of the ridiculous rumours he spreads about his invincibility.'

My throat dries up. I don't have the words to argue.

He snatches the quill from the scribe and scrawls something across the letter. 'Take that back to him!' He scrunches up the paper and throws it towards me. I pick it up and try to flatten it out against my leg.

'But everyone will die, my Lord.'

'What? Nonsense, child. This is ridiculous. My Generals tell me we are vastly superior and my spies talk of a disorganised, undisciplined rabble. We have nothing to fear. You're lucky I'm in a good mood today so I won't be feeding you to my dogs.' He turns to his guards. 'Now, get her out of here!'

'But –'

'Get her out before I change my mind!'

One guard takes my arms and another my legs. Kuchulyg turns to stomp off and in the briefest of moments our eyes meet.

Hold his gaze

I hold his gaze.

Do not blink

I stare and with the penetrating clarity of eagle vision I see him as meat, blood and bone, twitching nerve endings, erratic heartbeat, and weak muscle tissue.

See his fear

He doesn't scare me. He is a coward to his core. He blinks.

Chapter 28

A cloud of dust lifts as I land with a thud in the street, sore and bruised. It dawns on me just how close I came to being fed to the Gurkhan's dogs. Panic rises inside me. Even before I look up, I feel Sabira overhead. *Oh, sister, I tried, I really tried.*

Calm You me learn Not stop now
Turn tight
Fly low Ride wind
Soar tilt drop roll
You sharp Prey weak
Stalk him Sap him
This our hunt

I remember Atashka interrogating me any time I returned from a failed hunt with Sabira: *What did you learn? What would you do differently next time? How can you improve? What are you going to change?* He would make me think carefully and answer each question. *The choices you make will help you find out who you really are.* They're both right. I can't give up. I need to stop, sit and think, work it all out.

'Hello, you!' It's Mara. 'I heard through the Palace grapevine that you'd confronted the Gurkhan. Incredible how fast news travels when it's hot gossip. Though, to be honest I thought you'd be locked up, honest, I did. Or worse. Can't believe you're back out here. Old Kuchulyg must have been in a good mood, eh? Anyway, I'm ever so pleased to see you again. Funny really, I hardly know you, but I was missing you.'

Mara embraces me in an unrestrained hug. I really don't want to talk to her right now, after I've failed so dramatically. She rattles on, regardless.

'What happened to you inside the Palace? I want to hear all about everything, every tiny detail from the moment I left. And don't leave anything out. Did you –?'

She wasn't going to stop so I interrupted. 'I need to find Usen and Meder.' I start to cry.

'Oh, Gulzura. They're both safe, don't worry. Usen is being looked after by the ummah. I met him, and I have to say you didn't tell me how gorgeous he is, those eyes, and so talented with his music and poetry. Anyway, he was unwell, which is why he didn't come back for you on the day you arrived. It was his breathing. He's still a bit weak, but he'll be fine. I will ask Yajub or Nurdeen to fetch him.'

I should have known there was a good reason. I should have guessed that the dust and heat would set off one of his attacks.

'And Meder?' I ask.

'He's stabled safely. Usen can tell you exactly where. I don't know – you nomad folk! Anyone would think you were wed to that horse of yours.'

I nod, unable to speak as I choke back the sobs.

'Come on; we can't spend all day chatting in the street.' Mara links her arm in mine. 'The guards will back soon to check you've gone. Let's get something to eat then get ourselves over to the bathhouse. It would be good to just rest and chat a while before we go back. Once the others get home, we won't get a word in edgeways.'

'Bathhouse?'

'Wait and see.'

I don't have much choice other than to follow her.

The elderly woman at the entrance embraces Mara and, as she pulls her close, speaks softly into her ear. 'Hello, my Princess. How are you keeping? Is there anything you need?'

Mara answers equally quietly. 'I'm doing just fine, Bermet, but thank you for asking. Is there anyone here today I need to watch out for?'

'No. I know everyone: all trusted friends and loyal. You know we're all here for you if you ever need us – just ask.' She kisses Mara's cheek and pulls away. 'And, who, may I ask, is this?' she says, looking at me.

'This is my new friend, Gulzura, and can you believe this is the first time she's been in a bathhouse? She's fresh from the Palace. Quite incredible, I know.'

Bermet leans toward Mara and whispers something. Mara laughs. 'She's definitely one of us, I can assure you of that.'

The woman refuses to take the coins Mara hands her and passes over two pieces of cotton cloth, giving me a narrow-eyed look as I walk past.

'Princess?'

Mara shrugs. 'Stupid nickname, eh?'

She leads me into a room where we strip and cover ourselves with the piece of cotton. I am nervous about leaving my waist-bag, but Mara assures me it will be safe. I follow her into the next room, which is eight-sided, with stone benches arranged neatly on each of its tiled walls. Thin shards of sunlight shine through the slits in the domed roof. Mara turns a metal lever in the wall and, like a gift from the gods, water pours clean and clear out of the funnel below to fill a bucket. With no shame or embarrassment, she removes her cotton towel, picks up a brass bowl and then scoops the water all over herself, sighing with delight as the dust and grime wash off her and flow away down a hole in the floor.

'Come on, Gulzura, it's wonderful. Honestly, you'll love it. This is truly my favourite day of the week.'

'How does the water get here?' I am genuinely puzzled.

'All the water in the city comes through pipes directly from the river. I remember once, I had to hide out in those tunnels. Workmen go in and out every day to plug leaks but, I can tell you, I will never go back there again. Not for all the honey-soaked walnuts in the land. They are scary. Great if you like rats, spiders, slimy things and complete dark.' She fakes a shiver and a terrified face, then laughs.

I try to fill the bucket while holding the muslin over myself and it slips; then I slip trying to hold it up. Mara pretends not to notice and closes her eyes, smiling as the water washes over her.

'How do you keep clean in the mountains, then? Do you mind me asking? You don't have to answer, just that I'm really interested.'

'We have a special yurt where we heat a bucket of water on a small fire and wash in the steam that comes off it.' I don't confess how infrequent this is; nowadays, I only do it after my moonblood time. I take a big breath, remove my muslin and slosh a whole bucket of water over myself.

'How much water can I use?'

'As much as you want; it's endless. You know, sometimes I stay here doing this for so long my skin goes all wrinkly and then it takes ages for it to go normal again. I envy those women who work here: clean, fresh, cool in the summer; warm in the winter. I'd hardly call it work.'

Once we are both rinsed clean, we move into the next room which is full of chattering women and girls, washing themselves and their babies in great mounds of soapy suds. Maybe it's a city custom, but the women greet Mara quite formally and, without exception, they look warily at me. She seems to know them all and I watch and listen in silence as Mara reassures them that I am *one of them*. They exchange news which consists almost entirely of gossip about people I don't know, so I wash myself quietly and, once we are clean and dry, we set off to Mara's house.

'I can't wait to introduce you to my friends; you'll really like them,' she says.

Chapter 29

'You can't just bring a complete stranger back to the house without consulting the rest of us first.' I wake from a nap to hear a boy shouting in the room next door. 'You're putting us all at risk.'

'She needed rescuing. Don't you remember, Bortboi, what it felt like to be out there, on your own, the first time in the city, lost and alone?' Mara replies.

'Yes, I do, and I got on with my life on the streets. I learned how to survive, sleeping in corners and alleyways for many moons before I met you and the others.'

'You did, and bravo to you. But, there's a big difference. You're a boy! Do you have *any* idea what it's like to be on the streets alone as a girl?' Mara is shouting now.

'Alone? You were never alone! You've always had people looking out for you because you're *special*. The only reason I've survived this long is because I look out for myself. I don't trust people,' he yells.

'Well, I'll have you know, one of the reasons *I'm* still alive today is that I learned to trust my instincts. And my instincts tell me I can trust her,' Mara says, more calmly.

'You don't know anything about her. She might be a spy for all we know.'

'I have a feeling she's a good person, Bortboi. Let's just say it's intuition. I like her and I want her to stay. It won't be for long.'

'Well, relying on your intuition doesn't exactly fill me with confidence.'

'Don't worry. I won't tell her anything, I promise. Please give her a chance, get to know her yourself. If, in a few days, you still have your doubts, we'll think again.'

'Let's hope that's not too late,' he snaps, and a door bangs. I bite my lip; I don't want to be back out on the streets again.

'How are you doing?' Mara comes in and sees fear written all over my face. 'Oh dear. Did you just hear all that?'

'Would you like me to leave?' I whisper.

'No! Absolutely not.' Mara hugs me. 'You don't want to listen to him. He's just off on one of his rants. He's had a few nasty experiences and he's wary now. It's difficult to penetrate that. But, once you do, you're his friend forever. Don't worry, he'll come round, when he gets to know you.'

Before I get a chance to press her further, we hear a shout at the front door. Usen walks in. I leap up and wrap my arms around his waist so tightly he squirms.

'I've got the right place then?' He laughs. 'Hold on there, I can barely breathe.'

'Welcome, Usen.' Mara smiles flirtatiously, then leaves the room. 'I'll make tea.'

'Where's Meder?' I ask. 'How is he?'

'*I'm* fine, thanks.' Usen gives me a pretend-angry look. 'He's well and safe, missing you but getting fat on a city diet.'

'How are you?'

'Thank you for asking! I'm fine now. I'm so sorry I abandoned you. I collapsed at the stables. I have no recollection of the first two days after I left you. What *have* you been thinking about me all this time?'

I don't like to mention the words I'd called him. I squeeze his hand.

'Thank goodness you ended up here,' he says. 'What happened to you?'

When I tell him about my near escape from the slavers, he hangs his head in shame.

'I'm so, *so* sorry,' he says.

'I met Kuchulyg,' I say.

'I know. I heard. Did he listen? Did he take the message?'

'He read it and threw it on the ground. But I will get it to him. I will make him take notice.'

Mara bursts into the room with a dish of snacks. 'Right. Who wants something to eat?' She sits beside Usen. 'These are manti, which are dumplings filled with onion, cream and pumpkin; the triangular things are samsa and today they're filled with cheese and potato, I think. I can't remember what Rahmat told me. Just try them and if you don't like them, don't eat them. But, if you do, don't eat them all!'

'You eat well!' I exclaim.

'You wouldn't believe the waste that's thrown from the Palace kitchen, all perfectly edible. Meat, vegetables, fruit, sweets, pastries, pretty much anything we want and all the very best quality. We know the days and the times and we're ready, baskets in hand, to take first pickings. Anyway, Okean and Rahmat – they're pot washers, brothers, actually; don't know where they came from – they'll keep tasty morsels specially for me.'

I am in awe of Mara. She's so resourceful, so fearless, so happy and she seems to know everyone.

'Everything we own here has been retrieved from the rubbish tips at the back of the palace – carpets, wall hangings, candles, clothes, shoes. We live like kings and queens!'

'Where are your parents?' I ask. Usen shoots me a look that says I've been rude but Mara puts her hand on his arm, to reassure him.

'Oh, we're all orphans. No parents allowed here,' she replies, completely unbothered. 'There're four of us; I'm the only girl. Well, I *was* the only girl until you came along, Gulzura. You can sleep with me in my room. I've wanted a sister ever since I can remember and now look, I've got one.'

I like that. I imagine Sabira, were she still a girl, would be like Mara.

'We all have a different story of how we ended up here.' She pulls a sad face, then smiles and shrugs her shoulders. 'But here we are. There are people in the city who keep an eye on us, but you know, we look after each other, really, and even though it can be hard sometimes, we've managed quite well so far, as you can see.'

I wonder what my life would have been like without parents, without brothers, uncles, aunts and cousins. I watch Mara; nothing seems to stand between her and what she wants and I wonder if it's better to be alone but free than part of a family that protects you but tethers you.

It's not long before Nurdeen and Yajub arrive. They seem happy to meet me, particularly as they know Usen well. They chat and laugh and before long, everyone disappears into the kitchen, insisting I rest.

There's a knock at the door.

'Gulzura!' Aibek looks as surprised as I am.

Even though I've rehearsed this moment over and over again in my head, now that he's in front of me, I can't think what to say.

He rushes forward to hug me, then stops. 'Sorry. I shouldn't presume... I'm just so pleased to see you.'

'Hello!'

'What? Am I hearing things? You're talking? When did that happen?' He takes my hands, and his eyes widen with delight.

'It just... after Atashka.'

'I'm so sorry about your grandfather.' He looks genuinely upset. He hugs me again.

'I came to the city to find you,' he says. 'I missed you on the jailoo. I heard rumours but I didn't dare ask your clan for news. I thought if I came here, someone might know – and look, here you are, settled in with my favourite family of rejects!'

The others appear from the kitchen, carrying bowls and platefuls of boiled meat, vegetables and fresh flatbreads. We all sit in a circle and help ourselves.

'So, what exactly are you doing here in the city, nomad girl?' Bortboi's tone is openly hostile.

'Bortboi,' Mara snaps. 'Gulzura is our guest and we will treat her with the respect guests in our city deserve.' Bortboi lowers his gaze and mumbles an apology. There is no doubt who is in charge here.

With Usen's help, I give a faltering account of my story.

'So, you see, I must get Kuchulyg to surrender to Genghis Khan. There will be a massacre if I fail.'

'Well, a new leader would be welcome here: a vision we all share,' Nurdeen says. He glances pointedly at Mara, and everyone nods in agreement. I sense something awkward between Usen and Aibek, who don't seem to want to meet each other's eye.

Bortboi scoffs and leaves. I'm relieved he didn't press me further and before anyone else can speak, Usen interjects.

'I know you, don't I?' he says to Aibek, coldly.

'Yes, yes, I think you do.' Aibek looks down, his face turning a little pink.

'What?! How?' I ask.

Silence.

'Are you going to tell her, or would you like me to do it?' Usen spits out.

'I think it best if you tell,' Aibek mumbles.

'You know some of this story, Gulzura, and this looks the right moment to tell you the rest.'

'Can you start at the beginning for those of us who have no idea what's going on?' Mara asks.

Usen exhales. 'I was promised to a girl of Balta clan, in an effort by Father to make peace between us. Father sent me to them to fulfil my bride service. I set out with every intention of working hard for my new family. I was prepared to be tested by them and prove myself capable and worthy as a future son-in-law. But the gods worked against me from the outset. I had a breathing attack the day I arrived, and I could barely speak for the wheezing. Seeing my weakness, her brothers took full advantage and beat me up whenever they could. They said they were just play-fighting, finding out 'what I was made of', but the more bruised I got, the less I was able to defend myself.'

'They're a vicious lot,' Aibek says, and Usen shoots him a look.

'People started to call me lazy and useless because the coughing fits meant I couldn't help with much of the physical work. They joked that there weren't enough horses in the land for Father to offer to make up for my faults. I thought you were my friend, Aibek, but even you turned on me in the end.'

Everyone looks at Aibek, who is looking at the floor.

'It didn't take long,' Usen continues. 'Not even two moons, to reach a point when I decided I could not tolerate it any longer. What's more, the poor girl I was supposed to marry was just a child. She was terrified, and cowered whenever she saw me.'

Mara looks shocked and puts her hand on his.

'The final straw was your betrayal, Aibek.' Usen looks accusingly at Aibek, who returns the look with one of utter wretchedness.

'We were preparing for a raid to steal a bride from Ükü clan. I was forced to join the raiding party, to prove my manhood. Aibek, tell everyone what you did.'

Aibek doesn't look up and I stare at him, needing him to reassure me that none of this is true.

'I hid in an empty yurt,' Usen continues, 'as I didn't want to fight or kidnap a girl, and you' – Usen looks directly at Aibek – 'you found me and told her brothers where I was hiding. They beat me to a pulp for cowardice. You gave me away. I thought you were my friend, I trusted you – and you told them where to find me.'

'I don't know what to say,' he mumbles.

'Say it's not true,' I say. I am wide-eyed in disbelief.

'I don't have the words to say how sorry I am.'

'Aibek, why would you do that?' Nurdeen asks, shaking his head.

'I was a different person then. I'm ashamed now to think about the boy I was. So selfish, I could only think about myself, what would keep me in their favour, which was to let them know where you were hiding. I, too, was fighting for my place there. And it was pointless. But, being thrown out of my clan was the saving of me. I had to change. I had time to think about the kind of man I wanted to be. And long after I betrayed you, Usen, I thought about how it should have been different, how I should have behaved.'

Usen's jaw is clenched so hard that muscles twitch on the side of his face. I worry he might thump Aibek.

'I don't blame you for hating me, Usen.'

Usen stares hard.

'I have no excuse and I beg your forgiveness.'

'How did you end up in the city, Usen?' Mara asks, breaking the silence.

'When I lost Aibek's friendship, it was the end for me. As soon as I'd recovered from the beating, I went out one day, to check on the herds and I just kept going. I walked for days, barely stopping until I found myself at the city gates.'

'And that is where I have ended up too,' Aibek says. 'My attempts to prove myself in my clan only served to make me their next target. The gods made sure I was punished. I got my just reward for being unkind to you, Usen. Will you forgive me?'

Usen's face softens. 'I too have changed since those days; I have learned much from the ummah. My understanding of the Qur'an is that I should pardon you. No one is perfect, everyone is capable of wrongdoing, and I will forgive, as Allah would wish.'

Everyone exhales with relief. Except me.

'Besides, I have heard how you have been a good friend to my sister when she was alone and friendless.' Usen turns to me and sees my scowl.

'Come on, Gulzura, if I can forgive him, there is no need for you to bear a grudge. We are all on the same side now.'

Chapter 30

The next morning, I am reunited with Meder. I fling my arms around him. I never want to lose him again. I can see that he is well fed and being well looked after, but I can hardly bear to leave him to return to Mara's house.

In the evening, Usen and Aibek talk long into the night, arguing, joking, and, much to the relief of everyone, a friendship begins to emerge. At dinner the following day, our conversation is dominated by talk of forgiveness and understanding.

'I can forgive Aibek his faults. In fact, I would say I am glad he's not perfect. How unbearable it would be to be friends with someone almost god-like!'

Everyone laughs.

'But I will *never* forgive Kuchulyg,' I say. 'Revenge rules my every waking moment.'

The room goes silent.

'I will have no peace until he is dead.' My heart almost stops as I say this. I hadn't realised until this moment that that's what I was thinking. But it's true. I gave Kuchulyg a chance, and he didn't take it. The only way to avenge Atashka and save the Balasagun people – in fact, the whole of the Kara Khitai: *all* my people – is to eliminate the Gurkhan. And – oh, Lord Tengri, help me – I will do this. I will kill him.

'I thought you were just delivering a message?' Nurdeen says.

'Well, yes. Yes. That's my main purpose,' I say, quickly. 'And, I need to try again.'

'Take comfort that the gods will seek justice and retribution for Kuchulyg's deeds in another life. It's not the job for a... for someone who doesn't know the city,' Yajub says. I am almost certain he was going to say it's not a job for a girl.

'I need your help.' I want to ask them about the Three Hares, but Mara was so short with me when I showed her the symbol that I dare not risk it again.

Yajub is blunt. 'Forget it, Gulzura. I don't think you should be doing this. The idea that you can persuade Kuchulyg to submit to Genghis Khan is, well, quite honestly, it's ridiculous.'

I look Yajub straight in the eye. 'You don't know me.'

Usen picks up a komuz and runs his hands appreciatively over the instrument's smooth, juniper wood surface.

'May I?' he asks, to break the tension.

'Of course.' Nurdeen gives him a wide smile.

Usen balances the komuz in the crook of his right hip and thigh and strums a few practice chords before playing a tune and starting to sing. There is huge applause and shouts of 'More, more,' when he finishes.

'Let's try one that everyone knows.'

He starts another tune, and immediately Mara, Yajub and Nurdeen clap in rhythm and then join in, singing the chorus. I silently mouth the words, frightened that my voice will sound like a crow. Nurdeen and Mara get up and start to dance. With hands on hips, shoulders jerking back and forth, they move around each other in a circle, grinning broadly as they mimic each other's angular arm and hand movements. Usen picks up the pace, strumming and plucking the strings so fast now that they're almost a blur. Aibek takes his cue from the accelerating rhythm to stand, and reaches for my hand to join him.

'Oh, no!' I say, pulling away.

'Please?' His face is soft and pleading and hard to resist.

'I don't dance.'

'Everyone dances. Just stand up, relax and I will show you.'

I have never danced. No one has ever asked me.

I let him pull me up to standing. He faces me, holding my hands in his. 'Just copy what I do.'

He crosses his legs, then uncrosses, moving in little hops as he does so. I follow. Then he adds a small dip before changing direction. Once I have mastered the feet movements, he lets go of my hands and rolls his shoulders forward and back, making the same sharp, fast moves I've just seen Mara and Nurdeen do. I try to copy but get muddled and before I know it, I've trodden on his toes. He lifts his foot and hops about, pretending to cry. The others laugh and then take my hands so the four of us form a circle. Mara pulls me into the centre of the room, where we twirl around, hands raised high. Then the boys kneel and we dance around them. Before I know it, I am dancing without thinking. I let the music fill my body and allow my arms and legs to move with the rhythm. Soon, I am breathless, giddy and laughing.

Mara persuades Nurdeen to take over the komuz. 'Something slow and gentle, please!' she asks, as she boldly takes Usen's hand.

Usen blushes. As Nurdeen strikes up a ballad, Aibek holds out his arms wide and high, his eyes looking deeply into mine, inviting me in closer.

Girl be brave
Open wide heart
Let him in

My body surrenders to his embrace. My heart thumps like a shaman's drum as he holds me so close our bodies almost touch. He smells startlingly familiar, of clean earth and hot bread and honey. As he starts to move, swaying lightly, my body follows. We fit well together, our hips moving from side to side in unison, a hair's breadth apart. I look up; he is different. I thought I knew everything about him: how he scoops water from the river to drink with his left hand, how raw onion leaves make his tummy ache, how he skips wildly like a small child when he's happy, and how baby marmots playing in the sun make him laugh. But I see him now in a new light. His brown eyes are now the colour of roasted walnuts. His muscles, that have always been strong and taut, now offer safety and security. I blush with the desire of never wanting him to let me go. He moves his hand to the back of my neck and delicately traces the curve of my spine with his fingertips, sending a rapturous tremble through me. I look up and smile the widest smile of pure joy.

Nurdeen begins a new, faster tune. Aibek releases his hold and we link elbows and twirl around, just managing not to crash into Mara and Usen who are twirling in the opposite direction. I stumble, worrying that I've done something wrong and put him off and that's why he's let me go. Seeing my anxious face, he lifts me off the ground and slowly lowers me. As our bodies touch, an exhilarating energy surges through me, filling me with glowing light, from the very tips of my toes to the top of my head. My heart is beating to a new rhythm. I am changed. I have moulted and my new feathers take me soaring, higher than ever, over a world that has endless, glorious possibilities. Beads of sweat trickle down my spine as his lips brush my cheek. I look up to meet his gaze.

'I don't want this to end,' I whisper.

'It doesn't have to,' he replies.

But the evening does end as the music eventually peters out. I avoid Usen's eye for now; there's no doubt that tomorrow I will have to face his questions about what happened this evening between me and Aibek. Everyone collapses, exhausted, and falls asleep on various mattresses brought out and strewn haphazardly across the floor. I lie awake facing Aibek, watching his chest, still glistening with sweat, rise and fall gently with each sleeping breath. My body still tingles from the memory of how his hands and arms held me, firmly, yet with the softness of goose-down, as we danced. I reach out to touch those arms, as delicately as I can. He stirs but doesn't wake. I trace my fingertips along the length of the two long blue lines that hold his blood, his life force, on the inner side of his forearm. I reach a small tattoo that I've not seen before, toward the crook of his elbow. It's the same united Balta axe with snow leopard paw print that he carved onto the pendant for me.

I can't remember ever being happier.

Chapter 31

'Wakey, wakey, sleepy head.' Usen is prodding his finger into my ribs. 'It's time to get up. Everyone else has gone.'

I wake abruptly, cross, partly because Aibek has left without saying goodbye and partly because I've had a fitful night tossing and turning, unable to shake off the guilt of remembering that I am not in the city to enjoy myself. The gods gave me a task and I promised to fulfil it. Now, with the realisation that it goes far beyond the simple delivery of a message, the enormity of what I must do terrifies me. I ask Usen to accompany me on my morning visit to Meder.

'What am I doing here, Usen? It's fun here with Mara and her friends but what will happen if I don't do as the gods ask?' I'm deliberately vague about what that might be.

'Before we talk about that, what is going on between you and Aibek?'

I shake my head, annoyed that he's changed the subject. 'Nothing.'

'It didn't look like nothing. You are not a city girl. This is not our way.'

I don't meet his eye.

'I don't want you seeing him alone. Understand?'

The only thing I want right now *is* to see him alone, and to be back in his arms, but that will have to wait until I have worked out how I am to fulfil my mission.

'I think I should try to get back into the Palace.'

'No way, Gulzura. You'll just get caught again and Kuchulyg won't be so kind to you a second time. It's far too risky. You've tried and it didn't work.'

'But I have to. It's why we are here! The gods have ordered it.'

'We'll find another way. You are not going back into the Palace again. That's an order. Hear me?'

'Don't you remember what Bubu said? About the prophecy?'

He strides ahead muttering something about *sisters* under his breath.

Meder is tethered in a cool stall. He gives me a loud, welcoming whinny, and Usen gives him a pat before leaving. 'Don't be too long.'

As Meder slurps his water, I put my lips to his shoulder and talk quietly to him.

'Any day now, the Mongol Khan will obliterate the city. What am I to do?'

Meder lifts his head out of the bucket and rubs his wet muzzle up and down my leg to dry off.

'Oh, Meder, it's not funny.' I scratch his withers hard, so his lips quiver, which always makes me laugh.

Meder nickers softly, seeming to understand my dilemma. He stamps his feet and tosses his head, irritated by the flies gathering around him. Luckily, there is lavender just outside and I pick a big handful, bruise it between my palms and then rub it down his neck and shoulders in circular moves.

'I have to get the message through to Kuchulyg. But what if he doesn't listen? What if he has me fed to his dogs? What will happen if I kill him? What will happen if I don't? Maybe everyone's right about me, and I should just abandon the whole idea. But how would I face Bubu? And Father will marry me off as soon as he can and I will be condemned to endless drudgery – or worse, because if Kuchulyg doesn't surrender, Genghis Khan will kill us all anyway. And, besides, I promised Atashka I would avenge his death. But now I don't want anything except to be with Aibek. Oh, Meder, this is all so hard.'

Sabira, soaring high, hears me too.

Home waits you me
First we choose gods' task
Look   Who are you?

I groom Meder and in the long, sweeping strokes, a plan evolves.

Aibek is waiting for me when I get back to the orphans' house.

'How is Meder?' he asks.

'Getting fat!' I laugh.

'You need to give him a good gallop on the jailoo.'

'I want to. But I can't leave yet.'

'Please tell me you're not still thinking of confronting Kuchulyg again.'

'Not exactly. I have another idea.'

'What?'

I shake my head. I don't want to involve him.

'Really, Gulzura, it's too dangerous to oppose the Gurkhan.' He takes my hands in his and pulls me closer. My heartbeat picks up, and I fill with the sparks of a fire rekindled from the night before. 'If you fail, you'll end up in prison at best, and at worst... Kuchulyg is a cruel man who takes great pleasure in watching his enemies suffer long, drawn-out, painful deaths.'

'I don't plan to fail.'

'You can't take the risk.' He is adamant and the mood changes quickly.

'I have to. The clan wishes it. The gods wish it. It's my duty.'

'Your clan and the gods have put too great a burden on you. Besides, you have already shown remarkable courage and bravery. They will recognise this and absolve you of any further responsibility, I am quite certain.' He strokes a finger down my cheek and I ache to relax into his arms. '

'I made a promise to Mother Earth that if she saved me in the earth tremor, I would do her bidding. And, I owe Atashka.'

'It's foolish to think you can take on the Gurkhan by yourself.'

'Foolish?' I pull my hands out of his. 'Is that what you think of me?'

'You won't find peace until you can forgive and forget.'

'I will *never* forgive him,' I shout, angry that with so few words Aibek has smothered the fire in me.

'I can't stand back and watch you waste your life seeking revenge, when revenge is impossible. I've seen it before in bitter old men, who carry a hatred all their lives, never at peace. It will eat away at you, Gulzura, until it destroys you.'

'Bitter? Instead of criticising me, you could help!'

'I *will* help you! Come with me, let's return to the jailoo. We were so happy there.'

'If I return, we won't have a future together. I will be married off and we will never see each other again,' I say. He looks crestfallen. I'm so confused; I want to hit him and, at the same time, wrap my arms around him.

'I will do it with or without you.'

'Your stubbornness served you well when you were training Sabira, but now I'm truly afraid it will be your downfall.'

'Leave me alone. I don't need you. Go away!' I scream, in a voice I've not heard before.

'Really? You want me to leave?'

'Yes. Just go!'

He walks out, slamming the door behind him, and I wonder how, in the name of the gods, I managed to end up with the exact opposite of what I wanted. I have much to learn about how to use my new voice.

Chapter 32

'Gather round! I have a message.'

The people in the main square ignore me, giving me not even the briefest glance.

'An important message... for you all.'

I look up and see Sabira's reassuring silhouette in the clear blue sky. *Thank you. At least you're here for me.*

> *Kyuk Kyuk Kyuk*
> *Strong stay*
> *Speak true word*

'Listen to me.'

Nothing. No one stops. I am barely audible, even to myself, over the noisy hubbub. My voice is weak from a morning of wretched sobbing. My heart is torn in two.

'Why don't you stand on that plinth? You'll be heard much better there,' a scrawny beggar suggests and then disappears before I can thank him. I climb up and clear my throat. Nothing comes out. Silence.

> *Breathe brave breathe deep calm*
> *Your words now all to hear*
> *Kyuk Kyuk Kyuk*

Sabira flies down and, with a dramatic screech, lands beside me, wings outstretched, looking glorious, golden and dangerous. Everyone in the vicinity stops and I hear mutterings of astonishment. 'Who is this girl who has command of an eagle?' 'Messengers of the gods, they are!'

The people are a little afraid, but they are silent and I have their attention now.

'I have a story to tell you,' I begin tentatively. 'Listen to me, please. I am a poor nomad girl from the mountains. One day I was out tending the sheep and goats when our Lord of the Eternal Blue Sky delivered this beautiful eagle at my feet. She is my sister, my guide, and together we have come to the city to deliver a message.'

Sabira flaps her huge wings and calls out, so more and more people stop to listen and the square fills rapidly.

'A great army is on its way, led by the Mongol Genghis Khan. His message is simple: if we surrender and acknowledge him as our new leader, he will not harm a single one of us. But if we don't, he will raze this city, and every man, woman, child and animal will die in the process.'

There are gasps and mutterings in the audience.

'You may have heard rumours of the bloodthirsty brutality of the Mongol horde and their leader and I want to reassure you that they are greatly exaggerated. I have heard from the mouths of people who live under his leadership, and they say that in return for reasonable tribute, he has delivered a peace and security they've not known before. They live under laws that make all men equal, no matter their kinship or status. He's banned the use of torture and allows everyone freedom to worship whichever of the gods they choose.'

The audience are now nodding approval.

'I think what would appeal to you, above everything else, is that the Mongol Khan abhors the rich and powerful.'

Everyone knows exactly who I am referring to and applause breaks out, along with a few cheers.

Palace guards gallop in, slicing through the crowd.

'Clear the square! Orders of the Gurkhan! Clear the square!'

People scatter in all directions.

'Go, Sabira, go!'

She flies away as I jump off the plinth and run. I dart down a small alley, tucking myself in low behind a cart piled high with carrots. The clang of hooves on cobbles gets louder behind me and I turn briefly to see two mounted guards in pursuit. I dive into an open doorway and hide in the darkness, trying to calm my noisy breathing. The guards ride straight past. I check the alley is clear and slowly emerge. A foot soldier turns the corner, spots me and shouts.

'Here! She's here!'

He charges straight at me but he is slow and I dodge his outstretched arms easily with a quick sidestep. I keep running, turning left and right, ducking under a line of washing, jumping over children playing, narrowly avoiding a donkey cart, until I come to a dead end.

'This way. She went this way!'

Two guards, clearly fitter and faster than their friend, are closing in. My only hope is some steps up the side of a building at the top of the alley. I run up them three at a time to find a large, open terrace where a small boy is arranging wet mud bricks into neat rows to dry in the sun.

'Oi!' he shouts.

'Shhh.' I place my finger over my mouth. 'Please, I'm running from the guards. I need to hide.'

He nods and points to the edge of the terrace. Does he want me to jump off the roof?

'Up here. She can't have gone anywhere else.' It's the guards at the foot of the steps.

I look down onto a huge, cloth canopy extending from this building right across the street below to the building opposite, providing shade for the stallholders beneath.

'Jump!' the boy whispers.

There's nowhere to hide. I close my eyes, trust to the gods, and leap from the rooftop. I land in the billowing folds of the canopy and hold my breath, my heart pounding.

'Where is she?' I can hear the guards on the rooftop.

'Who?' the boy answers.

'The girl. The girl who ran up here. You must have seen her.'

'I don't know no girl,' the boy says and then shrieks, 'Ow!'

I flinch.

'She must have double-backed. How did we miss her?'

'Does it matter? We've lost her and we're going to have to find a good excuse, or we'll be up for a thrashing.'

There's a pause, then the boy leans over the side of the building. 'They've gone.'

I lie back and smile broadly, very pleased with myself. Who says I can't do this?

Aibek dared to call me *foolish*. Usen didn't think I was up to the job. It's only Sabira who believes in me. *Sabira? Where are you sister?* She's not overhead. I sit up on my elbows to get a better view of the sky and suddenly the canopy drops lower and there's a loud tearing sound. I scramble on my hands and knees over the undulating cloth and, before I can grab the wall, the fabric splits beneath me and I drop like a stone, straight onto one of the guards.

The shock stuns him, giving me time to roll out of his arms onto the ground. But he quickly comes to his senses and lifts me off my feet.

'Well, look what I've just caught. The gods have sent me a little gift.' He smiles and reveals a mouth full of rotting black teeth.

I lash out with a sharp, upward jab of my elbow and hear the sickening crunch of his nose breaking. He drops me to clutch his bleeding face and I dart between his legs, only to be met by two more guards who jump on me and pin me down. They tie my legs together and my hands behind my back. There's no hope of escape but still I can't give up. I twist and flail my body, snapping at them like a fox in the grip of an eagle, making it impossible for them to put me over the back of their horse. The last thing I see is a leather-gloved hand sweeping down at my head; then there is a searing pain and a flash of bright light.

Chapter 33

A high-pitched whooshing sound, like the edge of a waterfall, fills my ears and, with the one eye I'm able to open, I see blurry walls billowing like curtains. I lift my head no more than a whisker when an agonising pain shoots across my forehead. Darkness engulfs me.

It's pitch-black when I wake again. I tentatively explore my pounding head. My fingertips find a sticky patch of matted hair and I taste congealed blood. Am I dying? I'm not afraid, if I am. I know Atashka is waiting to greet me, and I shut my eyes, hoping that the end comes swiftly. *Oh, Great Lord Tengri, I am not fit for your task. I beg you don't let me suffer, take me quickly, and let another, stronger subject take up your request.*

'Oi, get up!' The voice is distant and I keep my eyes closed, hoping it will go away.

'Oi!' The man shouts louder and still I don't move. I hear the rattling of keys in a lock and the squeak of a door. His footsteps get close and then there's a nudge into my ribs. I open an eye and he retreats quickly.

'Right. Just checking on you.' He turns and leaves. I hear something skid across the floor. 'Breakfast.'

I close my eye and remain curled up. I am in no hurry to look around. The memory of those last few moments of freedom tumbles into my head and with it the shame of failure and the stomach-churning fear of reprisals to come. I survived the night but I hope the gods will take me before Kuchulyg has his fun.

'Is she alive?' a voice outside calls.

'Yeah. I checked,' another man answers.

'What? You went in?'

'Yeah. She's just a kid.'

'Well, I won't be going in there in a hurry. Damir told me he's had a good look at her and she's poxy! Do not touch unless you want your poker to drop off! Besides, she's a feisty little alley cat. He said it took two elite guards to pin her down, and Abishqa had to go home after she broke his nose!' The two men chuckle.

'Nasty man, that Abishqa. Never liked him. That'll make him think twice before taking on a girl,' the first man laughs.

'But what's a young waif of a girl doing here?' the second asks.

'The Gurkhan just wants her shut up for now.' He lowers his voice. 'Don't you know what's going on out there? Dissent is erupting all across the city and she was caught trying to stir it up. More and more people are talking about renouncing allegiance to our Leader and demanding a peaceful surrender to the Mongol Khan who's on his way as we speak, apparently. *Anyone* caught spreading this ridiculous idea is going to be locked up.'

'But she's so young. Look at her. What harm could that little bundle of bones in rags do?'

'He doesn't care who she is. He just wants her silenced. She's lucky he's not ordered her killed.'

'Yet...'

Their voices fade as they walk away.

A cool draught tickles my hands and I shuffle so it falls on my face. The relief from the stifling, fetid air feels as good as washing in a mountain stream. My tummy aches with hunger but the scummy surface and horde of flies on the breakfast dish make me gag.

Slowly, I check myself over. Despite painful evidence of a hefty strike to the side of my head, I still have all my teeth and nose in place and luckily didn't break my arms and legs falling through the street canopy.

The cell is triangular: two brick walls with a small, barred window high up, well beyond my reach. There's a wide archway on the third side, filled in with thick metal bars and a barred doorway. Large, uneven stone slabs cover the floor and the stench of urine and vomit fills my nostrils. I crawl over to the iron bars and give the door a shake, just in case it has accidentally been left open. It hasn't and it's secured by a large padlock. The bars are closely spaced with no hope of squeezing through. I take in the two long corridors that run from my cell, like the fork in two branches, each comprised of a series of doorways that look just like mine. The empty space echoes with the moans of people who I assume are prisoners like me.

I open out a blanket, lying in a corner, and throw it back immediately. It's crawling with fleas and stinks of vomit. I retch and shudder to think about those who've been here before me. In the other corner is a small bucket, filthy and fly-ridden. I sweep a few bits of dusty straw into a small heap and lie down. Exhaustion weighs down on me, accompanied by stabs of intense fear. I vow that if I ever get out of here, I will never again moan about bossy brothers, wind-chapped cheeks, or dung under my fingernails. My eyes are drawn to the tiny window and the small patch of sky. I stare up into the blueness. *Sabira, come to me. Please.*

Instead of her calming words, other voices call out inside my head: *You've failed again, you're useless. The gods are playing with you, can't you see that? You should have stayed on the jailoo where you know your place.* I open my mouth to shout out, 'Shut up!' Nothing. I have no voice. It's withdrawn to a familiar place, hidden deep inside me.

The lines between dream and reality blur as the day passes and I drift in and out of sleep. I'm home, on the jailoo, drinking in the delicious mountain air; it's peaceful, save for the sound of squabbling choughs on a nearby peak. Sabira is flying overhead as Meder and I gallop, bow and arrow poised to shoot. Kuchulyg is my target, alone, exposed in the grass. He does nothing to defend himself as I get closer. He doesn't need to; I am immobilised by his stare and my hand is unable to release the arrow.

The temperature rises, and the cell becomes like one of the kitchen ovens; sweat trickles down my cheeks and pools in the small wells above my collarbones. My drenched shirt sticks to my back and I'm desperately thirsty. Heat and hunger are sapping any energy I may have. I reach for the bowl, thinking that I will simply close my eyes, pinch my nostrils and eat, but it's empty. I'm not alone.

On the morning of the second day, I wake with a start as the cell door opens with a metallic jangling of keys and a thunderous clunk as the lock falls to the floor.

'Oi, girl! Move over to the far wall.'

I do as I'm told. If I wasn't so bruised and hungry, I might find it amusing that this huge man is intimidated by me. I can barely lift myself off the floor, and am completely defenceless, but I puff out my chest and give him a penetrating, narrow-eyed stare in an effort to confirm his worst thoughts.

'Here's your breakfast. Eat it quickly or the rats'll have it straight from the bowl.' He slides a wooden bowl across the flagstones, followed by a leather bottle, slams the door shut, relocks it and stomps off.

I fall upon the food, not noticing or caring what it is. The leather bottle contains water which I drink carefully, not knowing how long this ration will have to last.

Kyuk Kyuk Kyuk

Sabira is perched on the ledge outside, looking in through the bars.

Oh, Sabira, I'm so pleased to see you. Can you get through the bars? Stupid question – of course you can't. Oh, I wish I could touch you, smell you, feel you strong and sure on my arm. I need you, Sabira, more than ever. I need you.

I jump up toward the window, again and again, quite certain that if only I could put in a little more effort, I would reach her. I keep trying until my fingernails tear and bleed. I slump down, defeated.

No fall

This not break you
Gods test you
Ride dream winds Feel air free Gusts squall
Eyes sharp clear you hear you learn

She flies off. *Come back – I need you!* I curl into a ball and weep. I am truly abandoned if even my sister won't stay with me. Sabira's words jostle around in my tired head. The message is clear: the gods won't take me yet; they still want me to continue. But how? How am I supposed to achieve their wish locked up here? I think of Aibek's words: *the gods have put too great a burden on you.* He was right. I wish more than anything we hadn't argued.

Later in the afternoon, Sabira reappears and drops a small parcel through the bars. Frightened that the guards might see, I retreat to a corner and unfold the bright green leaf wrapping to reveal a delicious meal of vegetables and noodles. Someone outside knows I'm here. *Thank you, whoever you are.* I'm anxious, though, because Sabira is exposed on the window ledge, and if it were known she was helping me, I'm quite sure Kuchulyg would order his guards to shoot her down. *Go, Sabira, don't wait. Only visit at dawn or dusk to avoid the guards. Please be careful.*

I savour every bit of the food. Eventually, I'm left with just the bitter leaves. I can't risk the guards seeing them. I bundle them all together as tightly as I can in my fist and throw the lump toward the window in the hope they will go through the bars, but they bounce off and scatter across the floor. It's then that I remember the other occupants of my cell: the rats.

The leftover leaves tear easily into small pieces and once the last guard has gone for the night, just before it goes completely dark, I leave a small trail of green treats across the floor and wait. They are quick to pick up the scent and two skinny brown rats appear, pink noses first, sniffling their way cautiously across the flagstones. They gorge greedily, leaving not the slightest trace of my secret meal.

Chapter 34

The only way of keeping track of the passing days is the brief view of a comforting moon each night as it rises past my window. A sort of routine starts to form. The guards deliver food and water in the morning and evening, and it doesn't take long to find out which guards are kind, and which will deliver a sharp whack with a stick across my back or legs, given the slightest excuse. I don't talk to any of them. I don't look at any of them. I know each guard through the sound of their footsteps, the smell of their bodies and the way they give me my food. One repeatedly stands outside my cell and tells me what he wants to do to me; he talks in vivid detail and at great length in vile and terrifying ways. He never actually touches me; he doesn't have to. I lie curled as tightly as I can on the floor, hands over my ears, shaking with the fear that one day he might.

Day and night, there's no escape from the screams of other prisoners which echo through the corridors. In an effort to distract myself from this constant reminder of what lies ahead, I focus on training my rat friends, whom I name Keres and Kuban. It doesn't take long for them to trust and enjoy my company and me theirs. I whisper of my life on the jailoo, of meeting the messenger, of Kuchulyg, and of my miserable, impossible mission. Keres and Kuban listen attentively, waiting for their treats.

One day, I open the little, green parcel of food to find drawings scratched into the leaves: pictures of the funny people on the walls of Aibek's cave. My heart lifts; Aibek is thinking of me. But no sooner am I filled with the warm glow of remembering, than I am consumed by a crushing sadness that I will never see him again, and then a raging anger at being locked up.

As weeks pass, my resolve to fight is gradually eroded; the uncertainty of not knowing if today's the day it all ends, wears me down. How filthy I am; my hair is falling out, my skin flakes off in itchy patches. My body seems to know my fate and is conceding defeat. I thank Mother Earth for stopping my moonblood. Daydreams of riding on the jailoo, or being with Aibek, or flying free, are replaced by frightening visions of how my life might end in brutal and cruel ways. I start to believe physical torture would be preferable to the torture of being kept alone. I will not survive this and decide to take control over how I ascend to the heavens. I stop eating.

It's harder than I had anticipated, as stomach cramps and light-headedness increasingly dominate the next few days. At first, Sabira doesn't notice that I am getting thinner and my rat friends are getting fatter. And then, one day, she does.

Weak bruised shreds seep self-doubt
In you bird soul strong you
Find your bird strength
Fly

I close my eyes. Stretching our wings wide, we push off to catch an uplift and with a few slow, strong flaps rise high to meet a thermal. No effort, gliding, wingtip to wingtip. Balasagun below us; people unaware that we watch them, scurrying, busy, each with purpose, one purpose, to serve their master. As we leave the city, the wind buffets me with choppy blows. No sooner have we risen above the turbulence into a gentle breeze than we are mobbed by a horde of crows, squawking loud warnings of our presence. Sabira doesn't retaliate, but descends rapidly to pick up another thermal that takes us high out toward the mountains. We are hungry. Sabira flies over fat, lazy marmots, dozing on rocky outcrops, their soft tummies warming on the hot stone.

Not this prey

Why not? It would be so easy. Sabira flies ahead; I dip a wing, swivel my tail slightly and follow. Over mountain peaks capped white with snow, over barren valleys to the edge of a great forest. I smell the dog wolf before I see it. Sabira holds her position, poised on a current. I am beside her. We circle slowly, dropping in an ever-decreasing spiral. The wolf taunts a marmot between its front paws. The small creature trembles with fear before the wolf thumps a paw down on its back. The marmot squeezes out, only for the wolf to use its other paw to hold it down again. The marmot squeals and its family, standing on their hind legs at a safe distance, send out high-pitched whistles of alarm. The wolf repeatedly releases, re-catches and torments the marmot. He's plump; he did not catch this marmot to eat; he caught it to satisfy a different kind of hunger: a hunger that can never be sated. The hunger for power.

This our prey

Not the wolf! It's too dangerous. I have seen his jaws. I fear this animal the most.

We split up. Sabira flies low over the grass, directly into the path of the wolf to bait it. I fly high above, with the sun behind me, remaining unseen. The wolf is arrogantly preoccupied with teasing the marmot and fails to see the approaching danger. Flap, flap, glide. Flap, flap, glide. Lower, lower, silently riding the gentle hiss of the wind. I see the sweet spot on the back of his head and something inside me, an inner drive, an urge, takes charge. I tuck my beak into my chest, pull my wings in tightly to my sides and fall vertically, slicing through the air at breath-taking speed. At the very last moment, I pull my head back, stretch out my legs and like a bolt of lightning, strike the back of his skull. He falls immediately. The little marmot scurries off and Sabira curls her feet around the wolf's muzzle. I sink my talons into his head and ratchet them tighter and then snap my beak at the base of his skull, severing his backbone from his head. He sighs a last breath as his heart stops beating. Sabira and I rest on his warm, coarse-furred body, beaks open and panting hard.

Sabira rips into the wolf's chest, tearing apart the sinewy muscle to reveal his soft centre. With blood on my beak and hot flesh in my talons, I eat with my sister, side by side, in satisfied silence.

I wake refreshed, enlivened and excited by a new resolve. I will be patient. I will watch and wait. My moment will come and, when it does, the Gurkhan's power will not scare me.

And my moment comes sooner than I imagined. In the evening, a new guard arrives with my food and water. I sit at the back of the cell; eyes lowered as usual, when he addresses me.

'Hello,' he says.

I briefly raise my eyelids and he is smiling straight at me. Is this a trick? What does he want? I look down again.

'I'll be delivering your meals for a few days. Maybe you'll talk to me tomorrow. Bye.'

The following morning, he arrives again.

'Hello.' He places the wooden bowl carefully, considerately even, on the floor near me. 'I know the food is disgusting – they don't even give this to the animals – but it's all I can bring. I've added an extra spoonful.' I see him smiling kindly, pityingly. I have learned enough here to remain wary of such tactics.

'It's going to be hard for you to trust me. But I want you to know I'm here to help you.'

I've heard that line before. I don't move.

'My name is Damir and I want you to trust me. The first thing I did, when you arrived, was make sure the other guards wouldn't come anywhere near you.'

I look up at him.

'I told one of them you had the pox! I'm sorry. Of course, it was a lie, but I knew word would spread and it was the only thing I could think of to protect you from their lecherous ways.'

I venture an uncertain smile.

'I'm here to help you, although right now, I'm not sure *how* I can. The Palace is heavily guarded. At the moment, the best I can do is make sure you have enough to eat and drink. You look horribly thin.'

Sabira's food parcels are keeping me alive but, clearly, only just. I wrap my arms around my knees, uncertain of his motives.

'You are going to need all your strength when the chance of escape comes. And, you have to believe me, it *will* come. When it does, you need to be fighting fit.'

'Damir? Damir? Where've you got to?' A guard further down

the corridor calls. Damir retreats hurriedly, locking the door firmly behind him.

I take the bowl and force a mouthful down. It sits heavy and uncomfortable in my stomach. I heave, and it all comes up again.

The guards often overlap outside my cell and can't resist a gossip. They mostly discuss Palace affairs, or the weather, or problems at home.

'Haven't seen you in a while.'

'No, I've been on duty with the Gurkhan's messenger, riding out to all the chiefs of the Kara Khitai, handing out invitations to the great feast.'

'Great feast?'

'You haven't heard? There's going to be a big celebration for the anniversary of our *glorious* leader becoming Gurkhan. Three days of music, dancing, entertainment and a lot of drinking, for those invited.'

'Pah! A load of stinking-rich, swindling, grovelling toads, no doubt!'

'They'll all come, bowing and scraping, prostrating themselves at his feet, so they can eat the crumbs he drops and continue their corrupt existence at our expense.'

I listen intently. I had naively assumed that Kuchulyg's guards would be loyal. Except Damir, if I am to believe him. This new information is a welcome revelation.

'When is it?'

'It's to start on the night of the next full moon. There'll be no celebration for the likes of us, mind. Just more work.'

The two guards wander off on their patrols. I start to work on my next plan.

Chapter 35

Gods of sky and earth
Help now fast act
She strong Make her free to fly

It's mid-afternoon and although I can see dark clouds through the tiny window, a strange, orange glow lights my cell. Bells ring urgently. Voices shout in the streets and, although I can't make out what they are saying, I sense panic. Something is not right. I crouch, ready for whatever might come next.

The guards from both corridors run toward each other and meet outside my cell.

'That's the earthquake alarm! Quick, get out of here,' one says.

'We can't just abandon our posts!'

'Oh, yes we can. This building'll be one of the first to topple if it's a big quake. You can stay if you like, but I'm not risking it.'

The guard sprints down the corridor, leaving the other outside my cell.

'Right, quick, this is your moment.' It's Damir! 'Come on, quick now.'

He unlocks the large padlock and opens the door. I hesitate. He pulls me toward him.

'Gulzura, I am with the Three Hares. I'm here to get you out!'

I stay rooted. *Sabira, is this a trap?*

'Listen to me. I met your brother – Usen? – and he said to tell you that 'Meder is missing you'. I have no idea what that means and I didn't think I needed a code but he said you'd understand. Now do you trust me?'

If Usen trusts him, then I trust him.

He runs ahead, but my legs are weak and I fall behind after just a few paces. I'm light-headed and the desperate pleas for release from other prisoners, still locked in their cells, stop me in my tracks. I'm out of breath and struggling to make sense of what's happening. I collapse. Damir runs back and scoops me up into his arms. I want to ask him to unlock the other cells. My lips move but there's no sound.

'I need you to be strong. This is the only chance we've got of getting you out of here.' He stops and lowers me to the ground, then offers me his leather bottle. 'This will give you some strength, just for a short while – enough to get you going.'

I drink the bitter tonic and get a swift, euphoric rush to my head.

'Follow me down to ground level, then you're on your own. I'm sorry I can't risk being caught with you.'

I do exactly as I'm told and follow him along corridors and down numerous flights of stairs. Recognising the dung collectors' entrance, I pause briefly to catch my breath. I turn to thank Damir and ask him what I should do next, but he's gone.

The bells continue to ring and I peek out hesitantly from the big doorway to see chaos and confusion. Frightened people, shouting instructions, carrying whatever possessions they've grabbed, run past me, only to turn in panic and run back the other way. I close my eyes and, through my bare feet, feel the ground give a small shiver.

Remembering that the gods gave me Sabira in the last earthquake, I thank Mother Earth for helping me again. As Damir promised, no one pays me the slightest attention. But with so many people jostling, pushing and shoving to make their way out of the city, I am quickly lost and have little chance of finding my way to Mara's house. And is there any point in going there?

Father Sky fills the air with menacing clouds rising in high, flat-bottomed, plumes over the city. Cracks of thunder rumble all around. I see Sabira circling overhead. *Take me to Meder.* She flies off and I follow her path, as fast as I can, twisting and turning through narrow alleys. Spectacular bolts of lightning cause further panic and I bump into terrified people rushing towards the gates. Quite suddenly, I arrive at the stable.

'It's on fire! Get out!' A boy rushes toward me.

'Where's Meder?' I shout at him, glancing up to see smoke billowing from the stable roof and flames dancing around its edges. He tries to push past but I grab his jacket. 'You have to help me!'

The horses squeal in alarm, and hooves kick out wildly, striking the stable doors and stone floor.

'Quick, open the doors and let the horses out!' I release my grip on him and turn to fetch the water buckets.

'I ain't going in there. I'll be killed.' And he's gone before I can grab him again.

I run to the main stable doors and pull them open. Horses stampede out and through the entrance gates but Meder is not with them. I pour water from the filled buckets onto my coat and soak a scarf which I wrap over my mouth and nose. I take a deep breath and head in. The smoke is thick and black, stinging my eyes and making me cough. I can barely see but I hear his frantic squealing.

'I'm coming, boy, I'm here. Hold on for me.'

I reach his stall and open the door but his headcollar is tied too high for me to reach. He is wild-eyed, frothing from his mouth and flaring his nostrils, whinnying loudly and rearing. I find a block and drag it inside, as the heat of the fire and the clouds of smoke close in.

'I'm going to get you out. You have to trust me.'

I take off my coat and wrap it over his head and lead him forward. He stomps his legs and tries to rear up. 'Come, boy,' I sing; my voice is shaky and I stop to cough. But he comes and I get him out. We gulp in the fresh air and I collapse to the ground to retch and vomit.

'Thank the gods you are alive!' A man leans down to pick me up. Instinctively, I grab a stone and am just about to thrust it into his face when I see it's Aibek.

'I heard through the network that you'd escaped and I just knew you'd come straight for your horse.'

I want to reach out for him and pull him close but my body loses its courage and my arms don't move. His smile drops.

'Are you cross with me?' He looks genuinely surprised. 'Judging by the look of you, you had a narrow escape.' He reaches to wipe my face with his scarf. I wince and jump back, pushing his hand away.

'Sorry. I mean...' I don't want to sound like this. I want him to hold me, and I don't know how to ask for that. Tears well up. Through the thunder and the smoke, he moves closer and my body submits. I melt into his arms.

'Are you all right?' he asks.

'I am now,' I smile, and he leans down, hovering his lips over mine. I wrap my arms around him, urging him on. Our lips meet and the entire world stops; there is no sound, no pain, no past and no future, just him and me together in this moment of perfect, pure joy.

He pulls back and the moment is gone.

'We have to leave. As soon as the panic dies down, your absence will be noticed. Damir will do everything he can to cover your tracks, but they'll find out quickly enough. You have to leave the city now. I'll come with you. We'll go back to the jailoo.'

'You were right, Aibek, before. I should have gone back with you.'

The horses are skittish, spooking at every tremor, but we manage to weave in and out of the lanes, somehow avoiding the rushing people with their screaming children, until we are at the city gates which slowly open as we approach. A large crowd is demanding to be allowed through and the guards, overwhelmed by the mob, are letting them leave. A bolt of lightning strikes with a terrific boom and the ground shakes. The crowd goes wild, everyone clambering over each other, like ants escaping a flood.

Aibek and I stay mounted and push our horses on through the throng. Meder is jittery as people shove up against him. I bend forward and press my lips against a pulsating raised seam in his neck.

'Stay calm, please stay calm.'

As I raise myself, I spot a face that makes my stomach lurch: the prison guard who threatened me with his violent fantasies. Before I can disappear into the crowd, he shouts out, 'There she is, on the horse. The bay. Grab her!'

He shoulders his way through the crowd like a yak bull, knocking people right and left. He reaches me in alarmingly few steps and grips my calf in his large hand. I know exactly what he will do to me if I become his prisoner. Using the last of my strength, I kick out, making contact with his face. He roars and lunges forward, trying to pull me off Meder's back.

'Aibek! Aibek!' I shout. He glances over his shoulder, wheels his horse around and urges her back through the crush of people. He reaches me at the very moment that Sabira swoops in at full speed, wings outstretched, legs extended, talons spread wide, driving them into the guard's face. He drops me, and lets out a piercing scream. Sabira releases her grip. The guard staggers, blood pouring from his face. I urge Meder on through the gate, calling Aibek to follow.

I gallop at full speed in a straight line toward the distant mountains. When I reach a hidden dip by a river, I pull Meder to a halt, slide off, and land in an exhausted heap on the ground. He is foamy with sweat, his chest heaving.

'Thank you, boy.' I kiss his velvety muzzle and he nickers, rubbing his head against me. Sabira calls from above, circling round and round overhead. There is no sign of Aibek, but he must not be far behind. I strain my eyes toward the city silhouetted on the horizon, but can see no movement. The sun is setting and the light is fading. Sabira continues to circle overhead. I watch and I wait.

Chapter 36

He's coming! He's galloping toward me, reins in one hand, the other whacking his mare's rump and then – as he has done over and over throughout the past day and night – he passes me and disappears into a shimmering dust cloud that hangs over the distant horizon.

Dawn comes pink and hot and I remain where I've been all night, sitting on a small hillock, arms wrapped comfortingly around my knees, staring back at the hazy silhouette of the city. Why hasn't he come? My eyes, gritty with exhaustion, prickle as I look up to see Sabira returning from another exploratory flight.

Boy not come

He will come. I know he will. Sabira changes direction and flies away toward the mountains. When she returns, she is spent. She settles on a fallen tree, tucks her head into her wing, and sleeps for most of the day. I ache from the effort of escaping the city. I ache from the weariness of no sleep. Most of all, I ache from the loss of the boy I have fallen in love with.

Boy not come
We fly on

I can't leave. I won't leave. Not without Aibek. Some ill must have befallen him. I should ride back. He would do that for me, I know he would. He didn't abandon me when I was in prison. He stayed in the city and made sure I was fed.

But what can I do alone? I've failed in my mission, and I've failed Aibek. I will go home. I will be ridiculed and maybe punished for my failure, but what choice do I have? I will find a way to persuade the men of my clan to ride with me to the city. We will confront the Gurkhan. We will find Aibek.

'Yes, it's time to go home,' I say out loud and turn to Meder, and then, 'No! One more day. Maybe he's still trying to get to me. I can't leave.'

Boy not come
We go now

Sabira delivers a fresh rabbit which, without much thought, I skin, gut and butcher. I eat the meat raw, unable to summon the energy to start a fire. Meder nudges me, snorting lightly. I hold his head, and kiss his pink muzzle.

Another day and night pass until, reluctantly, I give in and we set off. Meder follows Sabira's flight path with no guidance from me. I slump over him like a corpse. What will I tell the clan? Maybe if Sabira catches some good game, they will think kindly of her, at least. Was it only three moons ago Usen and I travelled this way, so naïve, yet so full of hope and adventure? I feel wretched at the memory of the last time I saw him, wishing we had not argued, wishing I had left him with a hug or peck on the cheek.

I don't recognise the route, but Sabira circles continuously, ensuring we follow closely. I drift in and out of sleep.

Suddenly I am jolted awake, as Meder tenses, cocking his ears and flicking his tail. We are on the brow of a hill and, as my tired eyes focus, I see an astonishing sight. Below us is a camp: a city of yurts spread across the full width of the valley floor. I take up Meder's reins and circle him back below the brow. Sabira flies low and close.

Go brave Meet great Khan
Go soft tread Step much care

This is Genghis Khan's camp? Why have you brought me here? The hairs on the back of my neck rise and goosebumps tingle my skin. I'm simultaneously terrified and exhilarated.

Your task is now
Gods save you keep you trust you prize you
Quest needs you brave
Clan tale yours to make real

I turn Meder back toward the edge and look again into the valley. I have never seen so many yurts all in one place. Lower and flatter than our own, they are organised in neat lines and circles radiating from a huge central yurt. Banners and flags fly in every direction; cooking smoke rises in wispy trails; vast herds of horses and yak graze the outskirts of the encampment. I can't just walk in. I will be dead before the day ends.

And then my head fills with the faces of everyone I love in the city: Aibek, Usen, Mara and all the innocent people who will be killed when this camp packs up and moves forward as an army. I remember my dream of a city on fire, all its inhabitants screaming, trapped, burning to death. If I die at the hands of the Mongol army today, down in that valley, I will die trying to save them. I feel inside the sleeve of my chapan for the letter that Kuchulyg rejected. Maybe it will help.

I say a quick prayer to our Father of the Sky and Mother of the Earth, take a big breath and nudge my heels. 'Choo choo.'

Chapter 37

Out of nowhere, three riders, bows aimed directly at me, gallop into view. I hold my arms above my head in a sign of surrender and they circle around me, laughing. It's dangerous to approach the camp so boldly, but I'm relying on them feeling no threat from an unarmed girl.

'Well, what have we got here then?'

'Looks like we've caught ourselves a maiden.'

'I think she's ours for the day. What do you say, boys?'

'I say, let's have some fun!'

They are three Mongol men: one with a bent nose, one in a blue jacket and one with a simple topknot. Saying or doing the wrong thing now could lead to, at best, a quick death and, at worst, a very slow one. I glance up to the sky.

I here we side side
strong on guard

I look hard at them all.

'What are you doing here?' Blue Jacket asks.

I keep staring.

'Speak, girl! I said: what are you doing here?' Blue Jacket comes up close alongside and Meder sidesteps away.

'Impudent little brat. I say we give her a good thrashing. That'll make her talk,' Topknot jeers, trotting up on my other side.

'Here, take my whip.' Blue Jacket passes a leather bullwhip over Meder's neck, right under my nose, to Topknot. I pull back on Meder's reins and he reverses straight into Bent Nose's horse.

'Come on, lads, we're wasting time here, let's just despatch her and continue our patrol,' Bent Nose says.

A fourth man gallops up. 'What's going on? Who is this girl?'

He has elaborate tattoos down his face and neck and, although much younger than the others, has an immediate air of authority.

'She's not talking. I say we have some fun and then do away with her.' Topknot pokes me in the ribs with the whip. Meder tries to move but we're firmly wedged between the two horses.

'That's enough! I've warned you before. One more word and I'll have you all banished.' Tattoo Man nudges his horse beside me. I notice a familiar sign inked on his arm, just peeping out from his sleeve.

'What are you doing here?' he asks, gently.

It's a risk, but I reach into the sleeve of my chapan and pull out the small leather pouch to reveal the Three Hares symbol and, as I had hoped, the mood changes immediately.

'Isn't that Jebe's city gang?' Topknot says.

'Where did you get that?' Blue Jacket asks, staring wide-eyed at the symbol in my palm. He leans in and snatches the pouch, rips it open and pulls out the letter. He stares at it, turns it around, and then passes it to his friends.

'Here, give it to me!' Tattoo Man says.

He takes the scrap of paper, and his eyes scan the inky lines.

'She's a spy,' Bent Nose says. 'Slit her throat now and be done with it.'

Blue Jacket and Topknot whoop in agreement.

'Silence! All of you!' Tattoo Man says. 'I'm taking her back to camp.'

The other three look disappointed.

'You will continue the patrol. I want to know every detail of the landscape: every bump, hill and mountain; every river, lake and settlement. And don't come back until you've done it!'

They turn their horses and make for the hill I've just descended.

'You and I will take this document to our Lord Khan. He will decide what to do with you.'

My voice fails me again. I hope the Khan can see that in returning his original letter, marked by Kuchulyg's own hand, I am telling the truth when – if – I get to tell him my story. Surely, he will understand the risks I have taken on his behalf, and the great risk I'm taking now, riding alone into his camp? Surely, he will have mercy on me and on our people and on the city?

I think it unlikely Meder and I could out-gallop this man. He rides close beside me, which gives me the chance to study him more closely. His raven hair is plaited into tightly braided rows that snake over the top of his head. The sides are shaven clean, revealing a series of beautiful, intricate markings around his ears, across his cheeks and down his neck. His eyebrows are thick, his cheekbones high and he smells sweet and sour, of earth and metal. I'm looking for his story, but he has no visible scars; his skin is perfectly smooth and his nose unbroken. I see no indication whatsoever that he's ever been in combat or suffered hardship. He mistakes my interest as a sign I want to talk.

'I'm Toq. What's your name?'

I don't reply. I observe his easy manner, the unusual buckles on his boots, the lacing of his shirt under his jacket, until it dawns on me who he is, and I remember when I last heard his name.

The camp is calmly busy; children play; sheep, yak and horses graze. It looks and feels like a comfortable place, with some of the biggest yurts I've ever seen. It's hard to believe I am in the settlement of one of the most formidable armies anyone has ever heard of. Toq escorts me directly to a section occupied exclusively by single women.

'You stay here,' he says. 'I'll get Odval to look after you. She'll get you something to eat and drink. I will take your letter to the Khan.'

'Who have we got here, then?' A plump, round-faced, older woman looks me up and down. I'm relieved she speaks my language. She seems pleased to have a guest, and beckons the other women to join her. They all gather round, smiling generously, and she wraps an arm around my shoulder and sweeps me into her yurt. I shudder as I am reminded of Ruhsora and my narrow escape from the slavers. But then I remember that Sabira brought me here.

They good No harm you
Eat calm breathe
You speak They hear your tale

'Come now, child. You look half-starved. Before we set to finding out who you are, where you're from and why you're here, let's get you fed.'

I wait to see them eat from the same pot that I am served from. The bread and mutton stew on offer are delicious and make me think of home.

'What are we to call you?' Odval asks.

'Gulzura,' I croak.

'That's a beautiful name. My daughter will deliver her first baby next moon. If it's a girl, I will suggest Gulzura to her.'

I don't know what to say at this surprisingly generous gesture and stay quiet for fear I make a mistake. I know I need to make a good impression in the women's camp to ensure my survival. I finish my food in silence as they chatter, although I sense they are keen to ask questions as their eyes constantly flick to look at me.

'Excuse me?'

'Yes, Gulzura?'

'I want to see my horse.'

'Of course. Without our horses, we are nothing. You must check he's all right. But, once you've done that, come and find me again. You look like you need a good wash, some balm on those cuts and bruises, fresh clothes and then someone to brush out that beautiful hair and re-plait it Mongol-style!'

In the evening, so many women gather to eat that there's barely space for me. After the food is cleared, there is expectation in the air. I wonder if we are to be entertained and then realise, when I see all eyes on me, that I am the entertainment.

'Gulzura, we'd all love to hear your story,' Odval says.

I look around and remember how exciting it is when our clan has visitors, and how we relish their stories.

'I… I will try.'

'In your own time, child.'

'I am Gulzura, daughter of Jyral, Chief of Snow Leopard clan…'

They are completely silent; the only sound is a dog barking in the distance and the crackle of the fire. I take a deep breath. *Please let my voice be strong.*

'One day I was out shepherding and the ground shook…'

The words come, falteringly at first, and then more and more tumble out. The women are a keen audience and I am greatly encouraged by their 'oohs' and 'aahs' and the occasional gasp. My voice relaxes and I start to enjoy myself, adding extra dramatic detail, which they seem to love.

'... and I escaped with Meder, but...'

'What?' a woman asks. 'But what?' another says. 'Don't stop now!'

I look up. 'Aibek didn't make it. I don't know what has happened to him.'

They are quiet now.

'So, you see, it's not just about the prophecy any more...'

There is much chatter and then a torrent of questions. When I've satisfied their curiosity, we share stories about our daily lives. We marvel at the similarities and laugh a lot at the differences.

'Do tell me, please, about your Khan. What is he like?'

'It's a long story and I can see you're tired, so I'll do my best to give you the short version.' Odval settles back and all eyes turn to her.

'He was born clutching a blood clot in his right hand, a sign of his greatness to come. His mother named him Temujin and his early years were tough. His father was killed by a rival, and he and his mother and brothers were banished to live on the steppe. They should have died. But they survived, thanks to Temujin's ability to form strong friendships and clever alliances. He fell in love with a girl called Borta and married her, but she was kidnapped and when she returned, she was pregnant. Temujin nobly took on Jochi as his own son.'

I think about Aibek. How different his life might have been had his father accepted him as Genghis Khan accepted Jochi.

'Ultimately, Temujin united all the warring tribes and that is why we call him Genghis Khan, Universal Ruler.'

'How did he do that?'

'It's quite simple. He condemns privilege, he rewards loyalty. He brings defeated tribes under his protection.'

'But I've heard he's ruthless. I've heard he shows no mercy, obliterating entire cities, killing every living thing.'

'Yes, it's one of his tactics. He would much prefer to let everyone live in peace, but... any resistance is met by death. He has laid waste cities that tried to outwit him, or that held fast. In those cases, he is ruthless, killing with terrifying cruelty. But always allowing a thousand or so to flee unharmed. Their story spreads panic and terror, and other cities just surrender. No need to attack, no need for weapons, no need for anyone to die. He simply walks in and they let him.'

I don't know what to think about this. It feels dishonourable, like cheating, but it's also shrewd.

My head spins, trying to weigh up the rights and wrongs of a man whose success seems to rely on having two opposing natures.

'That's hardly the behaviour of a hero,' I say.

There are pained expressions and stifled gasps around the yurt and I suddenly realise that I've crossed a boundary. I bow my head.

'I'm so sorry. I am keen to learn. I don't mean to be disrespectful of your great leader.'

Odval smiles. 'I like your spirit, child. You are right to challenge.'

I like this woman, too. A lot.

'Once he's taken control of a city, he imposes his code of law. He lowers taxes for everyone and eliminates taxes for doctors and teachers. He won't tolerate religious persecution, and women have as much status as men. Is that enough to persuade you?'

Another woman speaks out. 'Before the Great Khan, we'd never known a time with no fighting, no war. But now we have peace. We go about our daily lives without the constant terror that we might be attacked at any time.'

I have never known peace. Thoughts, questions and ideas crash around inside my head and later, as I fall asleep, the doubts creep in. *Lord Tengri, is this my task? Am I doing right?*

Chapter 38

I offer to help with breakfast preparation and watch for any reaction as I take a knife to cut up the bread but there's none. I return it when I am finished, reassured that I could take it at any time if needed.

I am sent with a girl called Yisu to the river for water. A group of horsemen, glistening with sweat from a hard ride, passes us.

'Nothing! Where in God's name have they gone?' one of the men shouts.

'There was a raid a few nights ago,' Yisu explains. 'Two hundred horses gone, just like that!'

I'm astonished. It would take some bravery, or foolishness, to steal from these people.

'I pity whoever it is when they're found,' she continues. 'Problem is: the search parties have been out every day, in all directions and they seem to have disappeared into thin air. We can't move on until the horses have been found or replaced.'

When we return, the women are all busy around camp and I am left alone. Uncertain how far I am allowed to venture, I call Sabira to me for company. She flies overhead, telling me of the camp layout, of the movement of people and of their hidden weapons. I ask her to do something for me.

I wait the day out uneasily. There is no word from Toq.

Sabira comes to me in my dreams to take me flying. We rise quickly on a summer thermal and soar in ever-widening circles, higher and higher, until the ground below us takes on a curve where land meets sky. Suddenly, she tucks in her wings and descends rapidly. She has answered my request. Below us, in a tiny valley, surrounded by a circular wall of spiky, snow-capped mountains, are the Mongols' missing horses. It looks like they've been corralled here for collection in the future. I know this technique; I've heard stories of my clan doing the same.

'I know where the horses are.' I pat Yisu's leg to wake her.

'What? How?' she yawns. She turns over to return to her sleep.

'I just know. I need to go out with one of the search parties today.'

She opens her eyes again. 'You can talk to my father, he's organising the search, but I doubt he'll take you. Let me have a word with him, see if I can soften him up. You know how fathers can't resist a request from a loving daughter,' she winks. I have never had that power over my father.

Hasi is a small, craggy-faced man with deep dimples either side of a large smile.

'My daughter tells me you know where the horses are. How is that possible?'

'I have an eagle, and at night, in my dreams, sometimes I fly with her. Last night we flew together and she showed me where the horses are being held.'

He pauses, looking up to the sky. 'If this is true, you hold very special powers. Are you shamanic?'

'I don't think so.' I hesitate, unsure whether I can explain it, and, if I do, whether he will see it as a threat.

'Yes? I'm listening.'

'I have a special bond with my eagle. That's all.'

'Our berkutchi have noticed! You certainly have something that our eagle hunters don't have. Hard to put my finger on it, but it's, well, I've never seen the like before.' He pauses. 'It's a gamble, but as we've wasted days searching with no result, I'd say it's a gamble worth taking. You may join us today.'

'Thank you. I won't let you down.'

'Better get yourself some armour.'

Sabira flies low and close, guiding us along the narrow, concealed path that leads up and over the mountains that cradle the hidden valley. The leather chest armour weighs heavy and rubs uncomfortably around my arms and neck, and the conical metal hat doesn't fit properly, dropping over my eyes every time we canter. I daren't take it off or complain but I vow to lose it at the first sign of trouble.

At the crest, we look down to see the rustlers rounding up the horses ready to take them out. We are well placed to block their escape route.

'Nine of them and three of us,' Hasi says.

'Four.' I sit up tall and look him straight in the eye. 'Give me a bow.'

He looks unconvinced but hands over a bow and a quiver of arrows which I sling over my shoulder.

We descend the steep path and fan out across the valley floor at full gallop to encircle the robbers and the stolen horses. They are poorly prepared to fight and struggle to arm themselves before our arrows rain down on them. I line up three men in my sight, draw the bow back and, just before I let loose, I recognise one of them. It is Ilyas, Aibek's brother. He looks weedy and incompetent, and I feel unexpected pity for him. He doesn't deserve to die for trying to steal a few horses; the gods know this is what men must do, to survive.

Kill

My hand shakes. I cannot kill Aibek's brother. I fire at Ilyas's thigh, then shoot at another man, and again at a third, aiming only to disable. Ilyas and another robber fall to the ground, clutching their injuries, and the third lolls forward in his saddle. Hasi's men don't hesitate in shooting to kill as the marauders ride in circles, looking for an escape. In a matter of moments, the thieves are defeated and the Mongol men descend on the dead rustlers like ants on honey, stripping them of their meagre valuables. I glimpse one of them hacking a hand off to get at a ring and turn away in disgust at their savagery.

'They are poor specimens of men.' Hasi trots up beside me. 'A pathetic rabble. You did well, Gulzura. I'm impressed.'

I am horrified as his two companions despatch the injured robbers with a quick slice across their throats and then take their plaited hair with another. I open my mouth to shout *No*, but nothing comes out. Only one is left alive. It's not Ilyas. A sickness rises in my throat and I clutch Meder's neck.

'He'll go back and tell their clan what happened here,' Hasi says, misinterpreting my horror at their vicious brutality for disbelief that he's allowing one of the enemy to ride away, 'and they won't try it again!'

We drive the horses back to camp where Hasi is lauded, cheered and slapped on the back. He tells everyone of my skill with Sabira and how I helped, but I cannot join in the celebrations, and return quietly to the women's tent. I pray that Ilyas is at peace with his family in the heavens, and that when

Aibek finds out, he will forgive me. The savagery of the Mongol attack shocked me and when I think of this ferocious horde descending on Balasagun, an icy shiver runs down my spine.

I don't know exactly what I am going to do but I know I must wait for now and trust that word of my actions today will reach the Great Lord Khan.

Chapter 39

The Mongols' eagles screech pathetically, hooded and tethered to their wooden perches, unable to fly off to get their own breakfast. I crouch down to look more closely at the little silver bells tied to their jesses.

'They're pretty,' I say, and wait to see if I hear the birds reply. I don't, of course. Instead, I hear the men in the tent talking. I press my ear to the felt.

'Did you hear, her eagle told her where to find the stolen horses?'

'I've seen her flying that bird. No hood, no jesses! The eagle comes and goes as it pleases. She doesn't even feed it.'

'Yet she's its master.'

'No girl can control an eagle like that without help.'

'More like the eagle controls her. According to Hasi, the eagle guided the search party straight to the horses.'

'She must possess very special powers.'

'The kind of powers only granted by the gods.'

I smile. It won't be long now until the Great Khan summons me. I skip with the lightness and joy of a spring lamb to find Meder.

'He's a very fine horse.' Toq rubs his hand appreciatively over

Meder's glossy, golden back and down his leg. He grabs a fetlock to lift his foot and examine his hoof. I feel my hackles go up, like a dog, watching him touch Meder in such a familiar way.

'And a very patient one,' I add, hoping Meder doesn't kick out.

I curb my instinct to walk away, as being favoured by Toq probably increases my chances of seeing the Khan.

'I am Gulzura,' I introduce myself formally.

He smiles and I soften a little, remembering that, without his intervention, I would have been killed just a few days before.

'I must say, you've caused quite a stir around camp already. No-one's talking about anything but the girl with the eagle. Quite impressive!'

I blush at the flattery. 'She'll show you no mercy if you lay a finger on me.'

His eyes widen.

'I didn't mean...' I am unnerved now as words are tumbling from thoughts to voice. 'I mean, she's my friend and she protects me. Not my only friend, of course; there's Mara, and –'

'And is there a boyfriend, perhaps?'

'There's... Aibek...'

'Tell me...'

'He got caught in the city when I escaped. I'm so worried about what's happened to him. I won't rest until I know he's safe.'

Toq starts to run his hands over Meder again.

'We could do with more horses like this,' he says. 'Where did you get him?' He looks genuinely interested.

'My brothers have bred a magnificent herd from Fergana Valley stock. It would be an honour to have you visit and purchase a few.' I try to hide a laugh at the thought of this horde descending on my tiny clan with no notice.

'What's so funny?'

'Just the thought of my elder brothers wetting themselves in panic at the sight of a Mongol delegation galloping into camp!'

He looks amused. 'I doubt your clan would have enough horses for our demand, but we might just do it, to give you a laugh and your brothers the fright of their lives!'

He puts his arm around my shoulder and pulls me close. I pull away.

'I'm sorry,' he says. 'I'm just being friendly. It's our way...'

'Oh, but...' I step back. 'Tell me about your weapons.'

'Really?'

'Yes, really. I heard you were a terrifying army, but –'

'You have no idea, do you?'

I shake my head, relieved that I've distracted him.

'Here, come with me. I want to show you something.'

He holds out a hand and I'm not sure if he means me to take it or not. I don't.

'I won't bite!' He smiles widely. I smile and still I don't take his hand.

We walk through rows of yurts where the familiar morning smells of dung fuel fires and fresh bread make it feel like my own clan camp. A tiny ripple of homesickness crumples me. I wonder what my family might think if they knew I was in the heart of the Mongol camp. Surprised? Probably. Proud? I doubt it.

The sound of hammers beating hot metal brings me back to the present. Twenty or so blacksmiths are hard at work. Axes, lances, arrow heads and more are being heated and hammered into shape by men made of nothing but muscle, shiny with sweat. Short, long, straight and curved swords, single-ended and double-ended lances, and all sizes of head, chest, arm and leg armour are stacked up in vast piles. We pass under awnings where carpenters strip bark from freshly cut trees to make ladders, bows, arrow shafts and huge, carved pieces that I can't identify. In a large, open area, men are practising archery, hand-to-hand fighting and lancing bales of straw. Everywhere I look, preparations for battle are under way and the sheer size and scale leaves me speechless.

'Impressive, eh?'

I nod. I wonder how, in the name of the gods, I am going to stand in the way of this enormous army that is ready to advance on the city I am supposed to save?

'Have you ever seen a stone-thrower, or a siege machine?' Toq asks, walking faster. I shake my head; I don't know what he's talking about.

'We learn a lot from our captives. The Lord Khan takes great pride in learning from foreigners who can teach us new skills: engineers and metal workers and inventors, as well as poets and musicians. We're learning from captured Jin how to make the heaven-shaking thunder bomb. It explodes on impact, killing a great many people. It's quite something!'

We stop in front of a wood and metal contraption.

'This is a stone-thrower. Small stones are loaded there, in that box, and then a big stone is put into the sling, there.' He's pointing and I nod, keen not to look stupid. 'When the weighted end is released, the big stone is launched.' He swings his arm over his head and whistles. 'Bang!' he shouts. 'All gone!'

I am horrified. This is what awaits my friends.

'We'll soon have twenty of those ready to pummel that pathetic city to dust.'

'The people of Balasagun don't deserve this,' I say quietly. 'Most of them are opposed to the Gurkhan and would leap at the chance to swear allegiance to your Khan.'

'You have a kind heart. Our ways must seem so brutal to you.' He lifts my lowered chin slowly with a finger and I meet his gaze. 'And you have the most beautiful eyes.'

An arousing smell of hot metal and worn leather comes off him and my legs feel shaky; yet an uncomfortable ache grows in my chest.

'My friend Aibek is still in the city. He would support the Great Khan. If I return and get him out, he would help you, I'm quite certain.'

'The Gurkhan must be defeated.' He's not listening and pulls away. 'He sent a spy. Would you like to see him?'

I wouldn't really.

A locked, wooden crate lies on open ground and between the slats I can just make out someone bent double inside. The key hangs on a nearby post, taunting him, just out of reach.

'Don't get close, Gulzura. He spits like a grumpy camel.'

The prisoner has no room to move and is begging for a drink.

'Why are you keeping him?'

'Sometimes it's better to send a spy back alive with information than to kill them outright. But don't tell the Khan we're having our bit of fun tormenting him in the meantime.'

The man groans piteously and I turn my head so I don't have to look.

'I can see you've had enough of the savagery of war and fighting and spies. Have you had anything to eat yet this morning?'

Toq stops briefly at a yurt and emerges with a leather bag. Summer bulrushes line the banks of the river where he sets down a blanket and lays out a breakfast of fresh bread and apricot preserve. Questions and doubts fill my head: Hasn't he got work or duties? Is this a romantic gesture or just friendly? I don't want to be here but I cannot risk upsetting him. Maybe food will settle my nerves. Toq tears a chunk of bread from the loaf, dips it in the sticky golden jam and offers it to me. I put out my hand to take it.

'Let me feed you,' he says, and I open my mouth like a baby bird. He pops the bread between my lips and licks his own fingers.

My heart is pounding and I flush. He lifts my hand and runs his fingertips over my calluses. 'A hunter, eh?'

I pull my hand away quickly, embarrassed by the hard lumps that disfigure it.

He picks it up again and holds it closer to his eyes. 'Don't be shy, these are the marks of a warrior.' And he kisses them tenderly.

A warrior! No one has called me a warrior before!

'Now, tell me all about that eagle of yours. Your power over her is remarkable. I want to hear all about how you achieved that.'

We spend the rest of the morning beside the river. Sabira is unusually quiet and keeps her distance. Although Toq asks me endless questions, keen to learn every detail of my life and how Sabira and I work together, all I end up talking about is Aibek. The guilt of leaving him behind and the worry of not knowing what has happened to him are fierce and deep inside me.

'I can see this Aibek means a lot to you,' Toq says. 'I will send a spy to the city to find him, and invite him to join us here. Would that cheer you up?'

I am overwhelmed with relief and give Toq an impulsive hug.

> *Take care I warn*
> *He look kind but he cold*
> *Not hold your soft beat heart*

The sun tells me it's midday when I return to the women's camp, and find them preparing a meal.

'Can I help?' I start to chop and slice potatoes, watching the other women carefully to make sure my pieces are the same size and shape as theirs.

'Did I see you with Toq this morning?' a woman asks me. The others carry on with their work but go quiet.

'Yes. He took me to see the weaponry and the captured spy.' There's no point trying to hide anything from these women, who almost certainly know more than me about my time with Toq this morning.

'Typical of him, keen as ever to brag. Did he take credit?'

'No. Not at all. He just wanted me to see him.'

'That makes a change. You know, as General Jebe's son, he thought he was destined for greatness. But, like every soldier who serves under Genghis, he had to prove his worth. And, as you know, he failed.'

I've heard so many versions of this story, but I want to hear hers. 'What exactly happened?' I ask.

'No one really knows for certain – it's all been rather hushed up – but Toq returned from his mission to Balasagun with his tiny tail between his legs like a kicked dog,' one of the women giggles.

'Not just that. He'd been utterly humiliated by the Gurkhan. They shaved his head and beard and branded his cheek with a hot iron,' the first woman continues. 'Genghis was withering in his contempt and insisted on him having that elaborate tattoo to cover the facial scars, so he wasn't constantly reminded of the dishonour and embarrassment.'

'And now, in spite of everything, he's been made Head of the Keshig, the Khan's personal bodyguard.'

'Maybe it's so he can't get into any more trouble and the Khan can keep a close eye on him.'

'Yes, well, it doesn't seem to have damaged his sense of his own greatness!'

'I've heard he's not blessed with greatness in other areas though.' She wiggles her little finger and laughs. I squirm uncomfortably at this; it doesn't feel right. I'm not sure if I like Toq, but he's been kind to me.

As the days pass, I become increasingly impatient. Every morning I ask: 'Can I see Genghis Khan today?' and every morning I get the same answer. 'When the time's right, he'll ask for you.'

Finally, the invitation comes.

Chapter 40

'Don't just stand there gawping, come in!' a deep voice booms out over the chatter.

I close my mouth and step into the biggest yurt I have ever seen. Multi-coloured, embroidered and tasselled wall-hangings, depicting scenes of hunts, battles and family-life, line the walls. My bare feet sink into a soft carpet, richly coloured in reds and oranges, and I'm taken aback by the dazzling array of delicate, beautiful things decorating the court of the formidable Khan. Men and women are seated equally around the outer and inner edges of the circular table that fills the vast yurt. I am shown to a yak-skin cushion next to a large man with a shining, ruddy complexion, and a storm-cloud-grey beard. As I approach, he turns to smile at me and I catch a glint of copper tint in his long, dark hair.

'Come. Sit here.' He gestures to his right.

I lower myself hesitantly, annoyed with myself for not checking with Odval on the correct behaviour for this occasion. The man is wearing a crimson jacket with red fox fur edging the collar and cuffs. In his right ear is a large earring that glints in the soft light from the yak-oil lamps hanging at regular intervals on the walls. Is this the Khan? Unlikely; those around him are not deferential enough. I scan the room, urgently seeking Toq, or one of the women I know, but there is no-one I recognise.

'I've heard a lot about you, young lady. And, I have to say, I like what I'm hearing. Persistence, resilience, strong fighting temperament. Sounds like you have a true Mongol spirit. Are you sure you're not one of us?' He laughs from his belly.

The chatter stops and everyone joins in. My cheeks blush as heat surges from my chest to my face. I don't know what to say, and I'm not sure words would come anyway, so I look down into my lap.

'And I've heard all about your eagle and your special powers over her. Our army could do with women like you.'

I glance up without raising my head and all eyes in the room are focused on me. He is expecting a reply, but nothing comes out.

'You know, women are welcome in my army – as the proverb from the east goes: Women hold up half the sky.'

The yurt hums with murmurs of agreement.

'Lord Khan, you are right to welcome women warriors,' one man says, 'and from all that I've seen of this young woman's riding and archery skills, she would be much appreciated in our ranks.'

This *is* Genghis Khan. I take a deep breath and send a quick prayer to the gods that words will come. I look up at his face. Deep lines in his weathered, leathery skin appear to starburst from his eyes, enhancing their bewitching green colour. He catches me staring and I look down quickly and focus on the neat blue, yellow and red stitchwork of strange beasts that decorate the tablecloth. When I look up again, he is talking to someone else and I see Toq take a seat beside the man on the Khan's left. He smiles encouragingly at me.

'Father?' Toq addresses the man between him and the Khan.

'May I introduce Gulzura of the Snow Leopard Clan, daughter of Jyral and talented berkutchi. Gulzura, this is my father, Jebe, loyal General to our Great Khan.'

I bow my head.

'Genghis is right,' the General replies. 'We have much need of women warriors in our army. I've heard you are fearless and intelligent, with archery skills that would shame some of my men. Will you join us?'

Toq speaks before I can even attempt an answer. 'And, wouldn't you say, Father, that our berkutchi could learn a thing or two from the way she handles her eagle?'

'I would like to meet this eagle. Could I do that?'

I nod, frustrated that I am speechless, but encouraged as he smiles warmly at me.

The table is laden with meat stew and bread, plenty and more for everyone here. They drink kumiss, which they call airag, and, as the conversation gets louder and more heated, the flaps of the yurt roof are opened to let a welcome breeze drop over the company. I listen carefully as their strange accents make it hard to understand everything. They use words I don't know but try to remember so I can ask Odval or Toq later. The talk is all of war, and how they will sack Balasagun. The conversation bounces around quickly as Genghis seeks comment and listens intently with respect to each voice. Unlike the rowdiness that erupts after every meal where kumiss has been drunk in my clan, here, everyone is given time to voice their opinions and be heard. Suggestions pour forth on what they will do to the city; flood it, set fire to it, lay siege, cut off all supplies and watch the inhabitants starve to death. There is much guffawing and hooting as their ideas became more and more cruel.

'Enough, enough! It doesn't have to be like that.' I am as

surprised as everyone else as the words erupt from my mouth. But the yurt goes quiet and once again, all eyes are on me.

'Everyone is heard here; you don't need to shout,' Genghis says gently.

'My brother and my friends are in the city,' I gulp, desperate not to burst into tears. 'I don't want them to die.' My voice settles. This is my moment. 'It doesn't have to be like that.'

'So, do you have a plan, General Gulzura?' one of the men asks and they all laugh.

I have had a lifetime of my brothers' ribbing, and I remain straight-faced and deadly serious.

'It's not the people who are refusing to submit peacefully to you. It's their leader, whom most despise. If you show mercy, the people of Balasagun will willingly surrender and swear loyalty to you. Right now, they're terrified that you'll be worse than the Gurkhan Kuchulyg.'

'What ridiculous nonsense.'

I turn to glare at the man who interrupted.

'If you and your Generals take power and their lives continue as before, or even better than before, they'll be truly grateful and loyal to you. You'll reap rewards well beyond their meagre stashes of gold and silver. I think...'

My proposition prompts numerous simultaneous reactions. Some people are clearly horrified at the thought of going against their long-held, and successful, principle of showing no mercy to cities that don't offer immediate surrender. Others, clearly uncomfortable taking advice from a young girl they've never met before, speculate that I might be setting a trap.

'Silence! While you're all locking horns like rampant sheep, the girl has a proposal. She shows a brave spirit coming here. Let's hear her.' The Khan turns to me. 'Speak.'

I try to calm myself. The lives of my friends depend on what I say next.

'I...' My throat closes up. Then nothing. Silence.

'Don't be shy now – you can tell us.' The Khan leans in to listen but I have no voice. No! Why now? The gods are playing a brutal game with me and I can't do this anymore. I stumble out of the yurt before my humiliation can get any worse.

I run toward the river. Jebe, tired and a little drunk, lumbers after me.

'Slow down, Gulzura, I've had too much airag,' he gasps.

I stop. Something about the way he says my name reminds me of Atashka.

'Thank you.' He catches up, panting heavily. 'I can see that it was all a bit much for you in there, in front of the Khan and his men. But I would like to hear what you have to say and I'm happy to sit with you here and wait until you're ready.' He gestures to a fallen tree and we sit side by side on the knobbly trunk.

'I don't have a plan.' The words are a whisper. 'I just don't want to lose my friends.'

There's a long silence filled by the rushing water. Two owls hoot territorial warnings to each other.

'There are good people in that city,' I say. 'People who have done their best to disrupt Kuchulyg and his army. People who have risked their lives preparing the way for you and the Great Khan. Like the Three Hares. Like my orphan friends.'

'Mm,' he nods.

'They don't deserve to die. At least, not at the hands of those they would welcome.' My voice wavers.

'Did you know the Three Hares was my idea?'

He pulls up his sleeve to reveal the Three Hares symbol tattooed on his forearm, just like the one I'd seen on Toq.

'My approach to warfare has always been different from that of the Great Khan. Sometimes, I think the only reason he keeps me at his side is to be a counterbalance to his blood-thirsty ways. I've fought a great many battles under Genghis, and won most, but the loss of so many men never ceases to haunt me. I started the Three Hares underground network, as a bit of an experiment, really, to see if a ruler can be undermined and ultimately destroyed by more subtle tactics than open warfare. By creating networks among those who are oppressed or opposed to their rulers, we can incite unrest and dissent. The network also co-opts important local leaders, so when the time comes to fight, our enemy can't unite his people or defend his city at full capacity. So, you see, we can take a city with much less loss of life.' He pauses. 'And, from everything you've told us, it's working in Balasagun exactly as I'd planned. The oppressed Muslim majority are now ready to help us overthrow Kuchulyg.'

My stomach tightens. I inhale deeply, exhale slowly and let the words pour out, confident and strong. 'I know the city. I know the Palace Fortress. And I know the Gurkhan, a little. I don't know how yet, but I will make a plan. I will help you defeat him, without losing my friends.'

'That's it, your eagle spirit; that's more like the warrior I see in you.' He slaps me on the back – a little too hard, but I appreciate the gesture.

Chapter 41

I enter the river and gasp at the icy water. Meder stands on the bank, nibbling the buckthorn.

'Come on, boy, it's good for you.'

He pushes his head deeper into the thicket, enjoying the bright orange berries and alarming a little redstart. Sabira lands on a rock in the middle of the torrent flowing down from the Heavenly Mountains, clutching a grey pika, which she devours.

This is a welcome escape from the endless questioning. The women know that I had an audience with Jebe last night and have been interrogating me about every tiny detail. There's a heavy lump of dread in my stomach, knowing that the General is expecting me to come up with a plan to capture Balasagun.

Why did I tell Jebe that I would help him? I'm going to look like a halfwit again if I don't come up with something.

I wedge my feet against two rocks to brace myself. The icy water massages my back and neck and I warm up as hot blood rushes to my core.

You strong you keen you smart
Girl you see like bird
Look down sky to earth look far look close

'What do the gods want, Sabira?'

> *Seek out what you know*
> *Three hares spies lies dung girl*
> *War pacts tall walls false words*
> *You know all*
> *Now be brave*

My head fills with Sabira's words as the icy flow pummels and numbs my body. Three Hares, spy, secrets, friends, dung, friends, spy, Gurkhan. The words twist round each other, forming ideas then slipping away before I can understand them, spinning in ever-decreasing circles in the whirlpool in my head. And then, quite suddenly, the torrent subsides, and the words float calmly, orderly, to the surface, and land on the shore in a shape. The shape of a plan.

'I have a plan!' I shout, galloping toward Toq, who is on the practice ground, mounted with bow and arrow aimed at a target disc. 'Can I tell you about it? I'd like to know if it's good enough to present to your father.'

His arrow lands far from the centre. He curses, then canters up beside me.

'I'm just off to check out some new pastures for the livestock. Come with me and we can talk.' I follow him, wondering briefly why the head of the Khan's security elite hasn't anything better to do. We dismount on a piece of scrubland and he picks at the grass, rubbing it between his palms until a green juice oozes out, which he licks.

'Mm, this will do,' he says.

I would not have chosen this spot. The grass is poor, and the livestock will simply wander off to find somewhere better.

'May I tell you my plan?'

'Go on then. Though I have to say, I'm all for a full onslaught and total destruction of the city. After what that Gurkhan did to me, and now snubbing our Lord Khan too. There's no place for mercy there.' He spits and a green gob lands on the calf of my boot.

'We're going to kill Kuchulyg,' I say, proudly.

He scoffs. 'That's not much of a strategy.'

I laugh. 'There's more to it than that, of course. First –'

He interrupts. 'I hate that man. More than I've ever hated anyone.'

'Me too!'

'He deserves a long, agonisingly painful death.' Toq screws his eyes and pinches his lips. 'If I have anything to do with the attack, I will ensure he's kept alive to watch as we kill every living thing in that God-forsaken city.'

'If I have anything to do with it, *only* Kuchulyg will die. My friends don't deserve to die because of his failings.'

'Gulzura. Listen to me. You have much to learn about our ways. That is *not* how it will be done.'

'I'm following the lead your father took, with the Three Hares. If we use those tactics, we can ensure the safety of my friends, who are still in the city, and the safety of all the people who would be loyal to the Great Khan.'

'I don't agree with my father anymore.' He pulls down his sleeve ensuring the Three Hares tattoo is covered. 'Many think he's becoming old and weak and scared of fighting.'

'But he's a great General. Hasn't he proved himself over the years, shown his loyalty again and again?'

'All the more reason to stick with the ways which have proved successful. If we show weakness here, word will get out and our reputation will be ruined. Besides, we are Mongols and Mongols fight.' He puffs out his chest. 'That is what makes us who we are: fighting, bloody, brutal battles and winning.'

This goes against everything Odval so carefully explained about the lengths the Khan went to, to avoid fighting.

'But, if the majority of people in the city would gladly swear allegiance to your Khan, why would you kill them?'

'Because that's our way! It's always been our way, and you can't change that.' He stomps off to grab another handful of grass.

I don't follow. I don't want to tell him now, anyway. His gob of spit has dribbled down to my ankle, leaving a slimy green trail. He saunters back to me.

'I haven't told you yet about the news from the spy I sent to find your friend Aibek.'

My annoyance with him melts away.

'I'm so sorry; it's not good. I've been thinking how to tell you but' – he takes both my hands tenderly in his and looks deeply into my eyes – 'Aibek's not coming.'

'I don't believe it! What's stopping him?'

He bites his lower lip. 'I'm so sorry to be the one to tell you this but... he was killed while trying to escape the city.'

His words hit me like a blacksmith's hammer, smack in the gut. My legs buckle. Toq drops to his knees beside me, enveloping me in his leathery strength.

'I'm so sorry,' he whispers, stroking strands of hair from my tear-soaked cheeks.

The wound left inside me when Atashka died, which had been healing in the warmth and love of Aibek's friendship, is ripped open again to reveal a raw, gaping chasm. I cannot speak. I yield to the dark blanket of Toq's embrace.

'You're not alone, Gulzura. I will protect you,' he says, squeezing me tighter. 'We have each other and together we'll go forward to whatever the future holds for us.'

I can't breathe.

I need Sabira. She is nowhere to be seen. It's become increasingly obvious that she's not keen to come to me when Toq's nearby. He's reluctant to go, but I eventually persuade him to leave me. I clutch my amulet. *Sabira? Where are you?* An arrow-shaped flock of honking geese passes overhead and a marmot kicks out wet bedding to dry in the sun. Life around me continues unaffected and I start to sob again. I can't believe Aibek is dead. He was so close behind me at the city gates. I should have gone back for him. It's all my fault.

> *This man he spit words not true*
> *Boykindheart lives locked high*
> *He love he wait you love*

My head is spinning. Aibek's alive? I want to believe Sabira but why would Toq lie to me? Why would Sabira lie to me?

Somehow, I make my way back to my yurt, curl up on my mattress and shut my eyes tight.

I wait in the shadows outside the yurt where dinner is being served, until I see Toq approach, surrounded by his Keshig friends.

'Toq?' I emerge from the shadows. 'Can we talk… just you and me… before we eat?'

'Ah, wanted her all for yourself, eh? That's why you sent us packing when we found her,' Topknot laughs.

'Don't worry, when he's tired of her, we'll get a look in.' Bent Nose slaps Topknot on the back and they go into the yurt.

'Ignore them, it's just idle banter. Whatever is the matter? You look awful.'

I take a deep breath, unsure how he'll react to being challenged.

'Sabira tells me Aibek is alive. She's seen him. She says he's locked up. Somewhere high.'

'Of course she has!' He tilts his head reassuringly to mine and talks softly. 'Eagles travel between the world of men and the world of spirits and gods. I'm quite certain Sabira *has* seen him – in their world, up high, not ours down here.'

How silly of me; of course, that explains it. He's *locked in*, in the spirit world; the dead can never return to the world of living men. Nevertheless, a nagging doubt persists.

'She told me he awaits me... he loves me,' I whisper.

'He does, I'm quite certain of it. But not down here on the plains, the jailoo or in Mother Earth's mountains. He awaits you up there, in the heavenly sky with our Great Father. In fact, I have no doubt he's sitting enjoying *beshbarmak* with Lord Tengri himself, right now as we speak.' He nudges me, playfully.

It's a comfort to think of Aibek with the great God of the Sky and I smile, imagining him talking with Atashka, too.

At dinner, I am placed between Toq and Jebe. Jebe, like me, sits in silence, listening to the chatter. Toq gesticulates wildly, talking of a past adventure and lapping up the adulation of a group of even younger men. I dread that at any moment Jebe is going to ask me to tell him of my grand plan. But, he doesn't. He asks me how I am settling in; he asks why I prefer to ride without a saddle; he asks what Sabira's favourite food is until, without warning, I blurt out, 'I have a plan.' I have nothing to lose now. The worst that can happen is that they kill me, and I will join Aibek and Atashka. I feel untouchable.

He stops eating. 'I would like to hear it.'

Please, Lord Tengri, don't let my voice fail me now. 'The Gurkhan is hosting three nights of festivities, starting at the next full moon. All the Kara Khitai loyal to Kuchulyg, from right across the tribal lands, will be there, nicely rounded up and secured inside the city walls.'

'That would be a most favourable time to destroy the city.'

'No. It will be easier than that. I will release the spy Kuchulyg sent here, to send back a false story of Genghis Khan's motives and movements. The Gurkhan will relax at this news, and by the third night of revelry and over-indulgence, he and his party will be completely off-guard and unfit for a fight.'

'I like what I'm hearing. This is the vision of a skilled strategist. Tell me how do we gain entry to the city? It will still be guarded, surely?'

'Yes, but not strongly. Any guards not loyal to the Gurkhan will almost certainly take the opportunity to slouch off home. I'd like to suggest we use a tactic of yours.' Jebe raises an eyebrow. 'The feigned retreat. I've heard all about it in the women's tent and from your son. We send a small group of minimally armed men, who make a show of being disorganised and barely a threat, to taunt the soldiers who guard the watchtowers.'

'The men who do this run a great risk of being struck by an arrow,' Jebe says.

'Yes, it is a risk. But even the men loyal to the Gurkhan will be enjoying a drink or two, so their aim will be off and their common-sense dulled. They'll find it hard to ignore the taunts from your men, and they will be unable to resist the opportunity to bring some Mongol prisoners to the Gurkhan, a prize for which they would receive great praise.'

Jebe listens without interrupting.

'As the Gurkhan's guards exit the city gates, your men will gallop off toward a section of the river which is hidden in a deep gulley, impossible to see at night. They will hide there, while the same number of *different* men wait on the other side of the ravine as sitting bait. As the Gurkhan's men gallop to capture them, they will tumble straight down into the ravine and fall into the river at the bottom. Once they've gone, we'll get a message to the Three Hares to open up the gates for the entry of your army. They would do that, wouldn't they? Open the gates for us?'

'Indeed! That is an interesting use of the feigned retreat.'

'Once we're all inside, I will lead you and Toq into the Palace Fortress through a secret entrance. The Three Hares will know where any other supporters of Kuchulyg are staying. There will be no need to raze the city because by morning it will all be over. You'll have the Gurkhan and all those loyal to him killed or captured and you'll have complete control of Balasagun.'

'Thank you, Gulzura. You have thought this through well. Very well indeed!' He gives me another of his bone-shaking slaps on the back. 'It needs a few small refinements but, in essence, it is a most excellent plan.'

Jebe moves to sit beside the Lord Khan and has his ear for the rest of the meal.

'This is the perfect strategy!' The yurt goes quiet as Genghis Khan speaks. 'Jebe and our guest have a plan that enables me to depart with most of our men to join Subotai and Tolui. They are in great need of support in the campaign against the Shah Muhammad in Otrar if we are to destroy the Khwarizm Empire. I will leave twenty thousand men here with Jebe to take Balasagun and eliminate Kuchulyg.'

There's uproar and shouts of 'That's not enough to take on Balasagun and the Naiman usurper', 'Kuchulyg has more than thirty thousand men and the city advantage – how can we defeat him?', 'Our guest? You mean that girl? What can she possibly teach us about warfare?' I shrink into the shadows at the edge of the yurt.

'Enough!' the Khan roars. 'Are you all blind? This girl has a rare and beautiful gift. A gift only given by gods.'

The yurt quietens.

'The golden eagle has always been our connection with the spirit world. This girl and her eagle are heaven-sent. They're with us now for a reason and we run the risk of angering our Great Lord Tengri if we ignore them. Any man who believes they know better than the gods stand now and speak.'

In the silence, a clarity washes through me and my purpose is revealed. I am not only fighting for my friends anymore; I am fighting for what is right. I will save the city because this is what the gods command me do. It is my destiny.

Chapter 42

'Come and sit beside me.' Jebe has summoned me to join him for breakfast. He pours tea and offers me fresh flatbread.

'I woke early thinking about how this plan of yours might work and that led me to consider what happens once we've taken Balasagun.' He pauses. 'I would like to invite you to move west with us when we leave.'

'Oh, no, I don't think –'

'Hear me out. You have remarkable skills which we recognise as special and hold in high regard. I have heard talk of your bravery; your loyalty is evident and I have witnessed first-hand your ability in the art of war. Besides, we are all keen to learn how to use our eagles as you do. A future with us would see you valued and honoured.'

I feel my cheeks redden. I think how much I would like Mother, Father, Alik and Nurbek to hear his praise.

'Our plan is to put Toq on the throne in Samarkand, as soon as we've removed the Khwarizm Shah. The lad has had a few disappointments recently. He just needs the right moment to prove himself. But, let me tell you, I have absolutely no doubt he will make a great leader, one that will be spoken of in generations to come. I have a great wish to see the two of you together, side by side, as rulers in Samarkand.'

I look up, astonished.

'What a pair you would make.' He smiles widely and I am speechless. Me, queen of Samarkand? Is that what the gods want? Am I the new queen to be honoured, as told in the prophecy? Before I can think how to answer him, he pushes his breakfast away and changes the subject.

'We have precious little time, so I want to know everything about the city and the Palace Fortress. Can you describe how it's laid out? Entrances? Guard houses? Anything else that might help us navigate in the dark?'

I shake my head, reeling from his compliments and the future he has held out to me. It's one thing to know your way around a place, but quite another to explain it to a stranger. I don't have the words to describe everything I remember of the city.

'I can lead you when we get there,' I say, hesitantly.

'I'll need to know before then if we're to plan this properly. Can we send in a spy to steal maps?'

Then I remember the trader's drawings and wonder if I can make marks on paper to show where everything is, like he showed me.

'I will make a map.' My stomach churns in knots. The only time I have done this before was in the mud with a stick.

'Perfect,' he says. 'Dayir, fetch paper and pen.'

He wants me to do it right now, right here. Before I can think of an excuse to leave, the pen, ink and paper are laid out in front of me. I close my eyes and think about the shapes the trader's map used for mountains, nomad camps, rivers and forests. I take the pen, holding it exactly as I remember seeing, and dip it in the ink. I lift it out and two large drops fall onto the rug, staining it black. Jebe kindly moves his foot to cover the spots that are expanding rapidly on the felt.

I start with a large circle. 'These are the city walls.' I add smaller circles at regular intervals on the line. 'And, these are the watchtowers.' I add the main square and quickly realise that I've put it in the wrong place as the streets are now too bunched up and I don't have room for the Palace. I screw up the paper and start again. My second attempt is a little better but the Palace is now too small for me to add details like the dung entrance. I screw it up again.

'Take your time. You'll get there. And there's plenty of paper.'

After another couple of goes, I am happy that it's accurate. Jebe asks endless questions, digging deep into minute details, and I tell him everything I know. The bread has gone stale and the bees have given up trying to get into the jam pots before he is satisfied.

'Let's begin.' He summons his next-in-command and ten men appear. 'Tonight, before dawn, all our weaponry is to be moved out,' Jebe orders. 'Everything is to be taken to the hidden valley where we found our stolen horses.'

The men glance at each other with raised eyebrows.

'That's an order!'

Sabira takes me flying. She's impatient and it's hard to keep up as we fly at terrific speed on high winds directly to the city. We circle over the main entrance gate, and – to my surprise – I see Aibek. I'm certain it's him. He's lying injured on the ground in exactly the spot where I last saw him alive. I watch the guards pick him up and whisk him away. Then we fly to the tower, where I was imprisoned. And there he is. Locked up. Waiting. Waiting for me.

I wake trembling. I have to settle this. I rush out of the yurt to find Toq.

The sun has barely risen but he's on the practice grounds, horseback wrestling with Topknot. The horses circle tightly as the two men, bare-chested, grip each other's belts in a game of strength that will see one of them eventually thrown to the ground. Toq hangs precariously from his horse, while Topknot has both hands firmly on Toq's belt. He urges his horse to sidestep quickly and the momentum enables him to pull Toq clear off his horse onto the ground with a thud. Toq gets up quickly and greets me with a wide grin that makes my insides go woolly and soft.

'I came off deliberately when I saw you coming,' he says and Topknot scoffs.

'I won again, fair and square. Anyway, why stop for her? She's just trouble.'

He circles his horse around me, menacingly. 'Come to order us around, have you, General Gulzura? Sending us off to humiliate ourselves without a fight? Your idea of fun maybe?'

'Back off,' Toq orders and turns to me. 'Well, Gulzura, your plan has got everyone's attention and not in a good way.'

'No,' says Blue Jacket, who has joined us. 'There are lots of unhappy men this morning, including me and Altan,' he gestures at Topknot. 'What is our General up to, taking advice from a young woman and a stranger at that?'

I look at Toq. 'I need to talk to you.'

'Clear off, you two.'

They don't move, so he shouts, 'That's an order!'

Topknot and Blue Jacket wheel their horses a half circle on their back legs and gallop off.

'Now, what do you want to talk about?'

'Aibek.'

'Oh, not that again.' He folds his arms across his chest. 'Please, Gulzura, you have to stop –'

'Sabira took me flying last night and I saw Aibek. He *is* alive. He's a prisoner in the Palace Fortress, in the very tower where I was held. I'm so happy.'

'Sabira took you flying? What does that mean? You are talking nonsense. Anyway, I've had confirmation from another source that your friend was killed many days ago.' His eyes flash.

'Your spy must be mistaken. Maybe he's talking about another boy, a different boy, a different Aibek.'

'Are you doubting a Keshig spy? Seriously?'

'Well, no.' I'm pulled up short. 'No, of course not.'

> *Stay strong*
> *This man he sly words lie*
> *He dark shape casts on you*

'It's just that, well, Sabira has always guided me so carefully and truthfully in the past. She's shown me the way when I've been lost. I trust her. When she tells me that Aibek is alive, her voice is loud and clear.'

> *Boykindheart lives strong*

'My poor little love, this voice is just your mind playing tricks on you. I know that you want Aibek to be alive, and now you're confronted with the truth, your beautiful, delicate head just won't accept it. This is what is happening to you. Trust me.'

> *Hear me true I speak you*
> *Boykindheart beats strong love for you*

'I *do* hear her. Her voice is strong. I hear her now.'

Do I? Is that her voice or could I be imagining it? I don't know what's real anymore. I can't believe Sabira wasn't showing me the truth. But why would Toq lie?

'Are you really doubting my word and the word of my most trusted spies because you hear the voice of a *bird* in your head?' He chuckles and it does sound hard to believe when he says it like that. His face straightens and he looks sincerely into my eyes. 'I have no reason to lie to you. Anyway, the last time we talked about this, you said you wouldn't listen to that voice anymore.'

'Did I?' I don't remember saying that.

'Yes. For your own peace of mind, you must stop listening to voices that contradict the painful truth. Whatever it is that you're hearing, it's not Sabira, and it's lying to you.'

'But –'

Sabira, what is happening? Is it you talking to me? Am I being tricked? Did you not hear Jebe? He believes in Toq, he believes in me and he wants us to be together. I am to be queen, Sabira, queen of Samarkand and this is foretold by the gods. The prophecy: and you will honour a new queen. That's me, Sabira! That's my destiny!'

Toq interrupts me again.

'I can't bear to see you suffer like this. You have an important job ahead of you. I will be by your side, protecting you, helping you, and together we'll see the downfall of the Gurkhan.'

I hesitate, wondering why I feel so queasy, and my voice fails me.

'If your eagle keeps upsetting you, Gulzura, I can see to it that she leaves. Forever… if you like?'

Kill her? I shake my head furiously.

Man threat you me risk cleave us twin souls

Sabira flies away over the nearest ridge. Toq puts his arm firmly around my waist and walks me back to my yurt. I can't speak, and my head is whirling. I thought I could trust my instincts but maybe I can't. I thought I could trust the evidence of my own eyes – I saw Aibek, I know I saw him – but maybe I can't. I thought I could trust Sabira, but maybe I can't. I know she hates Toq; maybe she is trying to drive something between us and disrupt my destiny for some other purpose. Oh, how I wish, more than anything, that Bubu were here.

'You should know that there are a thousand men here who will fight each other over the chance to slit your throat if your plan fails,' Toq says. 'You must take great care. I will do everything I can to protect you. Stick with me, always.'

The spy in the cage is asleep as I approach, easily hidden in the dark afforded by a new moon. He wakes and recoils fearfully.

'Don't be afraid,' I whisper. 'I'm here to let you out. I'm an ally. I'm spying for our Gurkhan. I can't get back to Balasagun to report on what the Mongol army is planning, so I'm going to tell you everything and release you to tell the Gurkhan.'

I unlock the cage and he moans, trying to unfold his arms and legs that have been tightly curled up for many days.

'Shh. Quiet. If we're found, they'll slit both our throats.'

He's terribly thin and covered in sores. I help him up and he leans heavily on me as we walk around to test his legs.

'Now, listen. Good news – the Mongols are not the threat the Gurkhan thought they would be. They're not particularly interested in Balasagun, you see. Genghis Khan's real focus is the destruction of Shah Muhammad and the Khwarizm, far to the west, and he's leaving shortly for Bukhara to join his brothers and son on this campaign. General Jebe will remain here with just ten thousand men, certainly not enough to take Balasagun. So, you can tell the Gurkhan he has little to worry about. Besides, the men left behind are the ones Genghis doesn't want. They're exhausted and weakened from years of fighting wars in the east.'

The man places his hand across his heart, encouraged by this news.

'They have virtually no weaponry; just a few swords and pikes. Certainly not enough to take a city.'

'This information will greatly please our Gurkhan. Thank you. But, won't you come with me? We can escape together. You put yourself at considerable risk here with these barbarians.'

'I'm safe, at the moment, and will stay to gather more information while they still trust me.'

I fetch the man a horse and lead him to a small weapons store. He reassures himself that the Mongols are poorly equipped for a battle, then he leaves for Balasagun. The silk-thread-thin sliver of a new moon, just visible in the north-east, tells me there are fourteen days until we attack.

Chapter 43

My fingers are trembling so much that I struggle to buckle my pack which is strapped over Meder's rump. Toq insisted I ate some bread, and I knew I would need the energy to get through the night, but it wouldn't go down so I spat it out when he wasn't looking. Now I'm not sure if the pangs of nausea are from hunger or my jangling nerves. I curse as I remember the loss of my little knife and I vow to steal one at the earliest opportunity. I try not to think about dying tonight but the more I try, the more I think about it. I long to see Atashka, but then I think about a lingering, painful death and I shudder.

I don't know why I am so fearful. So far, my plan has gone well. Jebe has had news from the Three Hares that the Gurkhan believed every word of his returned spy and that the insurgents are prepared and ready for our arrival. I wait, impatiently, at the head of twenty thousand men on the periphery of the city, out of sight of the watchtowers on the walls, but close enough to charge through the gates once they are undefended.

'What's taking them so long?' Toq asks Jebe. 'The advance party should have returned by now.'

Jebe doesn't respond.

'I just want to get going. The waiting is unbearable,' I say, still fiddling with my pack.

'I remember how I felt before my first battle.' Toq puts his hand on my arm. 'Physically sick, couldn't keep anything down. Had to hide it of course, but felt dreadful.' I like that he's trying to make me feel better.

The wait is long and the moon rises, bright and shiny, hidden intermittently by fast-moving clouds. The air is humid and heavy with the prospect of a storm.

'Look, they're coming back!' a lookout shouts. I squint in the dark and just make out a cloud of dust in the distance.

'That's not a good sign.' Toq looks to Jebe for reassurance. 'It's all of them. Why not just a messenger?'

The lead horseman gallops to face Jebe. 'We've tried everything, General, and they won't come out. They're not as drunk, or keen to chase us, as we'd been led to believe.' He glances accusingly at me. 'Either we go back and try again tomorrow night or we think of something else.'

'I told you we shouldn't trust an outsider.' It's Blue Jacket. 'It's a plot. She's one of Kuchulyg's spies and she's playing a game with us; I'm sure of it.'

There's murmuring and agreement among the others.

'It *must* be this night,' I insist. 'If we wait until tomorrow, we run the risk that the party is over and the guests will have left.'

'The men are not happy. This is not what we agreed.' Jebe looks troubled. 'We know the Gurkhan to be clever and sneaky, so how can we be sure to trust you?'

My heart sinks. No, not now, not after everything is planned and ready.

'This is *not* a trick. Do you dare defy your Khan, who believes in me? Do you dare defy the gods who have sent me here?'

He looks at me. 'Then we need another way into the city. And quickly.'

Pipes gush Deep dark down Not seen that way

'There are tunnels from the river. They carry water into the city. In pipes. I don't know exactly how it works but I've heard about them. One of them goes to the bathhouse, I know that.'

'Why should we believe her? She was wrong about the guards on the walls.'

'Let's wait,' Toq says. 'We should be patient and lure them out as we planned. We know a feigned retreat works.'

Jebe strokes his thin little beard.

Moon bright and full
Clouds make shade Men sleep blind
Gods say now

'Tonight. It must be tonight!' I declare. 'Let me take you to the tunnel entrance. Once we're there, you can decide whether you want to go on or not.' I hope Sabira knows the way and can find it in the semi-dark. 'We only need one hundred men to enter,' I continue, 'to take out the guards on the city walls from within.'

'Leave us your eagle, then we'll trust you,' Blue Jacket shouts.

'I need her. Only she can guide us to the tunnel and into the city,' I say.

'Pah… just let me –'

'Enough! We will go!' Jebe says. At that very moment there's a deep growl of thunder in the distance, accompanied by an equally deep growl among the men.

Sabira directs us into a steep-sided canyon with a river flowing deep and fast along its floor. When we arrive at the tunnel entrance, it is partly flooded and we are soaked to the skin.

'Here? You cannot be serious.' Toq looks at the entrance. 'I'm not going in there. And neither are the men.'

'It's the only way to get into the city unseen,' I say.

'It's too dangerous.' Anger flashes across his face.

'I'll go first,' I say. I don't want to but I have a lot to prove. If we turn back now, my life will be more threatened in the Mongol camp, with twenty thousand disgruntled soldiers, than by attempting to get into the city.

'Thank you, Gulzura, for your help but you will stay here. It's not safe,' Jebe says quickly. 'We can make our own way now.'

'You'll need me at the other end,' I insist. I must go with them.

'You *will* stay here and that's my final word.'

His tone makes me realise no-one talks to the General like this without consequence. I stand my ground; the gods are on my side.

'I swear to you – if you leave me behind, I'll follow anyway.'

I fix Jebe's gaze, determined not to be the first to look away. His face softens then he gives me a broad grin.

'I can fight a Jin army of one hundred thousand armed men, but I cannot fight your eagle spirit.'

'I will guard the entrance,' Toq says. 'I need to organise for the horses to be corralled and guarded and then brought into the city once the fighting is over. You go on without me.'

'Please come with me,' I whisper, not wanting anyone to know how frightened I am. He enters the tunnel cautiously and returns rapidly with a horrified expression.

'I think it's perfectly safe. You go on ahead; there's much to be done here. I'll catch up with you before you know it.'

He's as scared as I am.

'Don't leave without a goodbye,' he says. 'You're not going anywhere without giving me a kiss.'

Before I can think of a reply, he pulls me urgently toward him and plants his lips directly on mine, kissing me hard. He pulls away as quickly and slaps me playfully across my backside. 'See you at the other end!' He winks and turns to order the men into a single line in front of the tunnel.

I gasp but before I can dwell on how unpleasant it was, Jebe appears.

'Our Great Khan wants you to have this as a small gift in appreciation of the bravery and loyalty you have shown.' He hands me a dark leather pouch. Inside is a knife with a bone handle carved with eagle wings either side, attached to a slim, sharp blade. I wrap my fingers behind the heel and swivel my wrist, watching as the talon-shaped tip reflects bright flashes of moonlight. It sits perfectly in my grip, and I know exactly what to do with it.

'Please thank the Great Khan and tell him I will do my best to always serve him faithfully.' I return the knife to its sheath and tuck it inside my sleeve.

'I will. Now, young lady, we'd better get going.'

We leave the horses with Toq's men. Someone puts an oil lamp into my hand and I wade into the tunnel. The tunnel entrance is small and, although I can just stand upright, I fear most of the men will have to crouch the entire way through. I have no idea how far it is and what obstacles we may face.

The small, flickering light only serves to reveal the full awfulness of our situation. The tunnel walls are lined with bricks, but many are dislodged and dangerous. The large clay pipe that runs along the floor is gently sloped to carry the river water into the city. It is half-submerged in the rising water, and there's little room either side of it for feet.

Most of the men have to strip off their thick layers of armour to squeeze inside and growls of dissent from way back in the single file reach me.

After the second cobweb wraps itself across my face, I walk with my hand stretched out in front of me. Something prickly scuttles across the back of my hand and up my sleeve and it takes all my effort not to scream. Then I tuck my hands inside my sleeves as protection. Jebe offers to lead but I decline. This is a test; what would the men think of me if I give up when faced with a few insects?

The water rises to my thighs as the tunnel splits again and again where smaller pipes branch off left and right. Each time, I choose to stay with the large pipe, convincing myself that this will go to the bath house. I have no way of knowing how long it's taking. The lamp splutters and goes out, leaving us in complete darkness.

'Send up another lamp!' Jebe orders, but it doesn't come. The darkness tricks me into seeing poisonous snakes in the water, scorpions on the walls and my thoughts are tormented by visions of emerging into a city already burned to the ground.

The water is waist-high now, and the air foul. The sound of men slipping and falling echoes up the tunnel and Jebe curses.

'I'm all for trying out novel ways to attack but this just might wipe us all out before we make it into the city. You are small, light and fast. This plan is not so good for the rest of us.'

Eventually, I see a pinprick of light ahead.

Jebe sees it too. 'We must have complete quiet now,' he whispers to the men behind him to pass back down the line.

The circle of light grows as we get nearer until it fills our vision and we pop out into a large, open moat, fully lit under the bright moon. I don't recognise where we are, but I do know we are not behind the bathhouse.

Chapter 44

Ten cloaked and hooded men appear from the shadows into the moonlight and line the bank opposite us. One steps forward.

'Who is your leader?'

Jebe stands in the water up to his waist, hand poised over his sword. 'I am. Who wishes to know?'

'We are the Three Hares.'

Jebe relaxes his hand and the man continues. 'Our spies have been following your journey into the city. A brave and shrewd tactic. The guards have no idea you're here.'

'We have this one to thank for that.' Jebe slaps me hard across the back. 'And you to thank, I believe, for securing her release from the prison.'

Once we're all out of the moat, the cloaked men apprise us of the current situation in the city – days and nights of partying, games, entertainment, food and much drink.

'We'd better move.' Jebe says, 'Lead on, now.'

'It's customary to release slaves on this kind of occasion,' says the man guiding us, 'but Kuchulyg has released not one. We cheered in the streets for his parade, knowing we were cheering his upcoming demise.'

'So much for the *great* city of Balasagun,' Jebe says. 'Two and a half thousand crossbows on the walls, two hundred siege engines in wait, and not one of them put to use. The weaponry sits idle while soldiers foolishly look out to the plains for the enemy. And yet here we are! Right in the heart of the all-powerful capital. A *most* excellent plan, Gulzura. Much better than the original.'

I brace myself for another slap, but he turns to the cloaked man instead. 'Now, let's go find the usurper who dares to snub our Khan. Tell me, where does he lie naked in his bed, comatose from drink?' Jebe lands a big slap on our guide's back and he stumbles forward.

'The Gurkhan and most of his supporters are sleeping in the Palace. The others are easy to spot; anyone dozing in a khazz-silk chemise under a camel-hair blanket is fair game.'

'How will Toq know where we are?' We planned how we would kill Kuchulyg together and I imagine he will be angry if we go ahead without him.

'There's no time to worry about that. We must press on.'

Jebe orders his men to follow the Three Hares north, south, east and west to launch a surprise attack on the guards on the wall from within. 'Once we've taken the city walls, we'll open the gates for the rest of our men and horses. Meanwhile, Gulzura, take me to the Palace.'

Sanzar greets us at the dung collectors' entrance.

'Thought I'd seen the last of you! Word spread quick of your escape. You're either mad or –'

'She's certainly not mad,' Jebe interrupts. 'Now, tell me all you can about where our enemies are in the Palace right now.'

Sanzar confirms what the Three Hares had told us at the moat. 'They're pretty much comatose. They're completely unaware of what's about to happen.'

'No leaks of information, then? Good,' Jebe says.

'The Three Hares have been preparing for this perfect moment for many years. It's an honour to meet you, Sir. Now the odds are in our favour. Now, for the first time, our power is superior. Now we know we'll win. Oh, this is sweet.' Sanzar lifts me up and twirls me around.

'Put her down, man! What do you think you're doing!'

'She's one of us, a dung collector and there's no shame in that. Even our true leader's only heir is one of us. The Gurkhan would never imagine his predecessor's daughter would stoop so low as to hide among the poorest of the poor doing the dirtiest job in the city. And that, Sir, is how we've kept her safe all these years, waiting for this moment.'

Sanzar's men lead Jebe's soldiers in small groups to different parts of the Palace, while I stay at Jebe's side. He is focused on the attack and keen to press on while we have the advantage. At the top of the first flight of steps from the cellar we encounter the Gurkhan's black-armoured, elite guards. Swords clash; men grunt and fall; blood is spilled. Jebe keeps me behind him. I want to fight too, but every time I step forward, he pushes me back aggressively. I'm pushed right up against a wall and, fearful of being crushed to death in the scrum, I dodge behind a large tapestry where I discover a door to one of the many secret passages. I feel my way along the unlit, low-ceilinged corridor until I emerge in a familiar space. *Sabira? Can you hear me?* I touch my amulet and close my eyes. *What to do? Go on alone?*

Quick sharp whip smart you no miss
High speed fist knife keen
Primed claw and beak
Eagle sister
Go hunt prey

I head toward the Gurkhan's private quarters: each turn, each set of steps, familiar. Just as I approach his bedroom, a woman emerges. It's Adel, the servant I'd worked so closely with during my time in the Palace. She stops in her tracks.

'Adel, it's me, Gulzura,' I whisper.

'Of course. My dear, what are you doing here?' She looks over her shoulder anxiously.

'I need to get into the Gurkhan's bedroom.' I immediately regret saying it. I don't know who I can trust.

Her eyes widen and she stumbles for words. 'Oh... I see. He's in his bed! I tell you what. I will wait outside and make sure no one enters, while you do what you need to do.' I sigh with relief.

'Thank you, Adel, I knew I could rely on you.'

'Go, dear, now, while he sleeps.' She opens the door and gestures inside.

I see the large lump of the man under the bedcover. The comfortable shape of the knife in my hand gives me confidence. I tiptoe toward the bed, praying the wooden floor doesn't creak. One step, two steps; my heart thumps hard. *Just think of him as prey. He's an animal and you are despatching him for his own sake and for the sake of all those who have suffered at his hand.* Three steps; I hold the knife out in front of me. Four steps; I'm at the bed. I raise my hand high, knife pointing downward, and clasp the other hand around it for extra weight. I breathe in deeply. On the exhale, I will put all my strength into the knife as I push it into the soft spot between the base of his skull and the top of his backbone. Just as I plunge the knife, he sighs loudly and turns over to face me, still asleep. It's not the Gurkhan. The knife lands in the pillow, missing him by a hair's breadth and I am left shaking. He farts loudly, and turns again, completely unaware how close he came to the end of his life.

I tiptoe back to the door and lift the latch slowly. It won't budge. I try again with more effort and still it won't move. Adel has locked me in. I am so stupid.

'Adel!' I whisper. 'Let me out.'

I put my ear to the door. Nothing. She's not there. I edge my way around the room, exploring every surface for another door. There's nothing under the wall hangings, nothing behind the chest. I check the window balconies for a way to climb down, but the walls are sheer: no grips, no ledges, nothing I can use.

Once hid now free
Look sharp
Trace of trail left in cleft
Dark shape shroud

I know there must be a secret passageway for the Gurkhan to escape this room, if necessary. I retrace my steps, running my fingers over every tiny crevice and gap in the stonework but nothing gives. *Think! It's here somewhere!* The man in the bed groans, lets out a foul belch, and turns again. The bedclothes slide off, revealing his half-naked, flabby body. My eyes are drawn to the silk bed-cover crumpled on the floor and then I see it: a small chink in the floorboards at the foot of the bed. I crawl over and lift the carpet to uncover a wooden trap door. It's heavy and the rusty hinges squeak as I lift it. I freeze, but he doesn't wake. I steal a lamp from the table go down the stone steps, having no idea where it will lead.

The tunnel has many smaller side passages, but I continue along the main route, imagining that it will emerge outside the Palace walls. Not where I need to be, but better than being stuck inside that room.

I am wrong, again. The tunnel ends with a door, bolted on my side, which opens up at the back of the kitchen. I emerge slowly, knife ready, but the room is empty and the huge fireplaces are just full of hot ashes. The sound of fighting, clashing swords and cursing echoes down the main staircase from the floor above. I edge up the staircase, my back flat against the wall. There's a guard at the top, facing away from me. I creep up, crouching cat-like, step by step, until I'm within touching distance. In one swift action I slice across both his calves, just above his boots. He drops immediately, screaming loudly. I jump on him, hold his hair tightly in one hand, pull his head back, but just can't bring myself to draw the knife across his throat. I roll him down the stairway and lock him into an ante-room.

Where is the Gurkhan? Where would he be if he's not in his bedroom? In another bedroom? In another part of the Palace?

Prey soft in drink-soaked sleep
Sweet bed scent and green lush walls nest he
Flesh bare like chick
You stab claw beak to kill quick

The garden. He will be in his favourite garden, on his daybed. I run from shadow to shadow, darting behind pillars, crouching in corners. I have practised for this moment over and over on the jailoo and now it's real. The thrill coursing through me is unimaginably better.

One of the elite guard stands at the entrance to the garden – a sign, I'm sure, that the Gurkhan is there. I approach silently until I reach striking distance, certain my technique will work again. But he turns and I'm in a terrible position, low on the walkway.

He launches himself on top of me and puts both his huge hands around my neck. He squeezes. I thrash my legs, trying to twist so I can kick him hard in the groin. I struggle to breathe as his grip tightens and then there is no more air. I can't breathe. My vision blurs.

I wake with fresh, cold air pouring into me and I suck it in deeply. I open my eyes and blink. Someone is leaning over me, pulling the weight off me. I blink again. He's helping me up. It's Aibek. I *am* dead and he's come to take me to Tengri. I smile.

'Hello, you,' he says.

'Hello,' I croak back. 'Am I dead?'

'You would have been had I not turned up just in time.'

'But you're dead!'

'No. I'm not dead and neither are you. We are both very alive. The guard is dead though.' He puts his arm around me and it feels full of the warm, pulsing blood of a living thing. 'Damir arranged to have me released as soon as the attack on the Palace Fortress began. He said you were here, and it looks like I found you just in time.'

I have so many questions, but there's no time. Distant screams, shouts and cries of the ongoing battle echo around the palace. 'Can you get dressed in the guard's outfit?' I ask him.

'I could but why?'

'I need you to stand guard here, at the garden entrance, while I go in and deal with the Gurkhan.'

'I am coming with you. You can't face him alone.'

'No. Please stay here. I have to do this on my own.'

'If I hear the slightest squeak, I'm coming straight in,' he says.

'Wait here. Make sure no one enters. I need to fetch something from the kitchen.'

Chapter 45

It's strangely peaceful as I enter the Gurkhan's private courtyard. Dressed in servant's clothes and carrying a tray, with a glass and a drink that I have prepared using the powder Bubu gave me, I approach him. He's dozing on a sumptuous day bed. A leaf rustles and my head swivels to see a vivid green beetle scuttling across it.

'Your drink, Sire.'

'Go away... dear gods, my head.'

But he takes it.

One gulp down he drinks
Slow to still
Cough cough clutch throat gasp
Mouth gape wide smile not smile wrenched wretched
I look round left right with sharp sight
Pearl buttons looped by cream soft cloth
Foul breath Flesh rot Recoil
No words No sound
Peace
Sweet rose and wild mint scent
He slur words Twist fear Make no sense
Wide fright eyes
Chest rise fall rise fall snarl

Small knife in small hand glints in gods-sent light
Forefinger talon digs flesh
Find bone gap
Precise angle
Thrust knife talon-pointed deep
Twist heart tight
His throat growls Skin cold grey
Not live Not corpse
Dark lips spit bright life force
Heart thumps blood
Mantle wings feather tips outstretched wide protect prey
Bite tear shred Peck bone shard Strip ripped flesh

Blue blood Red death

Silence

Power

Chapter 46

I wake in the courtyard in a crumpled heap. The memory of a dream, in which Sabira killed Kuchulyg, swirls in my head, but the sight of a gaping, bloody hole in the chest of the dead Gurkhan, and the taste of blood in my mouth, makes me suddenly retch. It was me. I killed him.

> *Quick sure hook beak knife claw*
> *Good first kill*
> *Eagle sister soar*
> *Sky proud Earth glad*
> *Gods give praise*
> *Now rise we earth air twins*

I shake with shock, exhilaration, disgust. I thrust my head into the gushing fountain and wash the caked blood from my face and hands.

I suddenly remember Aibek. I rush to open the gate, but he's not there. Has he abandoned me? Surely not. I need Mara, or Sabira. I must rest. I must find him. I can't think properly.

'Hey, Gulzura! Come!' A Mongol soldier runs toward me. 'Jebe sent me to find you.'

In the main hall, Jebe is briefing his most trusted men.

'Ah, Gulzura. Good to see you. The battle is won but Kuchulyg is missing.' Toq sidles up to me. I can't help but feel contempt for him. His armour is unmarked and his face fresh as if he had just woken from a pleasant sleep, while all around him are cut, bruised, bloodied and exhausted.

'He's dead.' I don't know what else to say.

'General, the Gurkhan has been killed.' A soldier bursts in. 'We found him in one of the gardens, knife to the heart. Looks like he was scavenged by rats too, the state of him.'

Jebe looks at me. He raises a questioning eyebrow and I nod.

'Silence please, so we may honour Gulzura.' He ushers me forward. 'With the courage and determination of an experienced and seasoned warrior, Gulzura pursued, hunted down and killed Kuchulyg. And, thanks to her, this morning the city of Balasagun awakens to a new order...' He turns me to face him. 'You and your eagle have been key to our success and their freedom. And for this, I will reward you. Your bravery, strong spirit, decisive actions – all undertaken with no concern for your personal safety – have earned you a place in our elite Baatuud. From this day forth you are Baatar, a hero, divinely blessed and heavenly inspired.'

Everyone cheers. I am both proud and revolted. I want to leave as quickly as I can and find my friends.

'That's truly a great honour.' Toq smiles but his face betrays his envy. 'I regret I was not at your side to protect you.'

'Aibek is alive,' I say quietly. 'You lied to me.'

'My messenger was wrong then?' He tries to put an arm around me. I shrug it off.

The melodic rise and fall of a muezzin, welcoming people back out of hiding to public prayer with *Allahu Akbar,* echoes around the city from the Burana Tower. Men and women of the Three Hares are out in force to spread news of the Gurkhan's death, the new regime and the changes that are being implemented with immediate effect: taxes lifted, fairer laws, open worship of all religions. Crowds on the street celebrate cautiously.

I hammer on Mara's door and it opens immediately. Her tiny house is crammed full of noisy people and I can barely make her out in the centre.

'Excuse me. Excuse me.' She pushes her way over. 'I am so very pleased to see you.' She hugs me tightly, jumping up and down. 'Oh, this is such a great day for us. I've been hearing all about your adventures, and how you helped bring this about. You are incredible, but actually I'm not that surprised. I knew all along how wonderful you are. To think my friend did this! You are the talk of the city, you know! You're quite the hero. Anyway, all these people have come –'

'Mara, I'm so happy to see you again but, before we celebrate, I have to ask. Have you seen Aibek? And where is Usen?'

'Usen has been travelling to and from the mountains and I haven't seen him for a while. I miss him terribly when he goes, we've become quite close, you know. I must tell you about it some time. So glad I met you and then because of you, I met him –'

'Aibek?' I interrupt anxiously.

'I haven't seen Aibek either. I'm sure he will make his way here, if he can, as soon as he finds out you're safe and well. You know, he's careful, no harm will come to him. He's clever, like you. Ducking and diving like a –'

'I'm sorry, Mara. I have to go. I have to find him.'

'It's still risky out there. The Mongols are rounding up the last of Kuchulyg's supporters. Some are trying to flee. Some have even dressed as Mongols, or what they think a Mongol looks like, but they're just guessing and they look ridiculous. You know, I saw one –'

'I know where he is now. Thank you. Thank you.' I take her hands and kiss her cheek.

I head straight for the Palace prison. Of course, he's locked up there again, taken by the Mongols this time, because he was dressed as a Palace Guard. My new Baatar status gives me access anywhere, I quickly discover, and entry to the prison is easy. I find him, sleeping on the floor, curled up in a small cell next to the one I had been in.

'Aibek! Aibek! It's me,' I say quietly, not wanting to frighten him.

'Gulzura.' He rubs his eyes. 'Did you kill the Gurkhan?'

I explain briefly, but avoid the details.

'Why didn't the Mongols just kill you when they saw you as a Palace guard?'

'I persuaded them I was a spy for the Three Hares and luckily they decided to lock me up, rather than kill me, just in case.'

'Guard!' I summon one of the Mongol soldiers. 'Release this man immediately. He's one of us.'

'Not without authorisation from the General or his son. They're in charge now.'

'I am Baatar. Do as I say.'

'Not without authorisation from the General or his son,' the soldier repeats.

I turn to Aibek. 'Don't worry, I'll talk to them and have you released before you know it.' Then to the guard, 'Get him food and water. Now!'

When the guard has gone, Aibek reaches through the bars for my hand.

'I want to say something…' His hand trembles and I flinch.

'Oh, no! Nothing bad. I just…'

I try to pull my hand back. I don't want to be close if he's going to tell me something I don't want to hear, but he holds it tighter and I make a fist.

'Gulzura, I want to tell you… I don't know how to say it.' He laughs and I'm confused; how can this be funny?

He uncurls my fingers, slowly. I close my eyes and he tickles my palm with his finger, making lines, squirls and dots across it. When he's finished, he puts my hand over his mouth, closes his eyes and puts a lingering kiss onto my palm. He curls my fingers back to seal it inside.

'There, I've told you,' he says.

'What?'

'When this is all over, you and I will be together, forever, and the first thing I will do is teach you to read!'

I have no words.

'In the meantime, would you like to know what I wrote?'

I nod.

'I love you.'

My heart leaps and I feel I could fly right out of the prison tower on the wings of this happiness to spread my joy across the city. I love him too. I hold my kissed palm to my lips and then take his hand and put a kiss into it for him to keep.

I am quite sure Jebe will release Aibek. But he proves elusive; every time I'm directed by someone to where they think he is, I am told he's just left. As I go up to the main hall for the third time, I see Toq.

'Can we talk?' I ask.

'Of course. I've always got time for you, my lovely.'

'Aibek has been put in prison. Your soldiers thought he was a

Palace guard. It's a terrible mistake. He was disguised because he was guarding the courtyard while I... I confronted the Gurkhan. They won't release him without an order from you or Jebe.'

'I heard he was there. But I also heard that he'd been found fighting for the Gurkhan. It won't be possible to release him, not until we find out the truth. I'm sorry to disappoint you.'

'Aibek would never betray me. Where's your father?'

'He's much too busy putting the new administration in place to deal with a petty matter like this. He needs to set off west as soon as possible, to join our Khan.'

I visit Aibek repeatedly, wearing a path between the prison and Toq, who continues to refuse his release. Each time I visit, I vow to tell Aibek about Ilyas, but the right moment never seems to arise, and when it does, I can't find the words. I fear he will be angry with me for not doing more to save him, even though he only ever spoke badly of his brother. Meanwhile, Jebe has returned to the Mongol camp to organise their departure for the West. Desperate, I try a new tactic and make doe eyes at Toq, smiling coyly, brushing my hand against his when we are close. Just when I think I'm making progress toward Aibek's release, I realise I have made a dreadful error of judgement.

'You really are the sweetest thing,' Toq says and strokes a finger along my jawline. 'I'd like you for my own. And you know it would please my father.'

He pulls me close and whispers into my ear, 'You are my princess and I can't – I won't – go on without you at my side.' He moves his hand to the back of my neck and traces the curve of my spine with his fingertips, sending an unpleasant shudder through me.

'You are a warrior and your rightful place is with the greatest army ever seen by the gods and our enemies. Together we'll go west. Imagine it. Think of the adventures we'll have.' His face lights up. 'We'll set off with my father before the next full moon...'

I look up at his elaborate neck tattoo to see a web of sinewy threads and I can't help feeling that I am a fly.

I manage to avoid him for a few days by spending time in the stables, but he catches me off guard, and tells me he's banning me from visiting Aibek at all.

'It's not doing you any good. It's pointless. You really should just forget him. He'll be out of the way shortly. We have our own plans now.'

'Out of the way? What do you mean?'

'There's to be a mass execution of the prisoners in the main square. We can't just keep them – they're expensive to feed and guard – and we need everyone in the city to know the enemy is completely defeated.'

I clap my hands over my ears, before he can tell me any more, and go straight to Aibek to break the news. We have to plan his escape.

Before I can speak, he says, 'I've had word from my people. My father has died.'

'I'm so sorry.'

'No, don't be. I'm not.'

'I need to tell you about... about Ilyas.'

'I know he is dead too. On some stupid raid, I heard; got what he deserved.'

I am unable to meet his eye.

'The clan want me back. Without Ilyas, they want me to lead them. And' – he looks utterly miserable – 'they have a marriage arranged for me.'

'To whom?'

'I don't know. To a girl from a clan we need to make peace with, I expect.'

I reach for my little stone pendant: the engraving of our clans' symbols entwined, a symbol of my hope that we would become entwined ourselves. Why do the gods want me to be Toq's queen when all I want is to be with Aibek? I look up, unable to speak.

'Gulzura, this is not what I want either, I promise you. But I swore that the day the clan invited me back, I would forgive them and return without bitterness.' He takes my hand through the bars and presses his lips into my palm. I cannot tell him what Toq has planned for him but I push my face up to the cold metal and whisper. 'I will not sleep until you are free.' My heart is broken. I have lost him, whatever the outcome now.

Chapter 47

The house is quiet when I burst in. Mara is staring out of the window.

'Mara, I have to get Aibek out. Do you know anyone who can help me?'

She looks at me blankly. 'I will help you. I will help you, but…'

She stops and, for the first time, she's lost for words.

'Take a deep breath,' I say. 'Tell me what's going on.'

She closes her eyes, breathes in, then opens them and it all pours out at full Mara speed.

'The tribe leader who was overthrown by Kuchulyg all those years ago – that was my father, and I am his only surviving heir – my mother, my brothers and my sister were all slaughtered when Kuchulyg usurped him – and I was taken in by the women at the bath house and then hidden among the Three Hares until I was old enough to live alone and now there's a lot of pressure on me to become leader of the Kara Khitai. All those people who were here earlier? They were trying to persuade me. The palace officials and courtiers all want a leader in place quickly, and they're looking at me! It's been a secret for so much of my life, and I've been longing for it, and preparing for it, knowing that it is my destiny. But I still can't quite believe that the day has come. This is it. It is happening. They're coming back to parade me through the streets to the Palace. I'm supposed to be getting ready.'

I look at her in astonishment. 'So, when the women in the bathhouse called you *Princess*, they actually meant you are a Princess?'

Mara smiles.

'And, when Sanzar called you Lady Maraim, he was using your real name?'

'Yes. People here would never let me forget.'

I look at my friend in a new light.

'They've always held the belief that one day I would take my father's place, what with not having anyone else left from my family. Of course, I have wished for it, secretly, but to be honest, I never really thought it would actually happen.'

'Why didn't you tell me?' I ask.

'Oh, Gulzura, I wanted to tell you, honest, I did. But I'd been sworn to secrecy for so long, I suppose I was just used to being silent on the matter. Please don't hate me for that.'

'Of course I don't hate you.' I hug her but I feel embarrassed that I didn't work it out.

'Even though I've secretly wished that one day this would happen,' she continues, 'now it *has*, I don't know if I want it. I'm happy here, with my little life, tucked away, unseen, and anyway, do I really want to be in the public eye, where every move I make is scrutinised by critics who comment but know nothing? And I know these people, I've met them in the street, on the dung heaps, at the bathhouse. I've been one of them!' She looks astonished at herself.

'So, what? You're saying you don't want to be leader?'

She true queen

Your task done
Gods are pleased

Oh. The new queen in the prophecy is not me – it is Mara! *She* is the woman who will secure the future prosperity of our tribe. Not me. The gods do not demand I marry Toq. I am released. My duty to the gods is complete.

'Mara, this is your destiny. You cannot fight this. The gods sent Sabira and me to help you. That was *my* destiny.' I laugh with relief for myself and with happiness for her.

'That's exactly what Oyun, the Mongol shaman, told me! His name means 'wisdom', apparently. He certainly was very wise and measured and he listened when I talked on and on; you know me. He reminded me of the prophecy, which to be honest, I'd forgotten all about. So, when you and Sabira showed up, I never gave it a thought. Anyway, he's going to hold a ceremonial ritual to get the gods' blessing and install me as the new leader. I hope he stays; I don't want him to leave when the Mongol army depart. I would like him at my side, like a kind of father, but not my father obviously. Anyway, he talked a lot about a prophecy coming true and you and Sabira. To be perfectly honest I couldn't really keep track of it all, but he made it quite clear that *you* are the reason I am here now. I have you to thank for this. He wants me at the Palace as soon as possible so I can prepare for the ceremony. He told me what will happen, and I don't think I can face it alone. You will be there, won't you? You must; I insist.'

She's holding my hands and pleading but I can't get a word in edgeways and she continues, 'It will be my first decree: there shall be no ceremony without Gulzura and Sabira! Anyway, Oyun said we must honour your eagle and I don't think we'll get Sabira there without you, will we?'

'Mara! You must become the leader – at once – and then your first decree can be to order Aibek's release. Otherwise, they will kill him.'

Mara's face falls. 'Oh, Gulzura, I can't. I have no power, it's all just ceremonial at the moment. There's to be a handover period – I don't know how long – while Genghis Khan ratifies my position, and while we await that, the prisoners are all under Toq's authority. I've been warned to be very careful not to tread on his toes.'

My heart clenches as I realise that in just one morning, I've lost my only friend, and my hope of freeing Aibek.

People arrive, keen to talk to Mara and she's swept away in the chatter. Usen appears at the same time and whisks me up into his arms.

'I am *very* pleased to see you,' Usen says. 'I've been back home, to let everyone know the news – I've been following your progress through Mara mostly, who hears it all from the Three Hares.'

'How is the family? Have they missed me?' I don't expect him to say yes, but I don't care. I'm thrilled to see him and punch his chest playfully.

'You should have seen their faces – it would have made you laugh: their mouths gaping in awe when I told them about your courage, the strength of your newfound voice, your audience with the Mongol Khan, your friendship with the General's son. To be honest, they're a little unsure you won't be too high and mighty for them when you return!' A little shiver runs down my spine. He smiles and leans down to me. 'There's some other news, important news.' He hesitates. 'I think you'll be pleased.' He waits again. 'Now that we have a new Khan, our clan is keen to make peace and trade agreements with other local clans. Surprisingly, Father has taken the Khan's lead in wanting the constant raiding and warring to stop. I think it suits him, now he's getting older.'

'So?'

'Well, as part of this new peace agreement, Father has arranged for you to be married as soon as possible. You'll be thrilled –'

'No! Absolutely not!' An icy shiver runs through me at the thought of a husband chosen for me for strategic reasons.

'Let me finish… it's going to be fine… it's –'

'No! Say no more, I won't hear of it. I would rather marry Toq.' I rush out and slam the door hard behind me.

'Gulzura! Gulzura!' I hear him chase after me, but I'm faster. He's shouting, but I can't hear him.

My head is spinning, my heart pounding and beads of sweat break out across my body. It's all too much to take in: Mara a princess, Aibek to be killed, Toq's proposal, an arranged marriage for me. All my hopes are dashed.

Meder whinnies as I open the half door. If my head wasn't ringing with Toq's warning: *it's not safe for you to venture outside the city walls*, I would gallop to the river where I would bathe in cold water and clear my head. Knowing it is unwise to displease Toq any more than I have already while I'm still trying to negotiate Aibek's release, I simply press my forehead to Meder's nose and rub my hands down either side of his neck, breathing in his warm, earthy smell.

Kyuk Kyuk Kyuk

'What am I to do, Sabira? Return and marry a man I don't know, or stay and marry a man I know well enough to know I don't want to marry him?'

Kyuk Kyuk Kyuk

'Imagine the power and status I would hold as queen of Samarkand. Travelling with the Great Khan, having adventures. It is beyond anything I have ever imagined. Would it be enough to allow me to learn, in time, to forgive Toq and live alongside him?'

Gods say you boykindheart life

'How can that be possible? Whatever I choose, Aibek *must* be freed to return to his clan, where he belongs. I have to accept that. And I have to live with the truth that... that I will never see him again.'

Meder nickers softly and, added to all the other heartbreak, I weep uncontrollably with the realisation that I have to let him go too.

Chapter 48

'I will marry you –' I say, and Toq's eyes shine with triumph '– if you release Aibek.'

He smiles. 'Of course, as a gesture of my commitment to you, I will release the boy.' He pulls me toward him. 'He must leave the city immediately and never return,' he adds. 'That's my condition.'

'That won't be a problem. Can you issue the order now?'

'All in good time, my darling. Now, let's celebrate our future.'

'All in good time, my darling,' I say and immediately regret it, as he winces at my tone. I cuddle in close to him, contritely.

'That's more like it,' he says and pulls me closer.

I yearn to feel the warm glow that I felt when Aibek held me but I don't, and when I close my eyes, all I see is Aibek's face. I jump back blinking quickly.

'Whatever's the matter?' he asks.

'Nothing.' Everything is the matter and I pray to the gods for those feelings to come.

'I'll be much happier once Aibek is released,' I add.

'In the name of the gods, you are quite ridiculous. I would never break a promise!' Anger flashes across his face, then disappears quickly behind a smile. 'I will write the order now, in my own hand, and you can give it to the prison guards yourself. Will that make you happy?'

I grab the note before the ink has dried and run through the Palace to the prison and show the guard Toq's order. I tell him to have Aibek escorted to the stables.

'Bring him in here!'

The guards push Aibek through the half-open gate. I step forward, holding Meder's reins.

'I can take it from here, thank you. I have his horse ready and will see to it he leaves the city as quickly as possible.'

They are reluctant to hand over their captive.

'Well, I wouldn't want to be in your shoes if Jebe finds out you've disobeyed one of his orders,' I bluff. 'Now, untie his hands. He can't be expected to ride out with his hands behind his back!'

They do as I say, and retreat.

'What's happening? No one has told me anything,' Aibek says.

'You must leave the city immediately. Go home to your clan and become the most brilliant and successful leader they have ever known, and don't try to come back. Ever!'

I try to smile but hot tears flood my eyes.

'I have no doubt I have you to thank for my release. How did you do it?'

I turn to stroke Meder, unable to meet his gaze.

'What did you have to do to get me out of prison?' He takes my forearms and chases my eyes with his as I look anywhere but at him. 'Gulzura look at me, what price have you paid?' he whispers.

I won't tell him. I can't tell him.

He steps toward me and moves his hands around my back, easing our bodies together. I feel giddy with the loveliness of having him so close again. He lifts my chin with his finger and leans down to kiss me. His lips meet mine tentatively, brushing them like a feather, and I press harder to let him know it's what I want too. He pulls me in tighter until we are a single body sharing an exquisite moment.

'I have loved you from the very first moment we met,' he says. 'That day you tumbled off the rocks and fell at my feet: cross, embarrassed and covered in eggy mess.'

I smile, remembering.

'I don't want to leave you,' he says quietly. 'I wish more than anything that this could have turned out differently.'

I nod. Me too.

'I will lead Balta clan in a new way and who knows, one day, gods willing, our paths will cross again. And, if not, I'll be waiting for you in the next world. We *will* be together again; I know we will. Until then, we must make peace with what the gods have chosen for us here and now.'

My chest heaves big, silent, sobs and we kiss, then wipe our tears from each other's cheeks.

I hand him the reins.

'I can't take Meder. I'll take any other horse, but not Meder. I know how much he means to you.'

I push the reins into his hand. I want Meder out of here, out of Toq's reach, and Aibek's the only person I would give him to.

I walk away. Meder whinnies a long, sad goodbye.

Chapter 49

The Palace is frantic with activity as the new administration is put in place and the Mongol army prepares to join Genghis Khan. Usen makes multiple visits to the Palace, begging to see me but I have the guards turn him away. I cannot face him trying to persuade me to marry one of Father's new allies. Eventually, I send him the message that I am marrying Toq and travelling west with the Mongols.

I try to see Mara, who has moved into rooms in the Palace, but the guards tell me she is much too busy. There's no response to numerous messages I send her. Toq is happiest when I remain in my room. Some days I don't even leave my bed. There's no sign of Sabira and I struggle to remember the last time I saw her.

I stand on the balcony and call for her. Her reply is distant, barely audible.

> *No fly Cage tight No see*
> *We cleaved souls*
> *I fly sky-bound to gods*

My stomach clenches and bile rises in my throat. No, no, he can't have her. Barely dressed, I burst through Toq's bedroom door without knocking.

'Where is she? Where is Sabira? Have you seen her, Toq?'

'Whoa there. What's all this?'

'I can't find Sabira. Have you seen her?'

'No, I haven't. I've been asleep… until you woke me.' He looks angry and I realise I've made a terrible mistake.

'I'm so sorry, Toq, go back to sleep. I should have waited.'

'Yes, you should. But, as you're in my room and I'm all awake now, come here and you can tell me all about your worries.' He grins and pats the bed beside him. I don't move.

'I'll see if breakfast is ready,' I say, backing out slowly. 'Shall I bring some to you on a tray?'

'I don't want breakfast, my darling, I want you.' He lunges forward and grabs my shirt, jerking me toward to the bed. I turn and twist quickly, forcing him to release me.

'You want to play, eh?' He's on all fours on the bed, moving left and right as I try to evade him.

'No, Toq. It's not right. We're not married yet.'

'Well, I'd like a little taste of the honey, to check it's sweet enough for me. Nothing wrong with that.'

He licks his lips. I turn to make a run for it, but in one swift move he leaps off the bed and he's in front of me, locking the door. 'Now, let's see who's going to win. I enjoy a challenge.'

He leaps toward me. I duck under his arm. I am much faster than him and easily avoid his clumsy advances. He tires quickly but he's lost face and I am frightened of the look in his eye.

'When we're married, you'll know who's in charge!' he snarls. 'I'll put a baby in you as soon as I can. Once you're a mother, there'll be none of this horse archery or eagle hunting, or wearing men's clothes. Your job will be to raise the next great General!'

An image of Mother flashes through my mind. *Be brave and fight for your dreams,* she told me. I have to get away. A knock at the door is a servant with Toq's breakfast. As soon as he opens it, I make my escape.

In the days that follow, Toq brings gifts: presents, he says, for a good wife; tokens of his love. He secures jangly silver bracelets around my wrists and ankles so I can be heard wherever I go.

There's still no sighting of Sabira and the occasional words I hear from her give me no cause to relax. As I head out to the orphans' house to seek their help, I am stopped by the guards at the Palace gates. They tell me they're under orders to prevent me from leaving, for my own safety. Toq appears quickly.

'My darling, where *are* you going?'

'Just to visit my friends. I miss them. I'll be back soon, my love.'

'No, no. You can't just wander out of the Palace. You have to stay here with me now. It's not safe for you out there. Anyone could harm you. Besides, you have me, I will protect you now.'

'But I am Baatar – your father gave me that status. No one would dare touch me.'

'Father is not here now,' he snarls. 'I am telling you it's *not* safe to venture outside the Palace. Come, why don't you do something more fitting for a future General's wife. Some needlework, perhaps?'

Obediently, I return to my room, where the guards lock my door from the outside. I wrap scarves around my noisy jewellery, go straight out to the balcony and climb down the wall, creeping silently from shady corner to shady corner. I won't be stopped from seeing my friends. But, just as I think I'm out of the Palace grounds, I'm caught by guards under Toq's orders and returned to him.

'I can see you need a lesson in obedience,' he says coldly, then signals to his guards who take me by the arm, and march me away. I break into a cold sweat as we approach the forge. A sickness rises as images flood my brain: my flesh being branded; heavy cuffs soldered around my hands and feet; my tongue removed and my toenails ripped out. I would put nothing past Toq. But the guards walk me straight on until we reach the back of the gardens.

I hear her pathetic cries before I see her.

The cage is too small; she can barely stretch out her wings. She is panting, thirsty and hungry, pecking at the bars, stomping up and down.

'*Let her out!*' I shout. 'You must release her.' I scrabble with the lock which won't release, then try to pull the cage bars apart. *I will get you out, Sabira, I will. Stay calm.*

Blood drips from my torn nails.

'Get away from the cage.' The largest guard kicks me sharply in the ribs and I roll away. 'We are under strict orders to keep her caged. He said just to make sure you see her.'

'Sabira is sent by the gods. Ultimately, you will have to answer to them.'

There is nothing but fear in their eyes.

Chapter 50

Cage bars harsh split us twins
Beak blood-blunt raw claw
In wind gust dream fly free
Rain tears blur sight no blink
Heart now click click tight chest
Soul-waste and wing-ache and twitch
Dreams stretch soar
Sharp head quick whip all sharp gone
No rest no end no breeze

No hope

I don't get out of bed when the guards, who enter without knocking, leave food. I have no energy to wash and dress. I simply stay under the covers. A quiet knock at the door sounds different. I sit up. The latch lifts slowly and the door opens. Damir looks in, cautiously.

'I'm not supposed to be here,' he whispers. 'But your friends are worried about you and begged me to find you.' He closes the door quietly and stays respectfully distant from the bed.

'Come in.' I beckon him to sit on a chair. 'It's good to see a friendly face. I had begun to wonder if there was anyone here not under Toq's influence. He has me trapped in this room and Sabira caged. I've promised to marry him, but he still won't let me out.'

'How can I help you?' he says.

'Do you think Mara will see me? I need to talk to her. I need her help.'

'I'm certain she will see you but not under Toq's eye. I will make arrangements. Be ready tonight. I will knock twice, wait, and knock once, so you know it's me.'

'But how will you –'

'That's not your worry,' he interrupts. 'Just be ready – I will take care of the rest.' He bows and leaves.

The day drags and then it's night and I lie in bed, ready to throw off the covers and run at a moment's notice. Damir knocks, as promised, and gives me directions to Mara's room. Then he stands guard at my door while I scamper barefoot, quiet as a mouse, along deserted corridors.

I knock gently. She nearly sends me flying with a huge embrace and a torrent of questions.

'Where have you been? Why haven't you come to see me? I look out for you all the time but they said you didn't want to see me. Is it that Toq that's kept you away? Word in the Palace is that you are to be his wife. That can't be right, can it? Tell me that's not true.'

There's so much I need to tell her, but the words just sit inside me.

'I've missed you.' I hug her tightly. 'How are you?'

'I'm all right. Still can't quite believe what's happening though. I spend almost all my days now with city officials – organisers and planners, important people, all asking me questions which I don't have the answers to. I had no idea how many decisions my father made on a daily basis. I go to sleep sometimes wishing I could just wake up back in our little house with Bortboi and Nurdeen and Yajub – and Usen, of course. Goodness, life was simple then. Anyway, enough about me, what are you still doing here?' she continues. 'I don't understand why you didn't leave with Aibek. He loves you so much and you are such a good match. You are the two halves of a very beautiful whole. The gods must have made you for each other. How come you let him go and you didn't go with him?' She stops to draw breath.

'Oh, Mara. I didn't want to let him go. Really, I didn't. Everything happened so fast. His father died and he had to return to his tribe because they have a marriage arranged for him. A new alliance with another clan. I couldn't bear to see that, Mara. I love him. I love him so much. Toq was going to have him killed, so I had to get him released. I had no choice, don't you see? Once I persuaded Toq to release him in return for my promise of marriage, I felt better. Also, Usen told me there is a husband lined up for me, too. I will not be returning home for that!'

'You idiot – I can't believe you don't know! Aibek's arranged marriage is to you!'

I look at her wide-eyed and I can't move.

'When Aibek's father died, Balta Clan and Snow Leopard Clan decided to forge a new alliance, to heal past wounds, and it was to be sealed with the marriage of you and Aibek! Usen was so excited he could barely contain himself; he knew how pleased you would be. Surely, he told you? Before he left, surely, he told you it was you and Aibek to be married?'

'No, he didn't.' I hang my head. 'I didn't let him.'

'So, you've seen Sabira now. If you make one more attempt to disobey me or leave me, I'll have her killed immediately,' Toq says.

'Why would I, my darling? I don't want to go back to be a shepherd on the jailoo, living a dull life with just sheep and goats for company. I want to travel west with you, be your queen, support you and raise young soldiers just like you.'

He looks sideways and I wonder if I've overdone it, but he smiles. 'That's more like it. My love. My warrior.'

'There is no need to keep Sabira caged. I am quite determined that my future is by your side. I have nothing to return to. Let's go forward together.'

'You should know our wedding is soon. Our shaman, Oyun, is preparing a ceremony to cleanse the city of its past, rid it of the old, bad spirits and get the gods' blessing. Our wedding will follow that. You should have a new dress; we'll get you out of those men's clothes. From that day on, you will be a lady of the court.'

He locks the door as he leaves. I curse under my breath.

Day after day, he visits and I make no progress toward getting Sabira released, and our wedding day is approaching fast. Eventually, I come up with a scheme and, with Damir's help, I make another night-time visit to Mara. We talk until dawn, throwing my idea around, back and forth, questioning its strengths and weaknesses, just as Jebe interrogated my attack strategy. And by the time day breaks, a plan is in place.

Chapter 51

'No! No!' I wail, prostrate at Toq's feet, howling in disbelief.

'It's decided. We won't disobey Oyun. He has spoken with the gods and this is their wish! Sabira is to be sacrificed to cleanse the city.'

'Not Sabira. Surely, the gods will accept a goat or a sheep. Anything but her!' I sob, clinging to his legs.

'It has to be the eagle. The eagle that helped bring about our victory. The gods want her back!'

I scream, become faint and fall to the floor. 'Not my eagle, no, no. No! Toq? You say you love me. Help me. Help her!'

He takes me in his arms. 'My darling, this is painful, I can see, but trust me. We cannot deny the gods. Oyun's ceremony will cleanse the city of its terrible past and welcome in a new era. You should be proud that your eagle is to be part of this.'

'No, no, no...'

'Come now, stop this nonsense. This is an honour.'

I bury my face in his shirt and my tears stain the blue silk.

He pushes me away. 'Take her to her room,' he orders, then leans in to whisper to me. 'You are making a ridiculous and embarrassing scene. Don't come out until you have calmed down.'

I hang limp in the guards' arms, struggling to breathe. They lay me on the bed but I fall to the floor and pray the most important prayer of my life. *Lord Tengri, Mother Eje, I beg for your protection here on earth or take me swiftly into the heavens. Only you know what my future holds and I am entirely at your mercy.*

> *Wings lift free   Fall to preen in place*
> *I no fear   She fire-brave   She bright-bold*

Toq bursts into my room the next morning, without knocking.

'Get dressed, my love. The ceremony is today, and I want you there, beside me.'

I groan and clutch my stomach. 'Oh, my darling, no. It's my moonblood time and I must remain here. I have cramps and am not in any state to be seen.'

'You've been complaining for days that you are shut in. Now I give you the chance to come out with me, you refuse!'

I pull back the bedcover and he looks in horror as I reveal blood-stained sheets. He doesn't notice the cut on my ankle.

'Go back to bed!' He slams the door behind him. I get up quickly, wash and dress, and it's not long before there's a knock, followed by three knocks, then two. It's Mara.

'Is it done?' I ask, breathless with excitement and fear.

'Yes. Oyun took very little persuading. He knows Toq well and has no respect for him. He talked with the gods, and as far as he's concerned, and he's quite clear about it, he believes that you and Sabira should be helped to leave the city as quickly as possible. So, it's happening. Today. It's so exciting.'

'Is she safe?' I am trembling. 'Where is she?'

'Oyun released her last night. He talked to her and says she knows our plan. That's what shamans do, don't they? They talk eagle and wolf and bear; they talk to our ancestors; they talk to the gods; Anyway, he says Sabira flew immediately out of the city, and I'm quite certain she's on her way back to the mountains to wait for you there.'

'How is he going to manage the ceremony without her?'

'With chicken blood and a few old eagle feathers. Toq will never know.'

I hug Mara tightly. 'I can't thank you enough for your help.'

'It's not over yet. We have to get you out of the Palace and out of the city.'

'Now?'

'Yes. I must leave you now as I have to be sitting right beside Toq at the ceremony. Oyun has given me a powder to slip into his drink which will make him incapable of talking sense, or moving very far. He'll appear drunk to everyone who sees him. I will flirt outrageously with him. Give him the impression that I'm his for the taking but, of course, I won't be. He'll never know. And, by the time he does know, it'll be too late. You'll be gone.'

A pang of guilt stabs my heart.

'It's too great a risk, Mara. I can't let you do this. What happens when he finds out he's been tricked?'

'Oh, don't talk nonsense. This is going to be so much fun. My guards will make sure no harm comes to me. And it's going to be a huge embarrassment for him. Can you imagine the humiliation, once everyone finds out he's been outwitted by a girl? He won't hang around; he'll be out of here faster than a blink of an eye. The Mongol army is ready to move west as soon as the official ceremony is done. Trust me, he'll be with them.'

She takes my hands. 'Are you listening?'

'Yes, I am.'

'So, as soon as you hear the first ring of the city bell – that's the signal the ceremony has begun – you must go to the stables, pick a horse, and leave as quickly as you can. I've asked for all the guards to be present at the ceremony. I told Toq's Keshig guard that the Three Hares have picked up rumours of a pro-Kuchulyg rebellion and that rebels will use the ceremony as an opportunity to assassinate me. So, you see, there'll be no one around to challenge you. I will make sure that I steal all the attention.'

She laughs.

'Look at us! Two girls from the dung heap.' She dances me around. 'Who'd have thought we'd come to this, eh? Me, Queen of Balasagun and you, Queen of the Balta Snow Leopard clan. Usen at my side, Aibek at yours. Just perfect!'

'Usen at your side? Does he know this?'

'Well, not yet, but I promise you I will do my utmost to get him there. He can't go back to life on the jailoo. He belongs in the city, with his poetry, his music, his reading. He belongs with me.'

'Do you think I can go back to my life as it was?'

'No! Not at all! You will be queen, and you will rule with Aibek, and your people will be lucky to have such a queen as you; quick-witted, determined, patient, compassionate and savage, when you need to be, and with the extraordinary ability to talk to an eagle!'

'Well, I will *not* be returning to tend the sheep and goats, that's for sure!'

'Just make the odd dung-cake, will you? For old times' sake!'

We fall into each other's arms. I don't want to lose this moment and I hold her close, enjoying her sisterly warmth and wishing we could be together forever. I am so grateful to her. I have no words to say how much I love her and how much I'll miss her. I might never see her again. We each have a new life to live, and mine could keep me on the jailoo for months or years – assuming I even make it home.

After a wait that feels like an eternity, I finally hear the bell. Mara is right: there are no guards, but I don't take any risks and run from pillar to doorway, making sure I am unobserved. As I enter the stables, a large boy jumps up from the ground to block my way.

'What you doing here?' he demands.

'I've been sent by the Keshig to say you can leave the horses and go to watch the ceremony.'

'I don't think so!' he says. 'My job is to guard the horses and that's what I'll do until I'm told not to, by someone who is not a girl.' He assesses me with an expression I recognise. I think how Mara would behave, and I twist my finger in my hair, like she does, smile coyly and walk toward him, making sure he sees me look him up and down.

'In that case, shall we take advantage of the fact that there's no one around?' I say, and he looks surprised but eager.

He bolts the door – 'We don't want anyone disturbing us' – and comes toward me, arms outstretched. I smile and hold his gaze, letting him wrap his arms around me. A shiver of disgust ripples through my body as his rough-fingered hands roam all over me. I push forward, making him walk backwards until he's up against the wall. I hold his hands and raise them up over his head, lean in to kiss him and whisper 'I'm sorry' as I thrust my knee sharply upwards, hard and fast. He doubles over, writhing in agony and unable to speak.

I have very little time to decide which horse will get me home and dart from stall to stall until I see a dark chestnut gelding who pricks up his ears and snorts a welcome.

'Come on, boy, you're off on an adventure.' I put a bridle on him, name him Kachu, and grab a bow and quiver of arrows. I jump over the boy, still writhing on the ground, as I run to the door and am sent flying when he reaches out and grabs my ankle. As he staggers to his feet, I raise the bow and fire an arrow, then another, each one landing in the fleshy calves of his legs. As I mount Kachu and gallop out, his screams ring in my ears. As we approach the gates, I slow down and prepare what I'm going to say but, thankfully, the guards are distracted, huddled around a betting game, and don't even look up as I pass through.

The plain lies ahead of us and in the distance are the jagged blue-grey outlines of the Heavenly Mountains. Freedom.

'This is it, boy. I'm going home.' A lightness inside me makes me laugh out loud. I imagine the look on Aibek's face when he sees me, how he will hold me and how we will kiss.

The drumming of my heartbeat in my ears is drowned by thunderous hooves and I turn to see a cloud of dust rising, from which emerge three Keshig guards galloping out of the city behind me.

I dig my heels hard into Kachu. 'Choo, choo.' But the guards' horses are bigger and faster and they start to catch up. *No. This cannot happen. Not now.* An arrow grazes Kachu's rump and I cling on as he rears and squeals. Another nicks my leg. If they were shooting to kill, I would be dead; they must want me alive. They gain ground rapidly and fan out, left, right and behind. I reach for my bow, load an arrow and drop it immediately as one of their arrows thumps into my shoulder. I gasp at the stabbing pain and have no choice but to pull it out. The wooden shaft snaps leaving the head in my flesh. I scream and load another arrow, firing right and hit a guard in the neck. He falls. Another arrow whizzes past me. I reload, fire behind and hit the next guard too, in the throat. I push Kachu on with my legs, swivel on his back, reload and fire left. I miss, and the final guard catches up with me quickly. He reaches out and grabs my coat, I turn Kachu in a tight circle and the guard is forced to let go of me as his horse gallops on. He wheels back. Reaching out he grabs a handful of my plait. He tugs hard and I fall backwards, half-hitting the ground, half-suspended by my hair in his grasp. I bump and scrape along, shrieking. Just as I think I can't take any more, I hear her.

Kyuk Kyuk Kyuk

Sabira screeches in, straight out of the sun, so the guard sees nothing until she lands in his face with her talons fully extended. I hear his scream as I am released from his grip. I stumble over to Kachu, mount, and kick him toward the mountain as fast as we can, away from the guard who is rolling in the dust, clutching his slashed face. Kachu's roaring breath tells me he really needs to rest, but I can't stop. I must get some distance. As we approach the river, we slow down and I look back. I can no longer see the guards. I lean forward and pat his sweat-soaked neck.

'Thank you, boy.' I look up into the sky. 'Thank you, sister.'

Fierce blood scrape Gold last sun Proud she rides
She keep clan safe
Boykindheart love her
She warm free heart love him
Wing tip hand tip lips kiss soft true
Dance the line from past to now and to the time to come
Clan kin all praise new queen
Air roars cold Snow flake fall to sharp white
Gods make safe shape for us to live in peace.

Acknowledgements

Eagle Sister has evolved over many years and I would like to thank the following people who have helped it on its journey: Aibek Kyibaev for introducing me to Kyrgyzstan, in particular the magical Son Kul lake, and helping me when I returned to explore the region on foot and on horseback; Berkutchi, Nurbek Chintemirov, for introducing me to his hunting golden eagle, Karaluk; the Kyrgyz Tien Shan nomad people who welcomed me into their yurts and fed me beshbarmak and mare's milk; Alan Gates who patiently answered all my questions about golden eagles; my Guardian writing group, who helped me get started; my Constellations writing group who helped me keep going; and my wonderful Editors, Claire Steele and Jill Glenn, of Constellations Literary Consultancy, who got me over the finish line with such kindness and patience. Special thanks to Claire for her unwavering optimism, gentle guidance and expert advice throughout. Big thanks too to my insightful and supportive readers: Rosemarie Hill, Gigi Joly, Tim Slader and Karen Banfield. Finally, special thanks to my gorgeous children, Cherry and Laurie, who have had to listen to me go on about Gulzura and her eagle for such a long time, read early drafts, talked through ideas and gave me so much encouragement all the way.

Constellations Press is a small independent press
committed to publishing works of fiction, memoir and essays.

We publish books that boldly reimagine society, and
that celebrate our diverse humanity, adding to the
total sum of the world's beauty.

constellationspress.co.uk